Mary Walkin Keane was ⌐   as
educated at the Convent   el
Hill, Limerick, featured in Kate O'Brien's *Land of Spices*. She now
lives in Canada, and makes frequent visits to Ireland.

  Mary Walkin Keane has been a secondary school teacher, and
lecturer on women and storytelling, myths, and the unconscious.
Her short stories have won her acclaim on both sides of the
Atlantic. *The Rose Tree* is her first novel.

THE
ROSE TREE

a novel

MARY WALKIN KEANE

BANTAM BOOKS
TORONTO • NEW YORK • LONDON • SYDNEY • AUCKLAND

THE ROSE TREE
A BANTAM BOOK 0 553 40651 5

First publication in Great Britain

PRINTING HISTORY
Bantam Books edition published 1994

This book is set in Gouldy Old Style

Bantam Books are published by Transworld Publishers Ltd,
61– 63 Uxbridge Road, Ealing, London W5 5SA,
in Australia by Transworld Publishers (Australia) Pty Ltd,
15– 25 Helles Avenue, Moorebank, NSW 2170,
and in New Zealand by Transworld Publishers (NZ) Ltd,
3 William Pickering Drive, Albany, Auckland.

Printed and bound in Great Britain by
Cox & Wyman Ltd, Reading, Berks.

For my family, both living and dead.

Thank you

Francesca Liversidge and all the team at Bantam for bringing me home.

Helen Heller and Daphne Hart, for accomplishing in weeks what I couldn't in years. And Aleda O'Connor for crossing our paths.

I would not know where to begin or end thanking the people in my life. There are a few, however, whose help was crucial:

Clive Jones and Darlene Madott, who edited early drafts and believed in this work long before I did.

Niall and Caroline Keane, without whom I would not have written a word.

And first, last, always: Tom Keane, who could give Orpheus lessons.

And set a rose-tree on her grave.
And now none living can
When they have plucked a rose there
Know where its roots began.
O my dear, O my dear.

– W.B. Yeats, "The Three Bushes"

THE
ROSE TREE

You want to know your story. You get up in the morning wondering and your last thoughts at night are questions. I can feel it in my bones.

All these years I have worried and fretted because there seemed no way I could ever speak. I wanted to tell you; I have told you a million times in dreams. Sometimes in nightmares you have answered back and condemned me.

Then one day the idea came – there was a way I could tell you. Not in dreams anymore. Nor in thoughts cast to the wind over the sea. Nor yet again to a damp pillow on your birthday. No, there was a way I could really tell you. It would carry a price, but at least I wouldn't have to carry the burden of your story in silence to the grave. You want to know and I do so dearly want to tell you.

It was at a funeral, of all places. I felt a peculiar fluttering the moment my father phoned with news of the death. I knew even then there was a Rubicon to be crossed. I thought I knew what I would find on the other side. I was so wrong. So very, very wrong.

I went to that funeral because I was compelled. Indeed, there were any amount of reasons I shouldn't: I didn't even know the woman anymore, it was a long way at virtually no notice, and I was supposed to be in front of my class at nine o'clock to teach. And anyway, I hate funerals. Morbid things, funerals.

But I went. Found myself driving down from Dublin, leaving my cosy flat in the hard grey of a March dawn. Driving through greystone towns: swimming past the rows of tall narrow windows in the rigidly cemented terraces. In any one I might have lived, and been lonely, and at home. Flashing in and out of towns of the living dead. And then passing the echoing grey slabs marking the rest of the dead. Yet these more alive somehow and heavily present because they now know the answers.

She is dead now and knows all about you. Knows the hold she might have had over me and how you might have changed everything once had I only told them all then.

I put the boot down, as my brother Harry says, and was coming in by the West End of Duneen by half past ten. Just in time for the eleven o'clock funeral mass. I call Duneen home out of habit although I have lived in Dublin twenty-one years now, nearly four more than the childhood years here. Imagine. And still I think of Dublin as a bus station I am passing through.

The West End . . . sounds like a great metropolis. Some metropolis. It has an East End too, a Main Street, and a Sea Road – any one of which you could walk through in ten minutes. You could, maybe you have. Maybe some force compels you to this place. In winter especially . . . like me. Like all its true children. And everywhere your empty footsteps ringing, triggering whispering sighs. Winter ghosts of decayed hotels. Ballrooms and salons bereft as the *Titanic*'s. Pasted over with rancid chip shops and black video hulks greedily waiting the influx of summer factory workers from the north. Poor Duneen – only a few miles from the border and two weeks of drinking or passion or Bingo away from the troubles to be had cheap. The beach is nothing to write home about. But then you don't come to Duneen for the beach. Or something to write home about, for that matter.

I thought I had all the time in the world to make mass, but I found myself in the middle of a traffic jam. A traffic jam in Duneen? In March? But of course . . . if I'd had the wits about me at all, I'd have expected it. Today's funeral would be no ordinary affair. This wasn't just any old woman's funeral; no, the social event of the season for the whole county. So much for the quiet walk by the sea beforehand; I couldn't even get near the town.

I eventually found myself a parking space up beyond the football grounds on the other side of the convent, but it was a good enough walk to the church.

There were still some seats inside because of all the devout mulling about among the crowd outside. Subdued greetings: Ah hello, I haven't seen you since – Jack Moran's funeral, was it? Always a sad day we meet again. That sort of thing. I kept my head well down, a scarf pulled over my face, more against recognition than against the biting March wind. I ducked into the church where I'd be safer from contact, picked out a seat at the back beside some people I definitely didn't know and sidled in. I hadn't been spotted yet and maybe I would be safe enough now.

Some hope. My knees hadn't hit the wood when the whispering behind me started:

"Would ya look. Wonders will never cease."

"What?"

"There – Róisín McGovern."

"You're right. It is too."

"Look at the getup."

"Never had the looks or the dress sense of the rest of them."

"What would she be now?"

"Must be forty."

"Looks every minute of it."

Well, *there* was a voice and a charitable disposition I'd know anywhere: Miss McAloon, the town's postmistress since before the war – the Crusades, I'd say myself. And I'd lay a heavy bet the other voice belonged to Mrs. Grimes. Fellow veterans of a thousand funerals. Passive spectators at other people's tragedies. And today's promising to be a real field day for them.

"Excuse me. Move along now. Over one now." It was the usher, the same old Shorty Flanagan. Hair still plastered back with Brylcreem, its parting power driven over his left ear. But twenty toothless years had permanently squashed his forehead down to his chin. No wonder he walks away every year with first prize at the town's funny-face contest. Gurning, I think its real name is. An idea stolen by the Chamber of Commerce from English television. To make a little change from sandcastle and fancy-dress competitions.

"Over now, please. We must keep the aisle seats free for the Children of Mary." Shorty was having himself a field day too, invisibly pushing the congregation in the direction he wanted it to go, dancing on his bandy little legs with importance.

The church was filling up fast. It was well past eleven now, and people were teeming in at all the entrances. A sudden proliferation of blue capes in the aisle signalled the arrival of the Children of Mary, diddled out of the pomp of formal procession by all the stragglers. They took up their positions at the aisle end of each row. Not without a few power struggles between them and some stubborn old crones who felt they had squatters' rights after warming those seats for themselves fifty or sixty years. But ably backed up by Shorty Flanagan, the Children of Mary stood triumphant in the end, an unlit candle held in every trembling hand.

Above my head, the organ gallery creaked under a full weight.

As if there had been a curtain call, the church swallowed in the last of the dawdlers and a rustling, whispering expectancy descended. Shorty made another huge fuss lighting the candle of the last Child of Mary. Then each one lit the candle of the other in front of her until the aisle was lined with eerie faces above the candles held decorously to chest.

Suddenly the congregation rumbled to its feet as the posse from the sacristy made its entrance. Of course, the bishop stole the show. Everyone was creaking up on toes to get a better look. He was fittingly sombre, greyer than I'd have expected. A prince of the church if ever I saw one.

"Doesn't he look magnificent," said Miss McAloon from behind me. "What more could any woman ask for her funeral?"

"It's a great turnout. Bigger even than Redmond's, the minister."

"Miles bigger. They're here from all over. Why wouldn't they? He's very well known since that time on the telly."

"If she could only see him."

"Isn't she looking down from a better place?"

If indeed she was, she saw an impressive sight. He was followed by a huge gaggle of cohorts—I lost count after twenty or so—priests of all ages and dimensions. And as if that weren't enough,

4

fidgeting and straining behind them came the entire fleet of altar boys. The group gathered at the steps of the altar facing the centre aisle, waiting.

He towered over them even without his mitre. Glacial he stood, alone in that huge crowd, wearing the simplest of white vestments.

From the organ gallery came the muted strains of a Bach fugue. No homegrown talent that. The normal fare ran more to Hail Holy Queen, Holy God, or a bad rendition of Panis Angelicus on really big occasions.

Every head turned to face the aisle at the sound of the coffin wheeled up from behind. The Children of Mary held their candles out protectively towards the body of their late sister, welcoming her home, illuminating her way onwards. How about a quick burst of Handel's *Arrival of the Queen of Sheba*? Or a few bars of the Nuns' Chorus? Now that would be appropriate – he used to be a great one for the choruses. Shut up, Róisín McGovern, dangerous ground. You're irreverent . . . blasphemous . . . or just a wee bit hysterical.

The bishop came down to meet the coffin, his face solemn. He placed his hands on the wood. His greeting was quiet, personal, not for public consumption. There were none of the theatrical one-liners for which he was renowned. No dramatic openers. If the crowd was hoping for his usual flair, it was disappointed. Yet as he mechanically recited the stock verses his mask slipped a little. His hands fidgeted with his alb, flicked through the pages of his breviary; his eyes scanned the crowd – here, there, resting nowhere, seeing nothing. The familiarity of the gestures sent a shock through me. Quite suddenly I was crying.

Crying, for God's sake. Snivelling here at a funeral without even a tissue to my name. Of all the stupid nonsensical reactions. It must be the funeral – morbid bloody things, funerals. I couldn't stop crying. It was worse than a fit of the giggles. What had I got to cry about? It wasn't as if I were chief mourner. As if I had any claim on the status of mourner at all. I didn't even like the woman.

The verses over, the priests shuffled themselves around and made their way to the chairs allotted them on either side of the

5

main altar. When the last altar boy was seated, the bishop followed and took his own place.

A bare-headed blonde girl genuflected and mounted the steps to the lectern. The token female . . . . Ah, that was better, no more stupid snivelling. Shut up, Róisín, and make yourself listen . . . .

"But when this mortal should have put on immortality, then shall be brought to pass the saying which is written. Death is swallowed up in victory. O death, where is thy victory? O death, where is thy sting? Now the sting of death is sin, and the strength of sin is the law . . . . " Who was she anyway? I didn't recognize her at all. Must be a cousin or something. She reads well. I wonder who she is. I've lost touch. It's been so long. It's all been so long.

"Wouldn't ya think she'd at least wear something on her head? Seein' it's a funeral . . . " whispered Miss McAloon loudly. "Up on the altar with that brassy head."

"My God, I give Thee thanks for what Thou givest and for what Thou takest away . . . . " Do I? Do I give thanks? O Lord, You took such a lot in Your time. "May He support us all the day long till the shades lengthen and the evening comes, and the busy world is hushed and the fever of life is over and our work is done; then in His mercy may He give us a safe lodging and a holy rest and peace at the last . . . . " And do I have to wait until the end for real peace? I thought I had it once or twice, but it's so hard to hold on to – there I was crying again. What was wrong with me; I was never like this. Must be the funeral . . . awful bloody things, funerals, anyway.

"We have loved her during life; let us not forget her in death . . . for the peace of God, which passes all understanding, cometh only to those who will accept the cross . . . . " Quite suddenly a wave of sunlight lifted first the words, then the stained-glass windows, then the whole church to a shattering brightness. I could see the patch in John the Baptist where my brother Harry broke it with his catapult. The colours flared briefly in the stations of the cross, executed in the style they call naive.

The sunlight waned, quick as it had come, and the church dimmed again. Over in the transepts, the last rays caught the heads of the little children from the convent school. All out in force. Of course they would be, wouldn't they? Because this funeral was no ordinary one. It wasn't every day a bishop concelebrated a local funeral. And certainly not a bishop who had sat in those self-same seats with the convent nuns in his own day.

Well, well. Talk about things changing and things staying the same: rows of little High Infants under the wimpled and slightly moustached countenance of Sister Columba. Old as Methuselah now, but definitely Sister Columba. She reached behind some heads to chastise a giddy one. It could have been me, it could have been yesterday.

Is there one there who will become famous? One infamous? And one who will not live to see either? Can that be me, Róisín McGovern, stuck at the back for my height? Bernadette Gibbons, centre of course, with the long white hair? That must be Lorcan Burke with the pudding cut and the plubby cheeks. And there's even a Ben. No one smiles, or nudges him, or casts him playful glances . . . . Ben.

It was then the revelation came: the beginning of your story was right there before me. There was indeed a way I could tell you after all these years. I knew it was for this moment alone I had come to the funeral. There I sat in the midst of all those sad funereal faces, mine suddenly beaming so inappropriately. No . . . oh no . . . so very appropriately.

7

I see Paris, I see France,
I see Fionnuala's underpants.

I could too see Fionnuala's underpants. They were knickers really. Pink.

My forehead was cool, down against the brass inkwell behind Lorcan Burke's back where Sister Columba couldn't see me. I loved my classroom: *Rang na Naíonán*, it said over the door, High Infants, in Béarla.

The room was sunny, with orange-afternoon wood, shiny and warm, worn from generations of elbows and seats.

I could hear the squeak of Sister Columba's shoes as she raised herself on her toes the odd time. And then after a little while, the squeak back down again. They were funny shoes only nuns and sometimes old ladies wore: black, of course, laced, with clubby thick heels and a design pinpricked on the fronts for decoration. You could hardly see anymore that Sister Columba's design used to be flowers because they were cracked into smiles everywhere from her tiptoeing up and down so much. But when she was cross she forgot how much she liked to tippytoe. Then the flowers just wrinkled and frowned as the hem of her habit shook.

I could hear a wasp fussing at the window. They die at this time of year, Daddy says. Poor wasp. Does he feel the heat of the sun and think the warm summer is still outside? All his wasp friends and cousins not dead but out there playing without him? Fionnuala moved and I couldn't see her knickers anymore. An awful hard name to spell, Fionnuala, the way Sister Columba spelled it.

I always spelled it *Finula* because that was the way it sounded, and, anyway, Fionnuala didn't mind if I got it wrong. I liked the name Fionnuala, but it wasn't as nice as my own – Róisín. *Ro-sheen*, it sounded . . . like *ocean* . . . a lovely shushing, whispery name . . . Róisín . . . not a bit like me. My mammy wanted to call me Adele, after her mother, but my daddy wanted to call me Róisín, and I don't know why he won for once, but I'm glad he did.

It was nice down there on the inkwell. With my one eye still resting on it, I swung the other one around as far as I could. Over to the cupboard with its label, *cófra*, hanging sideways. Even though it was far away my nose wrinkled with the sneezy smell of the chalk. On to the pictures of food: *arán, im, siúcra* . . . sugar. I loved *sh* words. *Shh-grr*. I said the sounds of it over and over to myself until they became quite strange. *Shh-grrr. Sshhhu-gr.*

Suddenly the voice of Sister Columba burst through the sugar.

"Ben Thompson, *cad tá im láimh agam?*"

My one eye still rested stubbornly on its inkwell; the other didn't want to leave its nice sugary place either but sailed around slowly until it saw Ben Thompson. Two desks over he stood, staring at the floor. His hand gripped the corner of his desk. I was sorry for that hand. It was far too big for its sleeve and the crack between the knuckles like a bare bottom.

"*Cad tá im láimh agam?*" the question came again.

I couldn't look anymore, not even with one eye. Please, God, please, just this once let Ben Thompson have an answer. If only he would answer, everything would be all right. Then he would be just like any of the other lads. Maybe even play football with them in the yard.

"All right, Ben Thompson, we'll try in English then. What have I got in my hand?"

"An apple," Ben muttered to the ground.

"Good. Now let's have that in Irish, please. That's not too difficult, is it? *Cad tá im láimh agam?*"

There was no sound at all then but the big old heavy clock like the one in hell that goes on for ever and ever no matter what. *Tick . . . mock . . . tick . . . mock.* Ticking and mocking Ben Thompson.

"*Úll*," I whispered because I couldn't stop myself. "*Úll*." He could hear me right well. Why wouldn't he answer?

"Róisín McGovern, how many times have I told you not to prompt? Go and stand with your face to the wall. Should we stay here until morning, Ben Thompson will answer."

I went, my face all bursting hot no matter how much I begged it not to. Six years old and a big baby with tears still.

Standing face to the wall wasn't so bad really . . . not as bad as outside the door anyway where Sister Ursula, the head nun, could easily see you. And today was Friday – it was nearly the weekend right this minute – but Sister Columba said we would be all kept in until Ben Thompson answered? Even if he took until morning. I knew Ben Thompson wouldn't answer. Not ever. And the whole school – even the whole town – would know that High Infants were kept in all night. And that it was all Róisín McGovern's fault for prompting.

This was altogether too much. I felt the hot urge threaten, then gather force. Oh God, no . . . please, please God. I glued my legs together, I crossed them over, but it was no use. The shameful wave burst and tumbled down, trickling all over my socks and second-best shoes, to spread in a dark steaming puddle around my feet.

There were gasps and snorts and a few sniggers. It was then the bell rang for the end of school.

"Oh for goodness sake, Róisín McGovern, why didn't you ask for *cead dul amach*?" said Sister Columba. She kept looking from me to the rest of the class to the door as if someone might come and deliver her from it all.

"Dear, oh dear," she said, squeezing and rubbing her hands together. "You know you only have to ask *cead dul amach*. You're not a baby." Suddenly she remembered the rest of the class and began to whoosh them out. "Well, don't just stand there gaping, children, off home with you now." She seemed to have forgotten all about Ben Thompson.

As for me, I stood frozen in misery. I tried to swallow all the salty tears and then the sticky stuff that started running in through my lips and down the back of my nose. Things would never ever be the same again. If I lived to be a hundred, I would still wake up every single morning with the shame and the sourness of this moment.

I trailed home, squelching and reeking, to Mammy. This was the worst thing I had ever done. She would hate me worse than ever now.

I stopped at our hall door. Ours was one of the biggest old houses in Main Street. Mammy said it must have been great when there were servants to heat it and clean its never-ending stairs. The street was a solid row of three-storey houses, the only way in through the front doors; ours was always left on the latch after school.

I stood on the hall mat inside the door, crying. It was nice to be inside the door at last where everybody couldn't see me. But there was still Mammy to go. "Immaculate" was the word people always used about Mammy's house, and to trail my offending self through it was unthinkable. So was calling her despair down to the hall door.

Just beside me was the downstairs parlour. We didn't use it very often; it was there Daddy gave grinds to students all the time after school and where he kept his books. Upstairs was the breakfast room we ate and lived in mostly, and up from that again were all the other rooms. A few steps down to the back from the hall was the basement kitchen and two rooms off it from the days when people had maids. I hated the darkness and the mice and the cobwebs down there, but I knew it was the only way to go.

I slipped off the oozy, smelly shoes and socks. I could only hope my feet themselves wouldn't stain the hall carpet. Down I went, carrying my disgrace across the cold dusty tiles and up the back wooden stairs into the old servery, our kitchen. Five more steps and I was up into the back of our living room. Mammy was usually lying down now, but today she was ironing something black: Daddy's dinner jacket – the dress dance! I'd forgotten all about it.

Relief flooded over me until I shook. Mammy loved dressing up for dances; she wouldn't be as bad today as another day.

"I wet the floor in school." I held my offerings out from me so they wouldn't do more damage. "I'm sorry, Mammy. It was an accident. I didn't mean it."

She just shook her head slowly and sighed: "I might have known. I might have known you would think of something to spoil today. I have looked forward to this day for months. Why does it always have to be you? Always you. Never Deirdre."

No, Deirdre would never do anything bad, let alone wet the floor in front of the whole class. She never did anything bad, right from not being born ugly and huge like me. My sister, Deirdre, seven years older than me and the living image of Mammy and her side of the family – the side with the looks.

Mammy was looking at my shoes, sodden and spread like two leaky boats. "Get them away from here. Just look at them, Róisín, your second best. Ruined. Well, they'll still have to do you, won't they, even if they do reek to high heaven? Maybe that will teach you if nothing else will."

Just then the hall door slammed. I could hear Deirdre flying up the stairs. Just bursting to tell. She made a face when she saw me there first. "The shame of it," she said. "It's all over the town."

"Tell them she has a kidney infection," said Mammy. "Maybe I should keep her home on Monday, what do you think? What came over her? Why did you do it?" They both turned on me.

I hadn't an answer. None that would please them anyway or make any difference.

"I suppose she thought she could last until the bell went," said Deirdre. "The right eejit." She came over beside me but not too close. "Ugh! Look at her. Every stitch ruined. She managed to get every last stitch she had on her."

Just then the rest of our family arrived: Daddy and my brother, Harry, from the Brothers' school. Daddy taught Latin and Maths at the Brothers' and Harry was in second year there, so they came home together whenever Harry didn't manage to dodge Daddy.

I tried to curl up behind my clothes and escape but Deirdre would not let me pass her. She told Daddy and Harry the big news. But they said nothing, only stood from foot to foot and looked at the ground. I knew that's what they'd do. I knew they at least wouldn't make it worse.

Daddy came up to my room when I had changed my things. "It'll blow over, Róisín. All be the same in a hundred years," he said.

See! I just knew it would take that long. I bawled all over again.

"Sorry, Róisín, wrong saying. How about a nine days' wonder? Do you think you could stand it nine days?"

"Maybe."

"Of course you could. Tell you what: how about a nice walk with me? Would you like that?"

Would I what. I loved walks with just Daddy.

"Come on, so. Your mammy needs a little rest."

Daddy never got cross unless we annoyed Mammy badly. Of course he never ever got cross with her, no matter what terrible things she sometimes said to him. Mammy was the best-looking girl in the university in Dublin in her day and she could have had anyone. Anyone. So of course when she picked my daddy, he realized how lucky he was and he never got cross with her no matter what. I knew the details of their yellowed newspaper wedding cutting by heart: the stunningly statuesque bride, her ivory silk and trailing roses, the dusty pink of her bridesmaids, the continental honeymoon, and charming home on the northwest coast. It sounded just like a fairy tale to me, and I sometimes held Daddy's hand on our walks by the sea and burned with the anger he never showed. How could she be mean to him? Wasn't it all a bride could ever want? Mirror, mirror, on the wall, and the prince loved her so and they lived happily ever after.

"I'm sorry, Daddy," I said to him as we slipped out of the house. I was afraid my disgrace would put Mammy in terrible humour for days. Sometimes Mammy was feeling so bad she had to go to her sister's in Dublin for a little rest. Nearly always around Easter and again when we'd be going back to school in September. She'd be better when she came back – for a while anyway – and then the tears and headaches and rests would start again.

"That's all right, Róisín, no harm done. You couldn't help it."

"Daddy, is it all my fault Mammy gets sad sometimes? Is it because I'm so bad?"

"Nonsense, Róisín. Everyone gets upset now and then. Life is not easy, you know."

"I'll try to be more like Deirdre," I said.

Mammy was always saying how Deirdre was so like she had been herself, a real O'Donnell. The O'Donnells had hands and feet so long and slender that shoes and gloves were very difficult to find narrow enough to fit. The McGoverns had what Mammy called platterpusses. "A fine, big, strong lump of an agricultural Irish girl," the song said. That was me and the McGoverns all over: not difficult to fit, just large. I was all McGovern. So were Daddy and Harry but they were not girls.

Daddy let me choose the way we'd go on our walk. I picked the cliff path back to the Fairy Bridges, of course. He even bought me a Turkish delight. He was always telling me about the year I was five – how every time I opened my mouth it was to beg for turkey's delight. That or a straw hat like Fionnuala's. Turkey's delight and a straw hat like Fionnuala's I wanted for my birthday. Turkey's delight and a straw hat like Fionnuala's, I scribbled to Santa Claus.

The only thing I didn't like about this story was the way he always used it to tell me that the older I got, the more I would realize people couldn't always have what they wanted. But today he didn't.

"Tell me about my name, Daddy."

"I've told you dozens of times already."

"Again Daddy." I squeezed his hand. "Just once more."

"Long ago, poets and musicians were forbidden to speak of Ireland. So instead they sang and told stories of Róisín Dubh."

"Little Dark Rose," I reminded him. "Like a code."

"Yes. Artists will always find a way of keeping the deepest hearts of people alive in troubled times. There were other names too."

But I wasn't interested in them because they weren't mine. "And you called me Róisín because of them."

"Oh no, I just liked the name and your Aunty Róisín is my favourite sister."

"What?" I stood, planted, because he had never told me this before.

"I only realized afterwards, Róisín."

"That's terrible," I wailed, desperate to be called after those lovely things.

"No," said Daddy. "Maybe it's even better this way."

But I was afraid the magic was gone. I was so miserable I was unable to move. He put his arms around me.

"It's all right, Róisín, really. It doesn't matter why you were given a name. Look at the chances against getting it. Pauline? Teresa? Angela? Mmm? Thousands of choices. Someone must have wanted you to get Róisín. Do you see?

"Things are never simple, Róisín. Nothing is as it seems. Look at where we live—how many places could you have been born? But this is your place. And what a magnificent place it is. Other districts are rich in minerals, precious stones—ours is rich in poets called William—" He pointed over the sandhills behind the golf links.

"Over there is the one you love now . . . . 'Up the airy mountain, down the rushy glen . . . . '" Then he swept his arm over the beach to the big mountain between us and Sligo. "Over there is the one you will love later . . . . 'But louder sang that ghost, What then?'"

I didn't think that was any good. Not like up the airy mountain. And little Bridget, dead with sorrow.

My father faced me to the cliff path and to the sea. He kept his arm around my shoulders and whispered:

> "Come away, O human child!
> To the waters and the wild
> With a faery, hand in hand,
> For the world's more full of weeping
>   than you can understand."

Now that was more like it. See, my daddy was cleverer himself than any poet. He knew I would never forget this awful day if I lived to be a hundred. And how did he know I was thinking the Fairy Bridges might help?

"Go, Róisín," he said smiling. "Off you go."

And I did. Ran the wall of death up the high bank of the golf links fence: *Up the airy mountain, down the rushy glen.* And then, avoiding cracks in the path: *We daren't go a-hunting For fear of little men.*

Away around by the golf links and high up over the sea. I stayed well ahead of him to get a few minutes looking down through the big hole in the ground at the Fairy Bridges. There you can feel the pounding and thumping of the sea right under your tummy as you lie; watch the waves rise and crash over the slippery lacy paths – the very ones the fairies who live there have to run along. If you're really quick, you might even see them dodge the boom-bubble suck in and out of the caves they sleep in when the sea is calm.

I turned to look for Daddy then; he had met up with Sergeant Egan and was walking up the path with him, swinging his walking stick. I wasn't too disappointed because although I liked having Daddy to myself, I also liked listening to him chat with Sergeant Egan: Went into the hospital hale and hearty only last Tuesday. You never know, do you. But there were business worries there. You're right. A white elephant that if ever I saw one. Where, Daddy, where? Show me the white elephant.

The tops of their heads bobbed towards me as they battled up the windy hill. My mother says the McGoverns always walk like that – the here's-me-head-and-me-arse-is-coming walk, Harry calls it.

"Magnificent, Raymond, isn't it?" said the sergeant then, looking back towards the town over the lonely curve of autumn beach. Sergeant Egan was ugly, all long and raw pink in the face, like the rabbit hanging at home on the hook in the pantry. The headless skinned one, of course; no one could be as ugly as the other one, hanging waiting in its icy cold fur to swing its sad face and clouded eyes at you.

"Magnificent it is, Paddy," said my father, looking back at the beach too, puffing a bit.

"I love it at this time of the year," Sergeant Egan said. His long face was wet with mist, sparkly beads of it standing on his shaggy

16

black brows. Paddy Eyebrows, we children called him, or Sergeant Eyebrows.

Magnificent? Were the two of them mad? And all the lovely summer things gone: the bright colours, the visitors, the amusements, the palmist. All the lovely summer things. The Dive-Bomber taken down, the tuppenny swimming pool boarded up, and the American Hamburger Kitchen. Nothing but cold, pee-smelly cement shelters left to play in. Magnificent?

"All bleached grey and wild again," said my father. "And so quickly. As if nature can't bear the false colours."

"Nature is right," said the sergeant. "But what else can we do? The town has no industry. No pulse. No choice but to tart itself up for the visitors."

"And worse it gets every year . . . ."

"Don't I know. Yet another pinball arcade. More slot machines, more hucksters –"

"A poor old used whore," said my father softly. "Raddled and tawdry."

I skipped off. Skipped off on those lovely strange words. *Raddled and tawdry, raddled and tawdry.* Like *addled* and *gaudy.* Those words I knew: *addled* was people who didn't always have the right answers even if they were grown up, and *gaudy* was too bright and something not quite right about it. Like the makeup on Miss McAloon, the postmistress: red claws with lumpy, bumpy knuckles behind them. Cakey powder stuck in the caves around her eyes and in the hangings of skin. And a red mouth painted on to try and make you think she had lips of her own.

> *Addled and gaudy, raddled and tawdry,*
> *Bright white elephants, hot addled tarts.*

Great skipping words. I loved words. Not all words, just words like that which sang in my head when I heard them. Not words Daddy put on his special teachery voice to explain: like the Fairy Bridges being marine erosion. Or a *bus* being *omnibus* and really meaning for us all. The stop was a *terminus* and two of them

17

termini. Words like that never sang in my ears, never made me want to skip and dance. Never made me forget for a minute that I wasn't ever going to speak to Ben Thompson again. No, not even after the nine days. Not ever. Not after a disgrace like that which was all his fault.

But one thing was lucky: if I had to be in disgrace, I could have picked a worse time, with Mammy and Daddy off to the dance. Joseph Tomelty was to be the guest of honour; he was down from the Abbey Theatre in Dublin to adjudicate the drama festival, and the dance was the highlight. Mammy liked plays too, and they had been to "Mungo's Mansion," "The Playboy of the Western World," and "Night Must Fall" during the past week. "Night Must Fall" was Mammy's favourite, and I think it would have been mine too: "Icy fingers down your spine," the program said.

Anyway, there was such excitement in our house that Mammy had almost forgotten about my trouble when we got home from the walk. Deirdre was ironing yet more starch into the dicky of Daddy's dress shirt with a handkerchief soaked in cold chalky water. Mammy took over and finished it herself, and then ran the iron over the yellow rustling of her own gorgeous dress – her primrose taffeta she called it.

No movie star in Harry's *Picture Show* magazines looked lovelier than my mammy that night. She wore her long black hair up, but softer than her usual French roll. Over her left ear she wore two yellow flowers which brought out the yellow in her own purply navy eyes. People often said my mother's eyes reminded them of pansies, and Daddy said Elizabeth Taylor was only trotting after her.

"She's the sweetest little rosebud that Texas ever knew.
Her eyes they shone like diamonds and sparkled like the dew.
You may talk about your Clementine or sing of Rosy Lee,
But the Yellow Rose of Texas is the only girl for me."

Daddy sang the words as he whirled Mammy around the living room before they went off. When he stopped, puffing out of breath

18

like a good-natured bear, he smiled and bowed to Mammy. Then he began to sing "The Man from Laramie," with his hand to his heart.

Mammy looked at him with a smile that wasn't a real smile. Don't say anything to him, I prayed, please God, make her not say anything. It wasn't fair. He looked so good and so safe and so nice in his black and white. I knew she thought his hair too bushy to be right, his cheeks too red, and she often called his hands and thighs hams.

But she said nothing tonight. He hung her white fur jacket around her shoulders, his hands patting awkwardly in a way I knew she hated, but she said nothing and off they went. How I wished it could always be like this.

Once they were gone, Deirdre remembered my trouble and she began to go on and on about it. I put my tongue out at her and my fingers in my ears and said Harry was the oldest and he was in charge. He told her shut up, and when she got no satisfaction from him she went up to her room.

But before she went she picked up her own picture off the mantelpiece and smiled at it for a long time. Then, with a na-na-na look at me, she put it back. I just knew she was thinking there would never be such a beautiful photograph of me.

That photograph was there on our mantelpiece as long as I remember. It was taken when she was about my age – she was thirteen now. In it she was wearing a blue cloud of a dress, with tons of dark smocking, and little ribbons around bunches of violets here and there. It was still up in our spare room but far too tight to do up on me; Mammy had it specially made when she was chosen to sing "My Sweet Little Alice Blue Gown" for Reverend Mother's feast day. She wore a straw bonnet with tiny velvet violets to match, tied under her chin off to one side with a violet bow. Everyone who came into our house looked at Deirdre in that photo and said how gorgeous she was and the living image of Mammy. They said she would be a real beauty when she grew up and give them all a run for their money.

It wasn't fair. No one ever told me I was a picture; there were no Alice blue gowns made for me, no straw hats strewn with flowers.

Fionnuala Fitzgerald in my class had the most beautiful straw hat. It was shaped like a Chinaman's hat, with a crown of coloured velvet flowers on top. When she first told me about it and that it tied under her chin with crimson velvet ribbons, I didn't know what colour crimson was. I hoped it might be like cream because maybe I could bear that. But when I actually saw the hat and that crimson was lovely bright red, I nearly cried right then and there I was so jealous. She wore the hat forward sometimes so the flowers showed the best; sometimes she wore it right down like a shield across her shoulders. Just as if she had run miles and miles out of a storybook and her hat had blown off with the effort.

I prayed every night for a straw hat like Fionnuala's. Because then I too would be a storybook girl, and there would be pictures of me on the mantelpiece in my Alice blue gown. And no one would dream of making me wear Harry's castoff coats again. I wouldn't have minded if they were Deirdre's, but her clothes would never look at the likes of me.

I stood on tiptoe outside Deirdre's bedroom door, longing to be asked in. Aching to be part of the dressing-table games she and Mammy went on with all the time. I sometimes stole empty cream jars and perfume bottles out of the waste-paper basket in Mammy's room and filled them with crushed rose petals and water, but they just made a stink instead of perfume.

"Go to bed, Róisín McGovern," shouted Deirdre, through her closed bedroom door. "I'll tell Mammy on you – what time you went to bed at. I'd have thought you made enough of a nuisance of yourself for one day."

So I went. And I did get ready for bed but I couldn't sleep. I could hear Deirdre pitter-pattering to Mammy's room and then back to her own. What was she doing? At last I couldn't stand it another minute and I went out once again to the toilet.

Deirdre's door was slightly open this time. Through it I could see her standing at her mirror, wearing an old purple ball gown of Mammy's. She had her hair piled up on her head. She had lipstick and rouge and everything on her. She looked at least nineteen. She was holding out the mauve net of the skirt whirling around la-la-ing to herself.

"I s'pose you think you're lovely," I shouted from the door. "Well, you're not." As it seemed to be an evening for singing tributes, I opened up my throat and bellowed:

> "After the ball was over
> Deirdre took out her glass eye;
> Put her false teeth in a basin,
> Locked up her bottle of dye;
> Put her cork leg in a corner,
> Hung up her hair on the wall.
> Then there was not much of Deirdre
> After the ball . . . ."

By the end I was shouting instead of singing, trying to annoy Deirdre, but she only smiled. She smiled at my hot, angry face and my solid lump of a body in the pink flannel pyjamas.

Then she too began to sing ever so softly and slowly:

> "Rafferty's pig was a wonderful animal,
> Built like a battleship solid and stout.
> Her appetite would have disgraced any cannibal;
> Ignorance was written all over her snout.
>
> The night she got loose there was such a commotion,
> Women were screaming and men turning pale.
> There was running and jumping, colliding and bumping
> And everyone making a grab at her tail."

I ran and slammed my bedroom door and stuck my fingers in my ears, but it was no good; I could still hear her annoying voice, raised higher now. I drummed my fingers in and out of my ears to mix up the sound, but it didn't matter because I knew all the words anyway. And knew how right they were. I was Rafferty's pig all right and no straw hat would ever make this sow's ear into a silk purse. Not ever. Little Dark Rose, indeed.

In spite of prayers for burst heating pipes, hurricanes, earthquakes, scarlet fever – anything that would keep the school closed the next Monday or me out of it – ten past nine found me unwillingly there and no disaster but the memory of my own.

Well, at least there was one thing I could do: I could carry out my promise never to speak to Ben Thompson again.

That would be easier said than done. It would mean facing the whole school at recreation in the yard during all the *sos* breaks. And that was something I hated at the best of times, never mind in the face of present shame.

Up to this, Ben Thompson and I always sat out *sos*. While the screaming and chasing, the jibes and rhymes went on outside the class window, Ben Thompson turned into a different person altogether in private. As soon as the others charged out to the *sos* bell, he would slide his slate out from underneath his desk. Without a word, and with the only smiles I ever saw on his face, his long thin fingers would begin to fly.

We all learned our drawing in class by chalking on slates. Try as we might, our tongues bitten in concentration, the results were pretty dismal compared to what was in our minds. The girls produced deformed fronts of houses, lopsided paths hanging in midair from their hall doors and three spiky flowers struggling on either side. The boys liked square cowboys, one spurred boot pointing east, the other west.

But Ben Thompson . . . Ben Thompson was different.

He drew fat donkeys that looked at me every bit as wisely as the real ones in the tinkers' fields. His roads all seemed to be going somewhere, with humpy bridges and sturdy stone walls that would stand up to the worst Atlantic gales. He drew round rosy people who carried their lives in their faces and in their bodies. Even my father couldn't touch Ben Thompson when it came to drawing. I thought he was the cleverest boy in the whole world.

But that was then. Before he ruined my life.

I wasn't going to play with him anymore, that was for sure and certain. There would be no more *sos* with Ben Thompson. Not on your life. It would be out to play for me from now on. Out to the barren playground, an acre of pocked cement.

Here we go gathering nuts in May, nuts in May, nuts in May. Here we go gathering nuts in May, on a cold and frosty morning. Ah no, that's no good; that's useless; nothing happens in that. Giant Steps is miles better. No, we played that yesterday. Red Light, Green Light? Naw. Tig? Oh yes, yes, Tig. We'll play Tig and Róisín's it.

"You're it, you're it," they all shouted, and obediently I lumbered after Bernadette Gibbons. Only I was too heavy, too tall, and too awkward. My body would never obey me, never run as fast as I wanted it to.

"Can't catch, can't catch," Bernadette Gibbons taunted and mocked in glee, flashing in and out under London Bridges and through farmers wanting wives. And I never once caught.

I tried skipping, patiently turning the rope for everyone else until at last it was my turn to jump in.

> *Cinderella dressed in yella*
> *Went out to meet her fella.*
> *How many kisses did she give him?*

It was a great rope for skipping we had then; Margie Duffy got it off her father's trawler. *Cinderella dressed in yella* . . . . I always meant to get to thirty kisses at least. But I wouldn't even have got to the first kiss when the circling axe sliced through my ankles. Out! Róisín McGovern! Out.

Maybe *sos* with Ben Thompson wasn't so bad after all; I went back to him.

He said nothing, just as if I'd never been away. Again he drew out the slate and his fingers flew. And again his face lost that look of having no one behind it; it took on a smile and a little pink. But let the first clanging of the coming-in bell be heard and Ben Thompson would change. Madly he'd start to scrub off the slate with his sleeve in case anyone might see what he'd drawn. Then back under the desk the slate would go, the smile slithering with it. And he'd call back as much of himself as he could, like a snail. Nothing left but a head of tatty red curls undefended.

"Honestly, Róisín McGovern," said Bernadette Gibbons one day, "I don't know why you bother with Ben Thompson. Don't you know he's the stupidest boy in the whole school?"

"He is not, Bernadette Gibbons. That's what you think."

Contradicting Bernadette Gibbons was dangerous. She was the nearest thing our class had to a film star, and so her opinions carried a lot of weight, particularly with the girls. I was no exception. Clouds of white-blonde hair waved and rippled down Bernadette Gibbons's back all the time, not just on a Sunday morning after rags on Saturday night. That hair was the inspiration for all our dreams. My own hair was long, too – if you pulled it. Let it go, though, and it sprang back to my ears in corkscrews. I struggled and struggled to get it into flowing ringlets like Bernadette's, but on me they always came out like tight spikes on the world's biggest hedgehog.

"He's the stupidest, thickest boy in the whole school," said Bernadette Gibbons again, with a flick of that white hair in my face.

"He is not. He can draw pictures better than anyone. As good as a book."

"Oh yeah? How is it we haven't seen any of them yet?"

"I have."

"You? Sure you wouldn't know a good picture from a hole in the ground."

"I would so. And he's not stupid."

"If he was any good, we'd see it in drawing class, Róisín McGovern. But he's as stupid there as he is everywhere else. He doesn't know B from a bull's foot. He disgraced the whole school

24

the day the inspector was here. He's nothing but an eejit and he'll be an eejit till the day he dies."

"He is not an eejit, Bernadette Gibbons. You're just jealous. You couldn't draw a line straight to save your life."

"Me, jealous? Of Ben Thompson? Well, that's a laugh. You must be as stupid as he is. You can't even play Tig."

"Sticks and stones – "

"You're as big as a mountain, Róisín McGovern."

"May break my bones – "

"You pissed on the floor."

"But words will – "

"You wear your brother's coat, Róisín McGovern."

"That's a lie, Bernadette Gibbons. It is not my brother's coat, it only looks like it. I hate you, Bernadette Gibbons – "

"Na-na-na . . . and I hate you back, Róisín McGovern. And it is so your brother's coat. And what's more, I'm telling."

She did too. She told every single person in the cloakroom who would listen. And then there were loud whispers behind bitten nails as to what other boys' clothes Róisín McGovern might be wearing unknown to everyone: whisper, whisper – underpants.

Yes, I hated Bernadette Gibbons. And I hated Mammy for making me wear that coat. "He's eight years older than you, no one will even remember it," she said. But she'd never have made Deirdre wear it. Not even if it wasn't miles too big for her. She'd never have made Deirdre wear that huge strealish boy's coat.

The more Bernadette teased, the more desperate I was to get rid of that coat. I tried missing my coat hook in the school cloakroom with it in hopes a bit of trampling might somehow make it unwearable. Not a chance. It was a ton weight, double seamed, and what Mammy called worsted. Which was the reason it had survived Harry in the first place and was too good to be given away. Brushed and dusted off it was as immortal as ever, dozens of winters ahead of it yet, three of them at least on me.

One morning after a worse show than usual by Bernadette Gibbons, I stayed behind in the cloakroom when the others all went to class. Late and miserable, I noticed Ben Thompson standing in a corner. I stopped crying long enough to stick out my tongue at him. Useless and silent and watching as always – it was all his fault anyway. I would never have had that fight with Bernadette Gibbons only for him. And it would never, ever end because I would be stuck with that lousy coat as long as I lived. I couldn't just "lose" it; everyone in the whole world knew whose it was now and who to return it to with millions of jokes. I was stuck with it. I put my tongue out at Ben Thompson again just for good measure. There was no end to my trouble and every bit of it was his fault.

And then Ben Thompson came over. Without a word he took the coat from me and walked towards the cloakroom door. He moved the coat already hanging on the hook nearest the door away and hung mine in its place. He looked at it for a minute and then he took a penknife out of his pocket – the kind you could win in some slot machines down by the amusements. He began to fiddle with one of the long, triangular hinges of the door. He loosened the screw and bent the sharp point at the end of the hinge back a bit. He ran his finger over the sharp part and smiled. Next he pinched up a piece of coat, and opening the door back, he began to thread it on the hinge. I caught on at last.

"Not there, Ben," I whispered. "She could mend it or put a badge on it there. Not that part. It'll have to be somewhere Mammy couldn't possibly fix."

I showed him where, and he took his penknife and poked his way into the material. Then he worked the hole he'd poked over the sharp end of the hinge. He pulled it tighter, making a bigger hole. We closed the cloakroom door and the strain on the coat was awful. We began to laugh: it was only when the door was closed you could really see what a mess the coat was in. And everybody was supposed to be on the other side of that closed door at class. You could go in and out, all right, if you had *cead dul amach*. You opened that door as you went in and closed it when you came

26

out. All day long people with *cead dul amach* came and went.

Suddenly I didn't care if it was a quarter past nine and I was dead late for class. After all, it was only a quarter past nine, and by half past three, with everybody opening and closing that door all day, Harry's coat was not going to be immortal anymore.

"Oh, Sister," I wailed to Sister Columba when I saw the damage to my good coat that afternoon. That was when she had finally managed to locate it after the cloakroom emptied. "Because I just couldn't find it, Sister . . . . It wasn't on my hook . . . . It wasn't on any of the hooks around . . . . It wasn't anywhere, Sister."

"Is this it, Róisín?"

"Yes, Sister. Oh yes. But what's wrong with it?"

"It seems to be caught on the hinge. Oh dear, it's been quite badly damaged."

"I'll be killed, Sister."

"It's not your fault, child. It just got caught on a loose hinge. It's nobody's fault. But why wasn't it on your own hook?"

"I don't know, Sister. It's awful heavy and it falls off the hook sometimes. I'm always finding it on the floor. Someone must have found it on the floor and just hung it there as they went out the door. I'll be killed, Sister."

"Don't be ridiculous, child. You couldn't help it."

"Mammy'll never believe me."

"Of course she will. I will send her a note."

"Oh thank you, Sister."

After that I liked Ben Thompson all over again. He drew pictures of my favourite songs and stories as I told him the words:

> "Down along the rocky shore
> Some make their home;
> They live on crispy pancakes
> Of yellow tide-foam . . . ."

And my very favourite part:

> "They stole little Bridget
> For seven years long;
> When she came down again
> Her friends were all gone.
> They took her lightly back,
> Between the night and morrow,
> They thought that she was fast asleep,
> But she was dead with sorrow.
> They have kept her ever since
> Deep within the lake,
> On a bed of flag-leaves,
> Waiting till she wake."

Ben drew them all for me. The little men weeping around Bridget. Green jackets, white caps. And white owls' feathers drooping and askew with all the weeping.

"Oh yes, Ben, yes. Just like our own Snow White," I said, enthralled that Ben drew the pictures just like the ones I had in my own head. Often Daddy, or a teacher, read us a story and I would be disgusted to see the illustrations afterwards and find they weren't a patch on what I had imagined.

Fionnuala Fitzgerald was the only other person who would play this, my favourite game, with me. And Lorcan Burke, sometimes. Ben didn't actually play it, except for the drawing during *sos*.

But Fionnuala played. Her mother used to give her permission to play at my house. She would have died if she'd known her precious darling was not at my house but climbing the island. No use telling her it was only a great big rock. Or that the worst which could happen would be getting cut off there by the tide for a few hours. You could be cold up there and hungry, maybe, but not in any danger. The climb up was what Lorcan Burke called a "dead cinch." Come to think of it, if girls could do anything at all, then that activity immediately became a dead cinch.

28

Anyway, the three of us loved the island. We could march around in the wind, screaming our heads off, and no one would ever hear us:

> "We daren't go a-hunting
> For fear of little men."

Fionnuala and I usually arrived first. We might be spotted on the way by Lorcan Burke, and in no time at all he'd be swarming up the back, more difficult face to meet us. We would each then insist on our own especially beloved bits, but nobody minded. Because all the bits were beloved – either favourites or favourite favourites.

Ben Thompson played without actually playing. He would allow us to catch sight of his red curls in the bushes, but could never be prevailed on to join us. There was one part that always seemed right for Ben Thompson:

> "High on the hilltop
> The old King sits;
> He is now so old and grey
> He's nigh on lost his wits."

Fionnuala and I would say those words and then Lorcan Burke joined in. We'd have whispered, but Lorcan would shout:

> "With a bridge of white mist
> Columbkill he crosses,
> On his stately journeys
> From Slieveleague to the Rosses."

As if to coax him, Lorcan Burke would run a few steps, drawing back his bow and arrow. We had a cache of props hidden on the island – things Lorcan Burke would not have been seen dead with at school: capes, crown, swords. Girl sort of things, dress-up things.

> "Or going up with music
> On cold starry nights,
> To sup with the Queen
> Of the gay Northern Lights."

Well, there was probably more chance of the Queen seeing Ben Thompson since no amount of asking would get him to join us. So we'd get on with it ourselves.

And even though my very favourite favourite was little Bridget being dead of sorrow, somehow it was always Fionnuala who played that part. I didn't mind. It was right it should have been her.

I went on hoping Ben Thompson would come and join us. First maybe on the island, then in the classroom. I kept waiting for the day he would show everyone, and not just me, exactly what he could do. The day when he would show Sister Columba he could draw fifty times better than she could; when he would begin to answer questions in class; when he would show them all that someone did live in Ben Thompson after all. But that someone was proud and would only come and go as Ben chose. He would come sometime, he would.

But he didn't. Instead, it all got worse and worse until Sister Columba stopped asking Ben Thompson questions altogether. And then the end came. I remember the day very well – it was the day we got our Christmas holidays.

First, the whole school went over to the church to see the crib and sing carols. Then we had prize-giving when we got back to our classrooms. I got second place in the class, after Fionnuala Fitzgerald, and that meant I got to pick the very picture I wanted: the one of Our Lady of Perpetual Succour. It had the most lovely colours: nearly all gold, with red and blue and green as well. It hadn't any plain white background anywhere in it and was framed in glass with lovely gold edging. I could hardly wait to show it to my daddy.

Bernadette Gibbons said it was gaudy, but that was just because there was only a tiny one of the Little Flower left for her turn, and it was nearly all white background. She said it was simple and elegant, but if it was all that nice, how was it no one picked it before her? It was not elegant at all – I bet it was the very last of the Christmas and feast-day cards Sister Columba had saved to make those prizes.

We had a party then with biscuits and cocoa, and we all brought presents for our nun. All the classes did that. I had Cusson's Apple Blossom Talcum Powder. Fionnuala Fitzgerald had black stockings to give Sister Columba, because her mother said they would be far more useful than all that soap and notepaper stuff and sweets she must be sick to death of.

But Sister Columba didn't open the presents in front of us, so we didn't know whether she was pleased with the stockings or not. Of course Fionnuala only told the girls about them and not the boys. We all giggled: we had never before considered Sister Columba might have legs that went all the way up and how she might keep up the stockings.

It really was about the best day ever in school so far, that day. I even brought pennies for the black babies. We had this box for the African missions, with a black baby on top – well, his head, anyway. And when you put in your penny the sharp thing you'd hit underneath would make his head go up and down, nodding his thanks. I had four pennies that day, and I only kept one for myself because it was nearly Christmas and you should be good to the black babies because you could easily have been one yourself.

And the best part: we got to dress up – to be witches and clowns and cowboys – oh, and everything.

It was close to going-home time when Fionnuala Fitzgerald turned white and said she was going to be sick. Sister Columba got her by the elbow and dragged her outside in an awful hurry. So we were left on our own and a bit giddy.

Crunchies O'Laughlin was especially giddy, having been kept back a year with the nuns when he could be with the Brothers – and still found himself last for the holy picture before Ben

Thompson. Crunchies' real name was Francis, but Proinsias in Irish. Proinsias rhymes beautifully with Crunchies, so that's what we called him.

But if he was behind us at schoolwork, he made up for it in boldness. He swept up a black cloak we had for dress-up and tossed it around himself. He tied a white handkerchief underneath around his face. There was no mistaking who he was meant to be.

"This class is the very worst I've come across in all my years of teaching." There was great uproar and laughing, banging the desks and stamping feet.

"You're all thick as double ditches," said Crunchies. More guffaws and sniggers, one eye on him, one on the door.

"Well, I declare to my stars, Ben Thompson," he said then, "but very smart you're looking today. And do you think now you could spell *cat* for us all?"

Giggles burst out behind hands everywhere.

"May God and His Holy Mother give me patience with the lot of you." That only brought more giggles.

I looked over at Ben Thompson. His head was down as always, hiding his face. But I could see his fists under the desk, with the knuckles white tight.

"Stop it," I heard my own voice. "Would you just stop it!"

"Well, if it isn't Miss Goody-goody herself," said Crunchies. "And how many times have I told you not to prompt Ben Thompson, Róisín McGovern?"

There were roars and cheers and claps.

"Oh, don't give out to Róisín McGovern, *Sister*." It was a girl's voice this time – I knew it was Bernadette Gibbons, even without looking. "She'll only wet the floor on you."

"Hey, give it up lads," roared Lorcan Burke from the window. "She's coming back; she's crossing the yard."

There was a mad scramble while everyone got settled again. There was only a bit of heavy breathing and the odd snort to be heard when Sister Columba walked in.

It was after that I gave up on Ben Thompson.

It wasn't just Ben Thompson, it was all boys. Lorcan Burke never spoke to us girls now if anyone was looking. And we were getting closer and closer to the end of the school year when we would go our separate ways: the boys to the Brothers' school, the girls remaining with the nuns in the convent. Already we were separating ourselves. The desks in our classroom were double desks; we all had to share. Girls now wanted to sit only with girls, boys with boys. And that's the way it was, except for Ben Thompson, who always had a whole desk to himself.

Primly we girls sat, gym-slips gathered in tight around and under us. To keep in the pleats, we said, but really it was to make sure no one could possibly ever see our knickers again.

Now it was only in punishment a girl would sit beside a boy. Being put beside a boy was for small things: not as bad as being put face to the wall and certainly not as bad as outside the door. It was for venial sins, like the time I was caught talking to Bernadette Gibbons:

"Róisín McGovern, what did you say?"

"Nothing, Sister."

"Don't add a lie to it, Miss. Tell the class immediately what was so important you had to take Bernadette Gibbons away from her tables."

"Nothing, Sister, honestly."

"Oh, really? Perhaps you might like to go to Sister Ursula's office and tell her this nothing of yours, would you?"

"I was just asking Bernadette if she'd play with me after school, Sister."

"I'll give you play if I catch you talking and disturbing my class again. Is that clear, my lady? Go and sit beside one of the boys now and we might get our tables done."

I looked around the classroom: Jimmy Lavelle was the only boy absent today, so his place beside Crunchies O'Laughlin was empty. There was no one beside Ben Thompson, of course.

Slowly I walked down to the bottom of the classroom. I stopped for a second as everyone pretended not to look, but some sniggered. Ben Thompson's head was down as usual, but I knew in a way he, too, was watching, he more than anyone.

I passed Ben Thompson's desk, walked up the next aisle, and perched on the very edge of the seat beside – but as far away as I could get from – Crunchies O'Laughlin.

If I have made that walk once in my mind since, I have made it a thousand times. And every time I cry for not sitting beside Ben Thompson. Because I lost a lot more than I saved that day.

I never saw Ben Thompson on the island again. And Lorcan, Fionnuala, and I gave up playing the game. We had not realized that part of the magic was being watched by the old King high on the hilltop. The old King had gone, with his music and his journeys to the Queen of the gay Northern Lights. He hadn't nigh on lost his wits – he had lost them.

All I could hope was that they were in the lake with Bridget. Waiting until she wake.

I knew something was gone forever. I wanted someone to hold me and tell me it would be all right – everything would be all right. There was no one. The only one I could think of who might help was Harry. Not that I thought for a minute Harry would hold on to me and comfort me. Far from it. But there was something comforting in his very rudeness.

I worshipped him. Never mind that while the nuns were cramming my head with hellfire at school, Harry was filling it with vampires and werewolves at home. Never mind that between them they were creating a horse of a most peculiar colour – one to unseat any poor child fool enough to ride it – and I took an almighty tumble. Never mind, never mind, I worshipped him.

The show-biz bug bit Harry very early in life and never let go its hold. As long and as far back as I can remember, his room bulged with paraphernalia from the world of cinema. He had every fan magazine that ever rolled off a press, and by age sixteen he had discovered that not only could he see all the films he ever wanted, he could actually be paid to do so. First he persuaded Mr. Twomey, the cinema owner, to let him help clean up the floors. For free admission he happily prised chewing gum off the seats and swept up cigarette butts and Yorkshire toffee wrappers.

But soon he was whispering to Mr. Twomey what publications might expand a manager's knowledge and so his profits. And then he was pointing out what films might be best suited to keeping Mr. Twomey's cinema packed with satisfied customers. In no time at all the films arriving in Duneen reflected the very macabre but profitably attuned mind of Harry McGovern. The cinema was thriving, everyone very happy with the arrangements, and no one more so than Harry. He was on the payroll now and part-time projectionist.

I landed head first by accident into Harry's strange world. It happened one day the whole family went on a shopping trip to the city. Well, at least Mammy and Deirdre were going shopping; Daddy was going paying and Harry and I were just going because that was the easiest thing to do with us. Harry tried to make good his escape the minute we got there, but Daddy had other plans for him:

"I want you to take Róisín to a film," said Daddy, collaring him firmly.

"But, Dad, I have a few things to do myself," said Harry.

No one wanted Róisín.

"Oh, yes?" said Daddy. "And what, might I ask, would they be?"

"Just a few things," said Harry, kicking the pavement as if he'd like it to be me.

"Fine, but you take her too. I want you to take her to see *The Great Day*. It's on at the Lyceum."

"What?" said Harry. "That's a lousy old tear-jerker, Dad."

"That may well be, but you'll do as you're told. I've heard it would be an excellent choice for her."

"But, Dad—"

"Not another word, Harry. Here's some extra money. Now off with you."

"Yeah, okay, Dad."

"Good lad. *The Great Day*, now mind."

Harry walked until we were out of sight; then he took off at a run through the sidestreets, me limping fatly up the rear. At last he stopped outside a cinema with this huge picture of a lovely little boy in a tasselled white suit, a bit like a prince's or a soldier's.

"Stay there a minute," said Harry to me as he disappeared in through the doors of the cinema. But I was afraid he'd leave me, so I followed him. He had collared a woman inside, just going through a door marked Private.

"Is the picture any good, Missus?" he said.

"Lovely," she said. "And is this your little sister? Aren't you the nice lad to be bringing your sister to the pictures. In this

36

day and age . . . well, well, sure there's hope for us yet. I – "

"Is it the one about the little fella who can't afford the suit for his First Communion?" said Harry, stopping her dead.

"It is," she said, smiling.

"And he loses his arm in some machine, trying to earn the price of a suit?"

"Don't spoil the end for her," said the woman.

"Cripes," said Harry in disgust. "I knew it was that bad. C'mon," he said, pulling me out the door of the cinema again.

"But . . . but . . . aren't we going to see it, Harry? Daddy said . . . ." I wanted to see the suit. I wanted to see the little boy. Most of all I wanted to see if they'd show him without the arm. I wanted to cry and cry for him.

"Ah no," said Harry. "That's a lousy film. You'd hate it. Anyway, we know the end now. What good is it when you know the end? I'll bring you somewhere much nicer, you'll see."

We were off and running again, me panting behind. I was gasping with a stitch in my side when Harry stopped at last and I struggled up to him.

This time we were at another cinema, but this one wasn't nearly as swanky. There were no pictures of lovely little boys here, only pictures of screaming women, and over the door in huge jaggedy sort of letters it said: I WAS A TEENAGE WEREWOLF.

"Listen carefully, Róisín," said Harry, holding my arm tight. "I'm going to tell that man inside if he stops us that you want to go to the toilet. You do that, and when you come out you're to walk straight on down past the sweets there and I'll be waiting with your ticket. Don't look at anybody and don't stop. They might make a mistake and think you're too small a girl to be going to the pictures."

I didn't know how they could think that because everyone said I was as big as an elephant. Far bigger than anyone else in my class. But I did as he told me and we went to the pictures. Harry seemed to enjoy it: he bit his nails all through and shushed me any time I asked him was it nearly over. I got so frightened once the *thing* came from that perfectly ordinary boy that I spent the rest of the time down on the floor with the popcorn, the lemonade bottles, and the Orange Maid wrappers.

I had nightmares for weeks afterwards. Harry told my parents he wasn't at all surprised; there had been a scene in *The Great Day* where the poor child in the film lost his arm in a machine. In his opinion it was enough to give any sensitive child nightmares. Meanwhile, he told me quietly that if I said anything to anyone about the werewolf, there were a few things he happened to know that Mammy and Daddy might be very interested to hear. He only had to mention a few – like the spot Lorcan Burke and I found where you could watch courting couples from, and the playing doctor he saw once – to have me on my knees in obedience. But pretend obedience – somehow I knew Harry would never tell things like that to Mammy and Daddy.

No, he was always threatening to tell on me and Lorcan Burke, but I knew he wouldn't. It was all part of the fun. He often let us into the cinema after school or on a Sunday, and during the summer he always told me if he saw Lorcan Burke heading for one of our secret places, so I could find him there.

No, Harry was not a cruel tormentor by nature. And in return for silence he showed me his secret drawer. He had found a magic compartment in his wardrobe by accident. He said it was for locking away jewellery and private treasures in the old days. You touched a certain spot and the drawer swung open. This he did, but he couldn't show me exactly where – then it wouldn't be secret anymore, would it?

Inside were Harry's private treasures. There were tricks and practical jokes, rubber rats and spiders, a tiny, rock-hard loaf a magician threw off a stage in Belfast once that Harry caught, and a ventriloquist's little dummy head, which moved its eyes and mouth when its knobs were pulled.

Harry said these weren't really his special treasures anymore, they were kids' stuff, and he might even give me some of them some time. There were only two things in the whole lot now he still liked: one was a skull that was an ashtray. It wore golden glasses, with two cigarette rests in the eyeholes. And then there was his all-time favourite: his pack of marked cards.

These cards looked exactly like any others to me. They were the same sort of dirty white colour, they had the jack and the king, the three and the joker: every card exactly the same as in any pack. Their backs were ordinary: navy swirls and flourishes and flowers. Try as I might, I couldn't see anything special at all about them. Then Harry showed me their exciting secret: if you looked at them closely, you could see that the centre of one of the flowers in the corner was in fact a clock. It didn't have numbers, of course, just little dots, but everyone knew where four on a clock would be and so on. If the card was an eight, the clock said eight, eleven the jack, twelve the queen, blank for the king, and one the ace. And the little flower clock was the same in all the corners, so you could read it no matter how the other person held his hand. Unless, of course, he held his cards glued together an inch from his nose, in which case Harry felt he wasn't the type to be parted from his money in any event, and would move on to greener pastures.

I told him this was stealing in case he didn't know, but he said he never took from anyone who didn't owe him or have it coming to him. He said he was sort of like Robin Hood.

Well, that would have been that – because try as I might, I could never find the way to open that drawer again – but one day Harry left his cards unattended when Mr. Twomey called him off suddenly. He had been playing cards with Deirdre. He seemed to be winning a lot and she losing, and finally she threw down her cards and flounced off in temper. It was soon after that Mr. Twomey called for Harry and off he went.

I took the cards and hid them in my bedroom. I only wanted them for a little while, just for one great morning in school well away from Harry's sight. But he came back with Mr. Twomey in double-quick time. He missed the cards immediately, said little, but set about trapping the thief his own way.

I was a fool to think I could get away with it, even for a minute. Not with Harry, of all people. Not with the nightly lessons from Boris Karloff, Vincent Price, and Lon Chaney . . . . He played cat and mouse with me and he had no shortage of ideas: lights would go off on me all by themselves, boards and doors creaked behind me, and I'd hear dragging, limping footsteps in the dark.

And then one night he went further: "Listen you," he said out of the corner of his mouth as I passed him to go up to bed. "Do you remember that werewolf in the film? D'you remember yon film I took you to?"

"I do," I whispered.

"Well, I didn't like to tell you this before," said Harry, "but I think now maybe you should be warned. He lives up there" – Harry pointed to the trapdoor in the top-landing ceiling.

We lived in a tall narrow house. There were three bedrooms on the top floor, but I had the only one which was occupied. Outside my door was the trapdoor to the attic. The rooms on either side of me were junk rooms, full of heavy old antiques that Mammy brought home from auctions or moved up from downstairs when she got something she liked better. Some day she would refinish those pieces, she said. And some day the unpopular ones would come back into style again and be worth a fortune, she said. Meanwhile, she just kept bringing more home and piling more up in the spare rooms beside me. Sometimes I played house with my dolls there, pretending this was my furnished mansion. But it was lonely up there, and, of course, having Bernadette Gibbons or even quiet Fionnuala would be the very worst thing for Mammy's headaches.

"The werewolf lives up there," continued Harry, nodding and jerking his thumb towards the trapdoor. "But he's not allowed to come down unless to take revenge on someone who's really askin' for it. Say someone tellin' lies or stealin' something that doesn't belong to her. It'd be only to someone terrible like that he'd be let down. So you don't have to worry. Still, it's best to know these things, isn't it? To be prepared in case, God forbid, he ever did get down. And you'd be the first to know, bein' nearest him. You'd know immediately because he always makes this noise – "

Harry screwed up his eyes for a minute and then slowly pulled out his chain of medals from under his shirt. He shook them softly and they made a quiet noise like that incense thing the altar boys swing during devotions.

Harry had made a big mistake: if only he'd left the noise the werewolf made to my imagination, he'd have been away with it. But what werewolf worth his salt would announce his arrival to the sound of Harry's Miraculous, his Saint Christopher, and his Lourdes? Honestly, it was as bad as Daddy trying to tell me you could buy babies for five pounds at the hospital. Didn't any half-wit know the tinkers never had five shillings, let alone five pounds, and they had more children than the old woman in the shoe. I knew for certain then Harry was playing a game with me. My fear took on a lovely shiver at the edges.

From then on I was nearly disappointed if there wasn't a glove tacked on the wall and sticking out behind my curtain; or a pair of boots, toes up and soles out from under the bed. I bit my nails waiting for the sound of Harry's medals to approach, the key to fall out of the lock, or the knob to turn slowly. I knew somehow that although Harry was supposed to be frightening me, I had the upper hand. I could no more have put words to it then than I could have understood it; but I needed no words for the lovely mix of excitement and dread as I turned off my bedroom light and dived for the safety of the bed, or closed the door on the blazing living room and broke my neck for the next light.

I did try and return the cards to Harry's room, but he was having none of it. Not for a minute was he going to give up the pleasure of catching the criminal himself. All he had to do was wait; when he was home he sat cross-legged on his bed, rereading his many movie magazines in case there were any little bits he might have missed the other times or at the cinema. And whenever Harry could be persuaded to leave his treasures and go out, he now locked his door.

I know he did because I used to watch him, waiting my chance to return the cards. Around the corner from my landing and down over the bannister I watched for hours, but he never gave me that chance. Once he did actually go off without locking his door, and I was already on the fourth step down when he came back whistling to himself without hardly a sound.

"Well, if it isn't the young one herself. And where are you off to with that guilty red face on you?"

"You mind your own business, Harry McGovern. Where I go and what I do is none of your business."

"Isn't it then? I wouldn't be too sure of that now, Miss. You might just have made it my business a while back there with those light fingers of yours, mightn't you?"

"That's a lie, Harry McGovern. I never touched your silly old cards. That's a terrible lie. And if you don't leave me alone, I'll tell Daddy on you."

"I don't think you will. Not with all I know about a young one who trots up to Holy Communion as if butter wouldn't melt in her mouth. Do you know that's sacrilege? And on top of stealing and lying, too. Three commandments, no less. Not to mention certain other ones."

I wasn't too sure what *sacrilege* was, but it sounded bad. Still, I'd take my chances: "Prove it first, Harry McGovern. And what's more, seeing as you're so fond of the commandments, I learned the eighth one, too, did you? Thou shalt not bear false witness against thy neighbour. That means you can't go around telling lies about people. And I bet it's much worse against your own sister than your neighbour any day."

But Harry had me a bit shook now. God and the commandments were a different proposition altogether. God was everywhere, not just in Hollywood. I'd rather a werewolf had it in for me any day than Him. And if God was fed up with you, the devil was always right behind on the lookout.

It didn't take him long to find me.

I woke up one morning shortly afterwards to a succession of strange noises. The sounds were coming from the unoccupied junk room next to mine: a shriek, followed by a fierce whacking sort of noise, and then a thump. The noises kept on like that, and first I hugged myself and wondered what delights Harry had dreamed up for me this time. Silly, stupid old Harry. Did he think

I didn't know that all werewolves and vampires have to be off home, like Cinderellas, before cock-crow? It was nearly broad daylight outside now. I smiled and yawned beneath the covers.

The noises continued, and it wasn't until I remembered that Harry had never been known to separate himself from his bed until noon – let alone in this dawn chill – that I began to be really frightened.

No, that was silly. There was nothing to be frightened of ever; I knew that. But there had to be some reason for the noises I was hearing. I would go calmly and quietly down the two flights to my parents' room and tell them something was wrong upstairs.

I set off downstairs. As I passed the open door to the spare room something zoomed at me in the half-light, whizzed past my cheek with black force, and disappeared over the door. Suddenly I had no doubt.

"Daddy! Oh, Daddy! It's the devil! He's upstairs and he's trying to get me."

I hurled myself at him as he came running up: "It's the devil, I tell you. Don't go in or he'll get you."

"Nonsense, Róisín," said Daddy. "It couldn't be anything like that. You wait here and I'll go and see."

I sat on my hunkers in the corner of the landing with my hands and my arms covering my head, afraid to look or even to listen. I nearly jumped out of my skin when something touched me: it was Daddy with a big black thing pressed between his palms. "Here's your devil, Róisín," he said. "It's only a poor old jackdaw that got trapped in the chimney. With no fires ever in those chimneys, God knows what's up there in the way of nests."

"Come on now, Róisín, and we'll set him free," said Daddy. We took the bird over to the window in my room. I opened it and Daddy set the bird gently on the sill, but he just sat there.

"Will he be all right?" I whispered.

"Of course he will," said Daddy. "He's just dazed; he doesn't realize he's free yet. He cracked a pane in the window next door, flying at it to escape. But better not mention that to Mammy, huh? We don't want to upset her anymore. I'll fix it on the QT."

I nodded. There seemed to be more and more things now we weren't to tell Mammy.

Then Daddy ran his fingers through his hair the way he always did when he was thinking. He smiled and picked up my arm and rubbed it against his sandpapery chin. His chin was always like that before he shaved in the morning. I loved my daddy: I would have been so good to him if I were married to him . . . .

Harry stopped me on the way to bed that night: "You know who that really was, don't you? No matter what Daddy says . . . he comes to his own now and again. Just to let them know he has them . . . earmarked. If Daddy hadn't got there when he did . . . . "

I began to shake inside. Harry had found my weak spot. No amount of makeup horror from Hollywood could really hurt, but the devil was different.

I tried to think of nice things in bed, but all I could see was me going to hell with the devil. I kept seeing the coloured pictures in my catechism of the happy white souls in heaven smiling under the clock that ticked *forever, forever, forever*. And the grey souls in the flames of purgatory with their tortured faces towards the clock that ticked *sometime, sometime, sometime*. But I now belonged to the black souls screaming under the clock of hell – *never, never, never*.

I remembered every awful story Father Redmond ever told us at the mission: the one about the girl who had committed mortal sin and then got a terrible sickness. She was dying and she knew it; she hadn't been to confession and she could feel the pits of hell closing in around her. Tossing, turning, and raging in fever, she screamed for her mother to get the priest. The mother did, but of course it was taking a while for him to come. The girl kept screaming, pleading with the priest to come and forgive her. Her mammy would say he was coming, he was just coming, she thought she could see him turning the corner this very minute – anything to try and pacify the poor girl. But she died before the priest could get to her to hear her confession, and where she went to didn't bear thinking about. I said fifteen Acts

44

of Contrition in case anything happened to me before I could get to confession myself.

And then I thought of all the lapsed Catholics Father Redmond told us about. And all the buses and cars waiting to knock them down and kill them before he and the other retreat priests could get to them to tell them the folly of their ways. Before a passerby could even whisper an Act of Contrition in their ears – just in case.

Then I thought of my own grandaunt Peggy. And the night she told me about when she was "visited" by no less a person than Saint Martin de Porres, although he was only Blessed then. He came one All Souls' Night, and of course she knew him immediately because he was black. He opened his arms wide and suddenly she could hear the wailing and screaming of purgatory. He more or less told her then she had no business toasting her toes by the fire on an All Souls' Night when there were visits to be made for the holy souls who – God help them – were toasting a lot more. On All Souls' Night you could gain an indulgence for the holy souls in purgatory by visiting a church and saying six Our Fathers, six Hail Marys, and six Glory Be's. The more of these visits you made, the more souls you got out of purgatory. So Aunty Peggy went back to the church there and then and had to be dragged out when they finally locked the doors for the night.

She always finished this story by saying that to the day she died she would never forget the sound of those poor souls in purgatory, and might God strike her dead that minute if she was telling me one word of a lie.

Yes, Harry hit on a very sore spot indeed when he brought the devil into it. He was quick to see just how near the mark he was and equally quick to hammer home his advantage.

He thought I might find his Inter-Cert Irish book interesting, so he showed me all the nice pictures. It was the story of Séadna, who sold his soul to the devil for three wishes. The devil – An Fear Dubh – liked to turn up at odd times in different forms to remind Séadna the time was coming near when he would be claiming him. In one picture you could see the tail and the hoof sticking

45

out under the fancy clothes. Harry saw to it also that I understood this story was written by a priest – An t-Athair Peadar O'Laoire. And he should certainly know what he was talking about.

As if that weren't enough, Harry brought up some fellow called Faust at the dinner table so Daddy could clear up a few points he didn't understand. Daddy said he was delighted Harry was at last showing some interest in areas more rewarding than the ones he usually wallowed in and spoke at length on the theme of selling one's soul to the devil.

"Well now," said Harry, as he collared me on the dark landing that night, "but isn't the devil a holy terror too? Dear, oh dear. Still, at least Séadna got value for his wishes: a purse that was never empty. And your man Faust didn't do too badly either – endless knowledge, everlasting youth, all big things to ask . . . wouldn't you say? Now, what I think is terrible is that there could be some might think it worth it for a lousy pack of marked cards . . . . "

I tried to blot out the words.

"Do you know what I'm going to do?" continued Harry softly. "Well, I'll tell you. On the Last Day, the Day of Judgement, when God is deciding who stands on His right with the blessed and who on His left with the cursed and damned . . . . I'll wait till then . . . I'll wait until He asks who stole Harry's cards . . . . And then . . . no matter where I am in that crowd, I'll elbow me way forward to see who it was . . . . "

It was too much. I could see that crowd parting like the Red Sea to show me, God, and Harry like three points of a triangle.

"It was me, Harry, it was me!" I hurled myself at his chest, clinging to him for dear life. "I'm sorry! I'm sorry! I'll never do anything bad again . . . . "

Harry was a bit shaken by the sudden strength of my remorse. He tried to prise me off him: "It's all right, I forgive ya this time. Look, will ya get off and leave me alone. I said it was all right. Sure, I knew it was you all along . . . . I was only havin' you on . . . . Will you whisht for God's sake or you'll have Daddy up – "

"But Harry, the devil . . . he has me marked for life now – "

"Don't be such a stupo. That was only an old jackdaw fell down the chimney . . . . Don't tell me you were ass enough to believe all that . . . . "

I looked at him from under the full weight of my misery. How did Harry know that wasn't the devil? No one could know that for sure. And if it was, he had me marked for life. And there was nothing Harry or Daddy or I could do about it now.

There weren't any second chances. There were none for Séadna and none for Faust, and there wouldn't be any for Róisín McGovern either.

Harry could forgive me until he was blue in the face and it wouldn't make any difference. If the devil had me, there was nothing he nor anyone else could do about it.

And what has the devil to do with you? I'll let you be the judge.

It's not easy trying to tell the truth. More difficult than I thought. I haven't the training for it.

There is one more thing that rises from those early years – just a moment on a beach, but it gives me shivers still. The loonies. Both secrets, sort of, they and the island. Everyone knew they were there, but they were still secret. Inseparable.

They never came again after the tragedy. We were never the same, either. There was no island after that. Fionnuala still went. Sometimes I went. But never Lorcan. Whatever magic had remained after Ben Thompson's withdrawal now disappeared completely.

It was only with Fionnuala, or maybe Lorcan, I'd watch the loonies. It wasn't a thing you would do with just anyone. We had watched them a few years now; crept around the edges of them, waiting, wondering. Although no one talked about it, their visits in September were as much part of the year's rituals as the Corpus Christi procession or the Soapbox Derby. Every year we waited and watched for them once September came.

And it's not quite true to say no one talked about them: grown-ups whispered to other grown-ups; children repeated and added to what they overheard. And then, of course, there was Miss McAloon – she never shut up about the loonies. "Mark my words," she'd say darkly. She was always saying things *darkly*. I used to read in stories about things being said darkly and I always thought of Miss McAloon. Every day, from behind the wooden bars of her post-office cage, she weighed and counted and tore and stamped, all the time making black predictions. No one escaped her gloomy forecasts, but never was she more moved to dire warnings than she was by the annual visit of the loonies.

My father called her Cassandra sometimes. I couldn't understand that at all. That was much too glamorous and beautiful a name for someone like Miss McAloon.

And, indeed, as far as names went, I certainly wasn't supposed to be calling them loonies. But exactly what I could call them wasn't certain either. It was just about this time the mental hospital, fifty miles away, was renamed Saint Gerard's; you were to forget it was called the Lunatic Asylum for the eighty-five years it stood before that.

Father O'Hehir it was changed the name. Names were important to him. You'd never catch him calling them loonies. But it was all very well for him, he had a way with words. He could talk about them at great length without calling them anything at all.

Yet even he was short of a few words the day the trouble Miss McAloon so consistently foresaw finally arrived. However, she reminded the town, maybe there was good cause for his discomfort.

Father O'Hehir was the one who had broken the silence; he had thumped the pulpit and asked what sort of a people could deny an outing to these, the gentlest of God's creatures, innocent as babes. The same sort of people who could turn a blind eye to the wickedness going on nightly in the sandhills all summer. Oh yes, a people who were silent in the face of God only knew what as long as the guesthouses were full and the cash registers ringing. But far from silent when it came to denying these poor unfortunates their little bit of an outing.

It was always September when the loonies were let in. The holiday season died on August the fifteenth – the holy day – as if someone shot it. But still the townspeople lived in hopes – you'd never know when there might be the odd late visitor. There was no sense at all in frightening them off with loonies, letting your charity take the bite out of your mouth.

And so it was well into September when the bus with the loonies rolled into the square. Out they wandered in aimless little groups for their day at the seaside – well, the remnants of the summer seaside. You could still see the odd garland of tin buckets and spades festooned hopefully outside a shop door, but the sound they made in the wind now was a lonely one. The sticks of peppermint rock were faded in shop windows and the sand already blown in little heaps in corners along the deserted seafront. The dew was icy cold on the grass in the mornings, and Phinny Moran was making his rounds with the fresh farm apples.

We were back in school on the day and well warned to come home straight. Out we sprayed like bullets from a machine gun the minute the bell went, but not to go home. No, but down to the seafront for a quick look at the loonies before our mothers got anxious. Some mothers got very anxious indeed; there would always be a few of the worst of them lined up outside the school wall, pretending they were just out for a walk.

My own mother was never there, of course. This was the time of year she went off to her sister's in Dublin. "A little rest," Daddy said. Always in September and then again before Easter. And after she'd come back she wouldn't have the headaches so badly for a while, and didn't lie down and rest so often for the sleep she said she missed at night.

But Fionnuala's mother was there. We knew she might be and were on the lookout for her. So I just walked out ahead and kept Mrs. Fitz distracted while Fionnuala slipped past.

You'd think Fionnuala could show a little gratitude, but no. She could get your goat sometimes just by doing absolutely nothing. Not joining in games you'd have stood on your head planning. Not ever being caught at anything. Not eating her sweets, but hoarding them. Once she kept a pretend sugar cigarette between her lips all day, when my packet was long gone. In the end I clamped her skull and chin together and made her bite. But she still had nine and three-quarters left.

"You're a mammy's pet, Fionnuala Fitzgerald," I said.

But that just got more of the same from her. Wouldn't say aye, yes, or no. Other kids would have pointed out that my mother never gave a hoot where I was, and that was much worse. But not Fionnuala.

I could not understand this at all, so I kept at her. Trying to make her shout the truth. To tell me how mean and lousy I really was. Then at least I'd know where I stood, and could nearly relax on familiar ground. But no, she would not be risen.

So I did the worst thing I could think of. I marched right up to their bakery door as we passed and shouted in:

> "Fitzgerald's bread would kill a man dead,
> Especially a man with a baldy head."

I only pretended I was shouting it actually in the door, because the last thing I wanted was Mr. Fitz out shaking the sweeping brush as he always did when he heard that rhyme.

Fionnuala still wouldn't say anything. She just kept on walking, her head down. I laughed. I shouldn't have, and I shouldn't have said that rhyme. Because I knew how she hated it. And she was funny about death – I think it was because of her mother.

Mrs. Fitzgerald owned the linens for the dead. Whenever someone died, Mrs. Fitz was sent for to lay out the body. I imagined her dressing the corpses, running around from one side of the bed to the other. On with the clothes for the wake, and then off when no one was looking anymore and they could close the coffin. The shroud worn to shreds from being yanked off reluctant bodies. And imagine washing it. Did she put it in with Mr. Fitz's shirts?

But Fionnuala said they all had their own shrouds, and Mrs. Fitz just did the bed and side linens. She showed them to me once, in their special drawer – glossy and cold as the marble of the high altar. All ironed and neatly folded in tissue and ready to go again at any moment.

"I suppose you don't even air them," I said. You could say the daftest things to Fionnuala and she would just let it go. "Catch your death of pneumonia in those yokes.

"I'm sorry, Fionnuala," I said suddenly. "I know I can be awful."

"You're always like this on the loonies' day."

I don't know why the loonies should make me think of cold and death like that, but they did. Of lonely bells tolling, and damp mists from the sea, and sad mothers' faces. Faces a thousand years old, doomed to wander forever dark grassy paths.

"Well, I'm sorry. Come on, Fionnuala," I said, "I'm sorry for teasing you." It never dawned once that she might have her own strange pictures in her head. And how mean it was of me to make hers worse trying to make my own better.

I took her arm and squeezed it to my side with my elbow until she nodded. I let her go then and we ran on.

Down by the right-of-way we ran towards the seafront. Along by the deserted shacks of the amusement park, ghosts of the summer just gone, and of all summers gone. Silent now after weeks of Tom Dooley hanging his head down, Frankie and Johnnie being lovers, and wardens throwing parties in the county jail. The skeletons of the Dive-Bomber and the swinging boats creaked and moaned in the wind. A loose shutter on the palmist's window clapped a reply.

We walked past the hobby-horses, frozen in mid-gallop for the winter behind painted boarding promising endless adventure next year. Past the Pongo hall and the other arcades where you could win fruit gums or pennies or try and guide the mechanical hand to pick up a ten-shilling note or a cigarette lighter.

We were dawdling. Getting ready for what had to happen next. Because any second now we might see the loonies.

Around by the bumpers we went looking for empty lemonade bottles to return for the twopence on them – more out of habit and for something to do, than from any real hope we'd find them so late in the year. Suddenly Fionnuala stopped and then moved closer to me.

"There they are, Róisín, look."

It was the loonies all right, a little cluster of them sitting on a bench staring out over the sea. Fionnuala took my arm and started to walk more quickly. The faster we walked, the sooner we'd be past.

"What good is this?" I hissed, digging in as she tried to scurry on, pulling me. "It's them we came to see. Slow down."

"Excuse me" – I marched right up to them, giddy, to keep away the fear – "but I wonder if you have the right time, please?"

They stared at us but no one answered. Loonies all right, you couldn't mistake them. Maybe it was their eyes: the way they wouldn't look at you, not right at you. They might look towards you, but not to listen or understand. Or was it the wrinkles? The wrinkles that seemed to be in all the wrong places.

And the clothes: they weren't fresh, not ironed or something. As if everyone were wearing everyone else's. Nothing seemed to fit properly or to match and the colours weren't right. Ordinary people always seemed to look as if their clothes were really part of them.

And then one of them actually did look at us. We turned tail and ran off.

Of course when something did finally happen Fionnuala wasn't there at all. No, at home, watched over by her mammy. It was one thing to sneak her past Mrs. Fitz for a quick look, but we knew she had only so long to get home before the Fitzes would have the guards out looking for her.

So Fionnuala missed the excitement, but I didn't. I was in the middle of it. With – of all people – Lorcan Burke.

Normally, boys wouldn't be seen dead with girls and vice versa. The Brothers' school and the convent glared at each other from opposite ends of the town like hostile encampments.

Lorcan Burke did talk to me sometimes. But only when there was no one around, of course. And mostly because the other boys ignored him. I couldn't figure out why – he always had the flashiest bicycle, the most expensive football, the biggest dynamo, the first pair of jeans. Sent by his father in England so Lorcan would be popular. But the lads just laughed at him and snatched his prizes to play with among themselves.

"Chicken," said Harry, when I asked him why Lorcan was not tough as the other lads. "Yella. Afraid of his own shadow. Afraid he'll get a belt of a ball or a dunt in a tackle. Mammy's boy."

But all the better. Because instead he sometimes came to me.

To the island. He wouldn't play Up the Airy Mountain anymore: now he liked to lie in the long grass, holding on to me. Lying on its flat grassy top, only Ben Bulben across the bay reached higher. No sounds but our breathing and the beating of our hearts and those of the wind and the sea below. Lorcan lying half over me in long silence. Like butterflies or mayflies resting on their one day of life. The sky going on forever overhead, long grass tickling my neck. Daisies and sweet clover out of the corner of my eye, the hot yellow glow of buttercups under his chin that meant love for sure. This was not a place for words. Nor, indeed, the playing-doctor touches of Lorcan's garage. Here we were a small part of a huge, wonderful, and mysteriously conspiratorial world. It commanded our respect.

Not like Twomey's cinema. That was a place for curiosity, not awe. We knew that we ruled the roost in Twomey's. We knew we were boss there, no matter how much we laughed or cried or screamed. But not so on the island – there was something on the island stronger than anything Twomey's could conjure.

Harry was part-time projectionist at Twomey's cinema and often let Lorcan in for ten Woodbines lifted from his mother's shop. Harry used to let me in on the promise of some job for him at home. He'd complain bitterly about the two of us crowding his tiny office, but the next Sunday he'd let us in again. And, there, we could watch the maestro plan and order what would split the sides, or milk the tears, or terrify the wits out of Duneen in the weeks to come.

A mug of stewed tea by his side, a Woodbine he'd never have dared smoke at home dangling from his lips, Harry pored over the form. Eyes squinting and brow furrowed against the smoke, while on every inch of wall space around curled yellowing stills of his favourite moments on the screen, Harry circled his choices. Vampires and werewolves were high on his list and Twomey's was thriving.

But it was one thing to talk to Lorcan Burke on the far end of a deserted beach and in the bowels of Twomey's where no one would ever know – quite another to do it in public. So, when I met him after dropping off Fionnuala at home, and he actually spoke to me in the middle of the street where people could see, I knew he must be desperate. Sure enough, he was.

"Hey, Róisín," he called in a loud whisper as I came out of Doyle's Grocery and Provisions with the messages.

"What do you want?" I said rudely, the normal tone of girl to hateful boy. We had good reason to be rude to boys.

"Do us a favour, will ya?"

"No."

"This is serious," he said.

"No catch?"

"What do you take me for?"

I didn't know. This was against all the rules.

"Wait till ya hear it at least. You'd think I was askin' your life's blood. I only want ya to drop home me schoolbag."

"Why?"

"Tell me mother I won't be home for a while. Tell her I have to help with the Harvest Festival Mass."

"Is that all?"

"Cross me heart. I'll give ya sixpence to do it."

I had a little snigger to myself, but quietly. Mrs. Burke was worse than Fionnuala's mother – Lorcan was another only darling.

I brought Lorcan's bag home to the little confectionery-tobacconist shop run by his mother. Sure enough, Mrs. Burke was not overjoyed. She wasn't moved to hand out a bar of chocolate in gratitude or anything. Instead, she quizzed me up and down as if I personally might have kidnapped Lorcan. But the Harvest Mass bit shut her up. Only a few altar boys were chosen for this honour and I could see Mrs. Burke was delighted Lorcan would be one of them. Her great love of religion was well known – I once heard Sergeant Egan betting Daddy it was exactly that which had propelled Mr. Burke to England forever, far more surely than the mail boat.

Lorcan was waiting for me in a lather of impatience down the street. "Good girl," he said. "Here's your sixpence. Jesus, if she hears I'm not only out of the Harvest, but barred from the sacristy for a month."

He began to run.

"What's the big rush?" I asked.

"Something's wrong up the town. I got wind of it on the way home. Ya comin'?"

Try and stop me.

We were not the only ones who had heard something. The bus to bring home the loonies stood in the square, swarmed around by half the town, pretending their presence was pure coincidence. Shopkeepers were busy outside their establishments, packing away the onions or the hardware for the evening. Or fiddling with blinds in the face of a cold, weak sun that wasn't about to fade anything. Housewives in their slippers and twinsets gossiped at their doors, hugging their chests, each hand up the other sleeve.

There were two women fussing around the busload of loonies – nurses, Mrs. Shanahan and Mrs. Lynch behind us decided.

The bus seemed full, but something was not quite right. The two nurses were going around in circles, bumping into each other up and down the aisle. Checking, counting heads as they went, then swapping places and starting again.

They whispered together, shook their heads, and then the young nurse with the freckles and the red hair came down the steps of the bus so fast she nearly tripped.

"What's keeping the guards?" she said. "Would somebody please get the guards?" There was a fair crowd by now, but nobody was moving. No one wanted to miss anything.

"Please," she begged. "We can't go. There's only the two of us here."

"Foxie Traynor went, Miss, a good ten minutes ago," shouted Mrs. Shanahan from the front door of Saint Dympna's, her guesthouse. "They should be here any minute."

The nurse kept looking all around the town square with worried eyes, not seeing whatever it was she wanted to see. The other nurse joined her at the door of the bus. They whispered and then they looked all around the square again. Then they whispered again and they shook their heads.

Sergeant Egan arrived: "What's all this now?"

"One of our patients is missing."

"Are you sure?"

"Yes. His name is McDermott."

"Where was he last?"

"No one remembers. No one has seen him since lunchtime. He's a young man, tall and dark."

"A young man, you say, Miss?"

"Yes. A schizophrenic."

"A *skitserfrenick?*" said Sergeant Egan, scratching the back of his head with the rim of his cap. As if he didn't know what to say next. "Seems to me there should be a doctor with you people. Where is he?"

"The doctors don't have time to come on outings like this. They are back at the hospital where they are needed. These patients don't need a doctor with them."

"Well, I don't know about that. They must need more than you think since one of them has managed to get himself missing. Tell me, Miss, he wouldn't . . . he wouldn't harm anyone, would he?"

"Of course not. None of these patients are . . . what nonsense . . . ."

"I see, Miss. Ah well, of course I knew that. But I just thought I'd be sure."

Just then Lorcan Burke nudged me and took off, jerking his head for me to follow him. I didn't really want to go, but in the end I did.

"Where are you going, Lorcan Burke? That was just getting interesting."

"Not likely," said Lorcan. "If your man's missing, he's missing and that's all there is to it. There'll be no more action there. I have a much better idea."

"Oh yeah?" I said, panting up Castle Street after him. "And is it any harm to ask what it is or where we're going?"

"Not at all," said Lorcan. "We're goin' to the library."

"Of course," I said. "Where the loony has Miss O'Donnell at gunpoint. Or is he just taking out an Agatha Christie?"

"Wait and see, Miss Smarty-pants. I'll put the laugh on the other side of your face for you."

We got to the library. If you could call a cluttered, musty cubbyhole at the back of the courthouse a library: bare dusty boards and rows of dark, dried-up spines with names you couldn't see, let alone read. And a path worn by me to the few Hardy Boys on the Juvenile shelf.

Miss O'Donnell, the librarian, sat in her box with her stamp in the middle of it all. Dispensing fines and request sheets for books you could fill out until you were blue in the face but you'd never see. She jumped up like a scalded cat when she saw us coming in and barred our way with a face on her that would have turned milk.

"Where do you think you two are going? Don't you know Juvenile day isn't until Saturday? And aren't you more than enough trouble then?"

I didn't know why we were there anymore than she did, so I left the talking to Lorcan.

"We'd like to have a look at the dictionary, Miss O'Donnell. We're stuck for a word in our homework."

"What's the word and I'll tell you," she said.

"It's not that easy," said Lorcan. "Look, we don't want to borrow a book or anything. We won't even touch one, we promise. We just want a look at the dictionary. Please?"

"You're not setting foot in this library until Saturday."

"Come on, Róisín. I suppose we could always ask your father. Then we can go and search for this *loony*."

"What loony?" said Miss O'Donnell. She reached out for Lorcan with a grip like a crab's.

"The one that's missing," said Lorcan. "Didn't you hear? We have to go now and search. Come on, Róisín."

"Take your time there a minute," she said. "Tell me what's going on and you can see the dictionary."

So Lorcan told her and then she had to give us the book. She tried to hang around us while we looked, but we kept moving away.

Lorcan had a bit of trouble finding the word, looking under *sci* first and then *ski* and then not recognizing it at all when he did at last come across it. Finally the light dawned.

"Look, Róisín, there it is." He stabbed the page with a dirty fingernail – "*Schizophrenia*. Isn't that just like the stupid way they'd spell it. Look what it says. 'Schizophrenia: A split personality . . . loss of touch with reality . . . introversion . . . .' "

"What's a split personality, Lorcan?" I asked, because it rang some sort of bell. "My father's always saying personality is everything."

Lorcan Burke looked at me with immeasurable pity and disgust. " 'What's a split personality,' she says. A girl who was told only a few Sundays ago. Well, I'll tell you again. Do you remember that werewolf in the matinée a couple of weeks ago?"

I did. Bells were ringing louder now.

"One minute he'd be an ordinary fella doin' his pushups in the gym?" said Lorcan. "And the next the hair'd be growing out of his ears?"

"That was only a film."

But Lorcan wasn't even listening. "Two personalities, they called it – a split personality."

"Ah go on, Lorcan Burke. Pull the other one."

"That is exactly what they called it."

"You surely don't believe all you hear in the pictures?"

"Do you think I would joke about a serious thing like this?" said Lorcan. "Do you not realize the danger this town is in? Maybe you didn't notice the next bit here either? 'Loss of touch with reality'? What about that? Do you know what that means?"

"No, I don't and I don't want to."

"It means not having the first clue what you're doing. Do you not remember your man in the film? He couldn't even remember strangling that poor girl."

Lorcan shut up then because he didn't know what the next bit meant. He flipped through the pages of the dictionary again, repeating the syllables as he went.

"In-tro-ver-sion. Here it is, Róisín, look. 'Introversion . . . turning in on one's self.' Oh my God, Róisín, what do you suppose the loony turns into on himself?"

59

I hadn't believed it until then and I don't think Lorcan did either. But now he could hardly hold the dictionary for shaking. And me – I had to hang on to the library shelf for support.

"They'd never let him out if he was like that, Lorcan. You heard the nurse. And Daddy said they'd never, they only let the harmless ones out."

"Supposing he's like your man in the film?" said Lorcan. "Remember how sly he was about the change? His own girlfriend didn't know. Not even his mother. Carted off on a stretcher when they told her, remember?"

"But that was only a film – "

"But nothing. There it is in front of you in the dictionary. And the nurse herself said what he had. You heard her. And now he's loose. And you know what? Sooner or later this loss of touch with reality, this change, is going to come over him and then watch out."

"Stop giving me the creeps, Lorcan Burke."

"We're the lucky ones, we'll be all right. At least we know what we're up against. You won't catch me out after dark for a while. And you're not to say a word to anyone, d'you hear? If your man found out we were on to him so fast, who d'you think he'd be after first?"

You wouldn't believe the stories flying around about the loony by the next morning. He was from Donegal – wouldn't you know it, weren't they all mad from inbreeding up there. No, it was because his father murdered his mother before his eyes when he was small and he was never right since. My father said it was nonsense and lies, and he was only a poor fellow got too much for his old mother to handle.

But no story about the loony could hold a candle to what we knew to be the truth. The worst thing was not being able to tell anyone. We knew they'd never believe us.

I clung to Lorcan Burke as if he were the saviour of mankind. He was like that doctor who used to arrive in the nick of time in the vampire films. Nobody would believe him either, but he just went right on doing what had to be done: dishing out crosses and garlic flowers. It wasn't his fault if the silly eejits couldn't stand the smell of the flowers or took off the crosses to wash their necks.

He was forever warning husbands not to leave their wives' bedrooms for a minute even, but that was no good either. They'd be off for the cocoa or something no matter how earnestly and loudly we implored them from the tenpenny seats. That left us no choice but to dive for cover because we knew exactly what was going to happen next, even if they didn't.

Well, I wasn't going to be caught out like that. Although there was never much talk about garlic flowers and crosses against werewolves, I was taking no chances. And, anyway, it was silver bullets you had to have to stop a werewolf. Where exactly were Lorcan Burke and I going to get any bullets, let alone a silver one? And how would we shoot it at him if we did? No, we'd have to hope for the best with crosses and garlic flowers.

I'd have loved to tell someone about this. But I had good reason to keep quiet. Once before I had tried talking about it. I had risked asking my mother about the loonies.

I wasn't daft enough to say it straight out. No, I asked, was being a loony anything like being possessed, like they sometimes were in the Gospels. I had thought I might be on fairly safe ground with the religion thrown in.

But my mother went absolutely mad. My hand was covering my stinging ear before I had even finished asking the question. "The very idea of it," my mother said. "As if Gracie had an evil bone in her body." And if I had the slightest notion of what mental torture was like, I'd have more sympathy and less talk of the devil.

What and under heaven was she talking about? What had Gracie to do with the loonies? Gracie, my cousin, who was years younger than the rest of Aunty Róisín's children, and Róisín keeping her a baby long past her time. All Gracie ever wanted to do was hold your hand and play dolls – and she thirteen since last Easter. But what had Gracie to do with the loonies? Grown-ups were strange; there was no accounting for the turns they could take. After that I knew when to keep quiet.

Except for one thing I had to know: I asked my father about garlic. If a simple thing like wearing garlic flowers could help, then I was not going to be found without. My father said garlic was sort of like an onion, and he imagined you'd have to go to Sligo or maybe even Dublin to buy it. But it was definitely like an onion. I asked him did onions have flowers, but he only said he worried about me sometimes. Other children gave up asking daft questions when they were half my age.

Well, he wasn't nearly as worried as I was myself, so I had a look in the big vegetable garden behind the convent. The onions were there, all right, drying on the garden path, not one flower among them. So I gave up then on the flowers, stole two onions for under my bed to be on the safe side, and put most of my faith in the cross on my rosary beads.

Lorcan Burke was every bit as bad as me. In fact, the crosses were his idea in the first place.

But there was one person delighted with this new turn of events: Mrs. Burke thought all her prayers were finally answered when she found Lorcan going to bed one night with his rosary beads around his neck. She had this favourite poem – a "recitation" she called it – which she trotted out at every hooley in the town. After Father O'Hehir's "Tangmalangaloo" usually. She'd be warming up – you could see her moving her lips to see if she could remember all the words, even before he finished. Her recitation was one about a widow whose son was a scoundrel, but in the end he turned his back on all his wicked ways to become a priest. You couldn't miss the line that Mrs. Burke liked best: *'Twas he who said the mass in black, the morning that she died*. She'd have tears in her eyes for that line, a fierce wobble in her voice, and such a look at Lorcan as would have the rest of us kids in fits laughing behind other people's backs. Lorcan would be purple, cursing and swearing at her under his breath not to get her hopes too high. Even the grown-ups laughed at her. But she didn't mind: at the very next get-together she'd do it all over again.

Lorcan Burke and I weren't the only ones with notions about the loony; everyone had some story. If he was at even half the windows he was reported at – watching ladies undressing – it said an awful lot for his energy and not much for his taste, my father said. He was seen leaping out of dark corners everywhere, pinching and chasing. Who else but he could have stolen certain things off Miss McAloon's clothesline? And no normal person could be responsible for the telephone calls besieging the unmarried ladies of the town.

"And that's where Christian charity gets you," Miss McAloon said darkly, looking towards Father O'Hehir's closed door.

She was not alone in deciding Father O'Hehir was to blame in the matter. Not at all – the whole town was agog to see what he had to say about this mess he had landed it in.

The church was packed to the rafters for mass, the ten o'clock on Sunday. You could feel the disappointment when he started on about the Sermon on the Mount and the great truths it held for us all. People looked sideways at each other, shook their heads, and there were low whispers. The coughing and the shuffling and the rustling got so bad that at last he was forced to throw in a few words about the thoughts uppermost in the minds of his congregation. "You don't need me to tell you how troubled we are in this peaceful little town." And he went on to say the same thing in ten different ways, as Harry put it. Father O'Hehir was as worried and helpless as the rest of us.

There was great grumbling and grousing done on the way home from mass about the lack of leadership, lack of answers, in fact, lack of any sort of effective activity about the loony. It was widely felt we could all be murdered in our beds. And let there be no mistake here, we could be and would be before anyone would lift a hand for us in Dublin.

Murdered in our beds, indeed, and they didn't know the half of it. I would hardly go outside the door, even in broad daylight; I couldn't get rid of a feeling that something more had to happen. I thought it was all those horror films I sneaked into. But Fionnuala Fitzgerald was as bad, if not worse, and she had never been to any. But there was something about what she had seen more frightening than any film.

"His name was Louis McDermott. My mother laid out his father," she said. "A few years ago now, but she remembers him well. He was very handsome. He was all right then. He won a scholarship to university."

"Stop." That was nearly worse somehow. Thinking he was once an ordinary boy. A brainy boy with dreams.

Fionnuala and I were on our way to school. It was a choppy, windy day. Already the sea and land had taken on the grey wild look they would wear for the winter. The look that said the town was ours again until next year's summer and visitors.

"Róisín, look!" Fionnuala gripped my arm suddenly. She was pointing to the beach. "Who's that?"

"Where?" I asked, peering blindly in the general direction.

"On the beach, look. It's a man."

"Oh yeah. He's really running, isn't he? I wonder what's up?"

"It's only Mister Duffy," said Fionnuala then, letting go of me. "Come on, we'll be late for school."

"Wait a minute," I said. "There has to be something up if he's running like that."

Margie Duffy's father was as strong as anyone we knew, a fisherman. But he was so winded he could hardly speak when he caught up with us at last.

"Kids . . . get the priest, would you? And the sergeant . . . . "

"Why?" I said.

"Christ . . . would you just go."

"What'll we tell them?"

"It's _him_," said Alfie Duffy. "Washed up . . . dead . . . . Go now."

"Jesus, Mary, and Joseph."

We didn't need to be told again. We were off and running.

"Fionnuala," I said, "drop your schoolbag here. That way we can run faster and have a good excuse to come back."

"Okay," she said. "Did you hear, Róisín? He's dead."

"Yes. I'll take the sergeant. Get Father O'Hehir, will you?"

"Right. See you back at the bags then."

I found the sergeant finishing off his breakfast at the barracks. He listened, threw his jacket over his braces, and was off.

On my way back, I had another thought: Lorcan Burke. I'd be a long time waiting for this sort of news again. I took the route between the Brothers' and his house and met him on his way to school.

"Gosh, thanks," he said, starting to run when I told him what was up. "You're not bad for a girl."

And so Lorcan Burke came back to the beach too. Father O'Hehir and Sergeant Egan were just arriving, having driven their cars as far as the seafront barriers and walked the last bit. Although the sergeant barely noticed me at the barracks, it was a different story when he spotted me and Fionnuala and Lorcan back on the prom.

"Clear off, kids," he said. "This is no place for children."

Of course, obedient Fionnuala was for off immediately and I wasn't much better. But Lorcan was going nowhere. He gripped his side and fell over the seafront wall. Not close enough to bother the grown-ups, but just near enough to catch what they said if he strained. "Can't move, Sergeant," gasped Lorcan. "Pain in me side from all the running. And the girls must be worse. Just give us a breather for a minute. We're dead from all the running. We'll be off as soon as we're able."

We took his lead and all hung over the wall, looking as if we neither knew nor cared what was happening, only to hold on to the little breath we had left.

"Are you sure it's him, Alfie?" came Father O'Hehir's voice.

"Of course I am, Father. Didn't the sergeant here say he was wearing a blue gansey under a tweed jacket when he went missing. Och, it's him all right. Been in about a week, I'd say."

"He must have gone in the very day he disappeared so," came Sergeant Egan's voice. "About a week, you'd say?"

"Aye, I would, Sergeant. A week, give or take. With all due respect, I've seen too many not to know. His own mother wouldn't know him now."

"May God rest his poor tortured soul," came Father O'Hehir's voice again. "The poor fellow. Well, we'd better go and say a few prayers for him, what? Where is he, Alfie? Are you up to bringing us yet or do you want to rest a while longer?"

"Hold on a minute there, Father," came Sergeant Egan's voice. "No sense in us all traipsing over. You go and say your few prayers, by all means, but I'd be better off making arrangements for the removal of the remains before the whole town is on top of us. I'll be after you as soon as I can."

"Not a bad idea that, Sergeant," said Alfie. "And if you're coming with cars and things, your best bet would be around by the back Strand Road. We'll be much nearer there than here. You'll find us not far from Cleary's Steps, about two hundred yards up from where I beach the boat. You can't miss us."

"All right, so that's what we'll do," said Father O'Hehir. "Just give me a few minutes to get my breviary from the car, will you, Alfie?"

"Take all the time you want, Father," said Alfie. "Sure your man is goin' nowhere. No disrespect intended, Father."

"No, no, of course not. Hey, kids!" We turned reluctantly towards his raised voice. "Off back to school now. This minute. Go on now, you're grand. On out of that and back to school."

We walked silently away as they all turned towards the barriers and the cars.

"Hey, slow down, will you?" whispered Lorcan Burke.

"Why?"

"Just slow down. And be ready when I tell you. Quick then, before they spot us. Look, those barriers are a good ten minutes away. . . . " He pointed to the yellow columns with the red gumdrop faces that glowed in the dark to keep the traffic off the congested seafront area. There was a time when they used to come down at the end of the summer season, but no one bothered any longer.

"NOW. Come on, Róisín," he said. "If we double back now, we could get a look at your man and nobody'd be a bit the wiser."

"We'd be caught. They'd see us."

"Not a bit of it. Not if we take the cliff path back to Cleary's

Steps. They'll never take that way. Anyway, they'll be at least twenty minutes yet. Just look at them yapping."

"You're off your head, Lorcan Burke. Now come on to school before they see what we're at. We'll be first up the town with the story."

"Not half the story we'd have if we get a quick look at your man. Aw, come on." He stood, poised to run, jerking his head first in the direction he wanted to go, then towards Fionnuala. "Tell me, does your woman talk at all?"

"Only when she has something worth saying. Will we go, Fionnuala?" I said, sure she'd say no.

"Yes," she said, "I'd like to."

Well, talk about wonders never ceasing . . . .

So we hurried back along the cliff path high over the sea and didn't stop running until we reached Cleary's Steps. There we paused, looking back over the beach towards the town. There was no sign we'd been spotted.

We turned our attention to the beach beneath us: our eyes skimming the black jagged rocks and the wet sand glistening after the morning tide. There was nothing else to be seen, yet.

Down the rotting wooden steps we went carefully, knowing where the really bad ones were and where the rail couldn't be trusted.

Between keeping cover and making speed and not really wanting to know anyway, none of us was looking too far ahead until we were actually down on the beach. There was plenty of cover from the rocks and the cliff, but it didn't matter because Alfie and the priest were only two dots in the distance.

And then we couldn't put it off any longer: we looked up the beach from Alfie Duffy's boat.

"Oh, holy Christ," said Lorcan.

We tiptoed towards the mound slowly, stopping to grab on to one another and then starting off again. No matter how slowly we went, we had to reach it eventually. All eyes locked on it all the way.

The sea made a greedy sucking noise as it lapped over the shins and then was dragged off them again. Playfully the water

67

fretted and gurgled around his mouth and the puffy red holes where his eyes would have been. He looked far too big and swollen for his clothes. As if you could jab him with a stick and horrible stuff would squirt out, like out of a rotten tomato.

And the hair – coarse black hair sprouted from his face . . . . One minute he'd be fine, the next, the hair'd be growing from his ears . . . .

"You were right," I whispered to Lorcan. "You were right. He's not human at all . . . . "

But I wasn't afraid, not the least little bit. No, I felt I was in some holy place where I had no right at all to be. The tears began to fall.

"Oh, the poor, poor fellow . . . . " I knelt in the tide beside him. "He must have been a good werewolf . . . . When he felt the change coming on he walked into the sea . . . . Don't tell anyone he was half changed, will you? Sure you won't tell, please, neither of you. We won't tell he was changed . . . Fionnuala?"

I turned anxiously towards her.

She knelt on the other side of the body, her hand on the poor puffy blackened one, her tears falling on the hairy rawness that used to be a face.

Like Mary in that statue you often seen in holy pictures. The white one. The one where she's kneeling, holding the dead body of Jesus.

"Lorcan?" I whispered. "You won't tell anyone either, will you? You won't ever tell anyone he was changed? Please don't tell on him. Promise?"

But Lorcan Burke surprised me even more.

Fully dressed, he splashed heedlessly into the tide. He fell to his knees in the water, where Father O'Hehir would never have gone, close to the savaged ear.

He leaned down.

"Oh my God, I am heartily sorry for having offended Thee . . . . "

Here, he started to sob and couldn't go on. Fionnuala and I joined hands and continued for him.

"I detest my sins above every other evil because they displease

68

Thee, my God, who art so infinitely good. And I promise . . . ."

We tailed off ourselves too, realizing there was no more earthly future for him to make promises.

"And anyway, God," Lorcan said, straining upwards from his crouch towards the sky, "it wasn't his fault, was it? You know that and we know that."

He swept his clenched fist behind him towards the town.

"It was ours, God, it was ours."

Lorcan Burke would not be consoled, would not be budged. The one who told us we could come only if we were quick and quiet.

In desperation, Fionnuala and I had to half drag, half carry Lorcan away.

No one ever encouraged us to tell the truth. Not the real truth. Not whenever it was nasty and interfered with goodness. And, of course, what truth interfered most with was sex, the only really bad sin.

Sin. Occasions of sin. Boys. How did we ever think there was sin at all until this one came along? Sins you might want to commit. Sins that preyed on your mind, a thing lying and stealing and cheating never did.

Boys happen in three stages. First the safe one, the one who will never grab you in a dark corner and show you what your obsession is all about. Next, the one who just might, given half a chance. And then the one who will break your heart if he doesn't.

It took my sister's wedding to wake me up to the game. I was in no hurry until then, neither my own nor indeed anyone else's idea of femme fatale. I could never imagine any boy off his food over me. Or me off my own, for that matter. Until Deirdre's wedding. That bloody wedding took over our lives for the best part of a year.

Deirdre was now a hostess for Aer Lingus, living in a flat in Dublin. There she had juggled a number of suitors with great success. These poor idiots lived and breathed in our house only in terms of what they had given Deirdre. There was the one who sealed the diamond earrings in her Easter egg, the one who gave her the doll with the real pearls around its neck, and the thrifty dentist who fashioned her a molar pendant out of discarded gold fillings. She was very careful to match each donor with his offerings so she would be sure to drip the appropriate gems on all occasions. Sometimes she dripped the wrong gems on purpose, to give a slow learner the right idea.

On the Saturday before Christmas in 1961, four astounded men – each of whom had been positive he was the only bright spot in Deirdre's rather mundane existence – learned in the *Irish Times* of her forthcoming marriage to a wealthy and well-known diplomat. (He was the one who liked to serve her martini on the rocks: high-carat, clear, brilliant rocks.)

The wedding was sole topic of conversation in Duneen from the very minute the engagement was announced. Dermot Comiskey was the lucky fiancé. He was a catch of course. He was already well known on radio, fighting for Georgian architecture. And he was one of the select invited to open the country's new television station on New Year's Eve. He was up and coming in political circles and was a distant cousin of the Guinness family.

As for Deirdre McGovern, she was home for Christmas, her finger weighted down by a sapphire outmatched only by the radiant sparkle in her eyes, according to page one of the *Champion*.

Suddenly the Chamber of Commerce, the Tourist Board – you name it – had an axe to grind. The wedding was news, good for the town.

"Over my dead body is she getting married in this town," said my mother. "We are not going to be a laughing stock for the whole country."

"Eligible diplomat weds culchie from the back of beyond," said my brother Harry, helpfully. "You can take the girl out of the bog . . . but where are you going to have the wedding?"

"Dublin. University Church," snapped my mother. "Rome, if needs be."

"Far too obvious," said Harry. "You'll have all the Sunday rags down here to see what we have to hide. Long exposés running up to the wedding: 'The Paths She Ran Barefoot Along,' that sort of thing. You do realize it will be trial by television, don't you? If you want a proper PR job, leave it to me . . . . "

Actually, Harry would have been the perfect choice. He would have organized that wedding as the show it was. He was already making a name for himself as an impresario in Dublin, where his early years in Twomey's cinema were standing him in good stead.

Daddy had packed him off to do a degree – any degree. But once in Dublin, Harry went from Premed in University College Dublin to First Arts, and finally to General Studies in Trinity, without ever passing any one paper of any one exam. My father was forced to give up on him, and Harry was free at last to do what he had been doing on the sly all along anyway. He had been quietly turning white elephants of theatres and cinemas in Dublin back into paying ventures. His real forte was an eye for an underrated performer or show on the sidelines of the action in London which he could import cheaply for a hit in Dublin. His reputation was growing.

But, of course, Mammy and Deirdre weren't about to hand the event of the century over to Harry. This wedding was Mammy's raison d'être; this was her reward for producing and rearing such a uniquely beautiful daughter. Sheila McGovern would show these redneck peasants a thing or two. This was a wedding people would remember, and no one would say the McGoverns did not know how to do things properly.

It was this sense of a girl's worth being apparent only in the calibre of male she could attract that began to gnaw away at me. Without having the faintest idea what I was about, I set out to have one person at least at that wedding whose heart would beat faster when it beheld the unlikely stimulus of the large, unlovely, unwieldy sister of the bride. The wedding was set for October – so I had ten months.

I cast Lorcan Burke in the role of the smitten. Mostly because he was the only boy in the whole world who had ever actually spoken to me.

What dubious connection I once had with Lorcan Burke had long disappeared in reality, but in imagination loomed large. I had never forgotten the magic of secret summer days on our island, and I decided he hadn't either. It was merely cruel convention keeping us apart.

If any communication between the sexes were normal, this would probably not have happened. But the height of romantic contact was letting the air out of the boys' bicycles on the way out of Legion of Mary meetings, while they had their evening study period in the

Brothers'. This brought response of pulling hair, catapulted missiles, or tripping in passing – all taken as signs of fervid devotion.

But my big chance would be at the New Year's social just coming around. This was the first approved mixed gathering for boys and girls in the town, a bonus umbrella celebration for single-sex organizations: the Junior Legion of Mary, the Sodality, the Pioneers, and the Patricians. It was to be a very innocent affair with games, races, and contests. Having pretended for all these years that there was very little reason why boys are boys and girls girls, Father O'Hehir was not about to abandon caution altogether and admit there might be any fun in dancing.

It was only the thought of this night that kept me going through a dreadful Christmas of Dermot-and-Deirdre worship at our house.

"A toast to Sheila," said Dermot, raising his champagne glass to Mammy after the engagement party dinner on Christmas Eve. "To Sheila, without whom there would have been no light in my life . . . . " He smiled besottedly, first at Mammy, then at Deirdre.

"He has a book in his suitcase," Harry whispered to me under cover of the twittering delight. "What to say to mothers-in-law, prime ministers, and television interviewers . . . . To our hostess . . . to Sheila," finished Harry loudly when I started to giggle.

There we sat like an illustration from *Good Wives* in that drawing room, well mannered among the ashes-of-roses brocades, shadowy grey velvets, and fringed lamps. All that was missing was a caption: Deirdre Announces Her Forthcoming Marriage.

"Anyone for a walk?" Harry said heavily.

I jumped up and so did Daddy. The three of us left the overpowering stuffiness of that room for the sharp clarity of the frosty night. Hardly a word was spoken as we climbed high over the night sea. There was something strangely conspiratorial about it all: the three of us stopping now and then in silent accord; no sound but the soft huffs of warm breath and the gentle lapping far below. A denial of the artificial celebrations at home. Something blessedly real and normal.

There was nothing blessed about my thoughts of Lorcan Burke as I watched him later serving midnight mass. At communion he held the paten under my chin for Father O'Hehir, and I inhaled him through a haze of incense, pungent Christmas evergreens, candlelight, and soft carols. I couldn't wait for the New Year's social.

What if it finally arrived and Lorcan wasn't there? It just didn't bear thinking about. For whom then the red dress I had painstakingly let out and down to fit me? I loved that dress on Deirdre; it was red-and-grey check, with red buttons all down the front, a huge swinging skirt, and wide belt that buckled at the back. Deirdre had worn it over four stiff slips. I had those too, but they were limper now in spite of all the secret rinsing in Bernadette Gibbons's house in pounds of stolen sugar.

Still, I thought I was lovely when I came downstairs to make my entrance at tea-time on the evening of the social. The skirt wasn't quite so wide now because Sister Agnes in Domestic Science had helped me to cut a panel out of it to make the bodice big enough to fit. I stood at the breakfast-room door and waited for Mammy to say something nice to me, as she always did when Deirdre wore that dress.

She burst into little light laughs; Deirdre and Dermot were not long gone back to Dublin and she was still in her easily amused amn't-I-so-much-fun moods. "Róisín, dear, oh dear, what are we going to do with you?" She shook her head and smiled a helpless "What did I tell you?" at Daddy. "It's no good, Róisín, dear. You can't wear those slips at your size. You look like a giant tomato. Take them off."

I blushed red as the dress and turned away. From the top of the stairs I could hear her still laughing with Daddy. "Oh dear, a ship in full sail," she said. "Red sails in the sunset," she said.

I took off the stiff slips, but the dress wasn't as nice at all without them. I decided I'd put them all on again after I'd had tea with them and said goodbye, just before I left.

Down I went and sat at the table with no slips on, but she still didn't say one thing about any bit of me looking nice: not my hair, not the dress, nor even the shoes I had polished three times. She just went on talking to Daddy about Deirdre and Dermot and the wedding and where they might honeymoon and live. So I got my own back on her: I let the big wide belt with the buckle at the back score all the varnish on her good mahogany chair. I knew well it was doing it; I could feel it every time I moved. I moved far more than I had to. I knew I couldn't be blamed, because how was I to see what was going on behind me, and anyway, she was the one herself who bought the dress with the buckle at the back for Deirdre.

I put on all the slips again and headed off for the social with Bernadette Gibbons. More like a huge red backdrop for her than actually with her. She had a brand new Twist dress; I didn't even know they were the new fashion until Deirdre came home with one too. It was so much neater than my mountainous tent. I wished I had left the slips at home.

Lorcan Burke was there all right. He nodded coolly to us from the boys' corner.

The chairs in the hall were all lined up around the walls. The girls were talking and giggling in clutches but not attentive to one another. While they pecked away at the air around each other, their eyes darted constantly. Mostly towards the doors to see who was coming in. And around the one corner the boys were huddled as far into as they could get.

Bernadette went into the Ladies and I tried to follow. You couldn't get within six bodies of the mirror, so I had to make do with the ancient glass-panelled door at the entrance that said No Jiving or Jitterbugging. I couldn't really see myself in it, but maybe that was just as well.

Inside the Ladies itself the excitement was rampant:

"Angela Whelan has makeup on."

"And a bra. You can see it right through her blouse."

"I bet she has hankies in it."

"Did you see Róisín McGovern's dress?" said someone when the giggling died down.

"You mean the marquee?"

Well, that was the last straw: I ripped off all those awful slips and hung them under my coat. When Bernadette was ready, I followed her out into the hall again. I wished I had someone there not as pretty as Bernadette to stand with. Fionnuala Fitzgerald, maybe. Only her mam and dad had stuck her away in boarding school.

We were standing there a few minutes when who should slink out of his corner and sidle over but Lorcan Burke. I gripped Bernadette's arm, but she pinched my hand really viciously until I let go.

"Hello, Lorcan," I said, pleased he could brave the stares to speak to us.

"Hello, Róisín," he said, sliding his eyes quickly over the red expanse and away. I never thought there could be different ways to say hello until that minute when Lorcan half closed his eyes and breathed it out to Bernadette. And she said it right back in a voice she never used on me. It was Bernadette he stood beside, Bernadette he whispered to. Then he walked back to his corner, whistling.

She looked straight in front of her then with a silly smile on her face, as if she were sleepwalking. She wouldn't talk about anything, not even Angela Whelan's makeup or bra or her own lovely dress. She just hugged her arms tight, and I might as well have been talking to myself for all the heed she paid.

Soon it was time to start – time to pick the boys' names. Father O'Hehir didn't want any picking and choosing of partners with all that entailed, so he put all the boys' names in a hat. Each girl would then pick her prize, a champion for the evening's festivities. Otherwise, there was every likelihood the boys would never leave their corner.

Bernadette's turn came before mine, as she was G. She floated up those steps to the stage. Her long blonde hair was loose to her hips and she flicked it out of the way as she turned to face the crowd. She fluttered a slim arm towards the hat with the names. She rustled the contents a little and then raised her selection. She read it to herself and then blushed slightly – Bernadette always blushed daintily, pink and pretty, whereas I bloomed red and patchy. My neck and ears blushed the most and for longest.

"Lorcan Burke," read Bernadette aloud, and squeezed her lips together so the dimples showed best.

My turn came and I rolled up those steps a huge ball of red fire. I got Jimmy Lavelle, who couldn't keep the disappointed look off his face.

All the games of Tig in High Infants came back to haunt me that evening. I was a useless elephant in the three-legged, I broke the egg for the egg-and-spoon before the race even started, and everyone roared laughing at the spectacle I made as Jimmy struggled under the billowing weight of his gigantic red encumbrance in the wheelbarrow race. It was awful; the only good thing all evening was general knowledge, which I won because I remembered William Thackeray's middle name was Makepeace.

As if things weren't bad enough, Bernadette Gibbons dug her nails into my arm in the cloakroom getting our coats after it was over.

"You'll never believe it, Róisín."

"What? Let go of me, you're hurting me."

"It's Lorcan," she sighed.

"Lorcan who?" I said sourly.

"He asked me to go with him. Honestly. You won't believe this: it was Lorcan made out the names for Father O'Hehir. Well, he kept his own name back. Yes, and then he slipped it to me before I went up to pick. Can you imagine anything more romantic? Oh, Róisín, I'm going with him. Lorcan Burke has asked me to go with him . . . ."

To go with him. She's going with him. Bernadette Gibbons is going with Lorcan Burke. Pass it on.

Well, someone would ask Róisín McGovern to go with him too. He would. Just let them all wait and see. But who? Lorcan Burke was practically the only boy in the world who would speak to me, let alone might ask me to go with him.

It was all wrong. It was awful. Lorcan Burke was mine. Or maybe Fionnuala's. I could bear that. But not Bernadette Gibbons. Lorcan Burke belonged to the island and Bernadette Gibbons did not. She would have just laughed at little Bridget, dead with sorrow. Would have kicked the leaves from her grave and rolled around in fits at Lorcan's kingly raiment.

It was all wrong. How could he?

"Very easily," said Harry. Harry went out of his way to tell me when he saw them at the pictures. How the pair of them made smoke rise better than anything on the screen. How he had to fight the projector to make it show the film instead of following Burke's hand. "Honestly, you'd want to see it, Róisín."

"Shut up you, Harry McGovern."

"Oooh, is that the way the wind blows? Well now, what's sauce for the goose is sauce for the gander. Why don't you get your own Russian hands and Roman fingers?"

"And why don't you speak English?" I answered sourly. You'd have to have seen whatever film Harry saw last to keep up with him. Pidgin, bad proverbs, clichés – or maybe the warnings of Charlton Heston wrapped around the come-hithers of Mae West – God knows what mood he'd be in. And it was worse now he was away most of the time and I was out of practice.

"Ah, but you understand me all the same, *ma petite* gooseberry. *Ma petite montagne.*"

I did. I knew all right. I didn't need anyone telling me what was going on with Lorcan Burke and Bernadette Gibbons. And somehow it seemed the last betrayal of the island.

I wondered what I could do and I made up my mind. If I could not have Lorcan Burke, I would have the only other inhabitant of the island. I would have Ben Thompson.

The minute I hit on it, it felt right. Because deep down I never stopped hoping Ben Thompson would blossom. Miserable guilt for hurting him publicly haunted me still. I would make up for all that forever now.

The Lone Ranger, the other lads called him. And the bike he was never off – Silver. "It's the Lone Ranger. Hi yo, Silver!" You could see the lads out slapping their flanks, encouraging his mortified progress down Main Street. Still, a nickname was not a bad thing in itself, surely. It was proof of some normality.

Yet I knew there would always be something different about Ben Thompson. I looked at him and saw velvety skin, soft and tender – too soft for a boy. Eyes piercing as a cat's for the millisecond you could catch them. To me, he was like the hero in a fairy tale – only his happy ever after was in some other story. And I wanted to do my level best to get him there. I didn't as much fall in love as want to jump on Silver with him and pedal like the hammers for Tír na n-Óg.

And there was no way I was going to let him down this time.

Ben Thompson liked me. He smiled whenever he met me. Always. And he never did at Bernadette, or even Fionnuala.

And he had finally chosen to show his drawing at school: the Art teacher in the Brothers' told my father that Ben Thompson was the most talented student he had seen in forty years in the classroom.

But the best thing of all about Ben Thompson was that I knew he would never hurt. He would never turn his back deliberately on me. He would not laugh and he would not ask someone else to go with him right in front of my eyes.

There was only one flaw in this logic: just as Ben Thompson would never ask anyone else to go with him, neither would he ask me. And God knows I tried to make him.

He liked me. I know he did. He smiled and blushed puce and then pedalled his bike off furiously every time he saw me. But he always smiled and said hello. It was that bike – he was always on that blessed bike . . . . How could he stop pedalling just like that, get off the bike, and start talking to me or any girl.

I played the cancelling names game all over my schoolbooks – the one where you cross out the letters you can find in both names. You cancel them out and count the ones you are left with. *Love, like, hate, adore, kiss, court, marry* . . . . And you get that Ben Thompson adores Róisín McGovern and she's going to marry him. And if you do Benjamin Thompson, you get that he loves me and I court him. And if you do Benjamin Joseph Thompson – which I remember is his full name from roll call – and Róisín Adele McGovern, which is mine, you get that he kisses me and I adore him, and what more proof do you want? I didn't know his confirmation name, but I'd ask him when he stopped his bike to talk to me. Which he would. Any day now.

Ben Thompson was gorgeous-looking, really, when you came to think about it. Every bit as nice as Lorcan Burke, if not nicer. Lorcan Burke had gin-bottle shoulders. I heard my father saying it once – "gin-bottle shoulders, just like his mother's."

"Bernadette?"

"Mmm?" Bernadette Gibbons was always mooning about these days; honestly, she'd sicken you.

"Do you think Ben Thompson is nice-looking?"

"Your taste was always in your mouth, Róisín McGovern," she sighed deeply. "That fella is an eejit now and he'll be an eejit until the day he dies. He'll never pass any exam known to man. Lorcan says he hasn't a hope in hell of getting the Inter."

Lorcan says, Lorcan says, I mimicked her in my mind. If she could only see herself.

"An artist, if you don't mind," said Bernadette. "An artist. Now I ask you. Van Gogh, the lads call him – after some painter fella. Poor eejit . . . Lorcan says it's the best of a few names they have for him . . . ."

Lorcan says. Lorcan says. Wouldn't I have loved to be able to stick "Lorcan says" in front of every second thing I said. Or Ben says. Anybody says.

Well, Bernadette Gibbons was wrong. She was wrong when we were kids and she was wrong now, and I was worse to be listening to her. They were all wrong. One day Ben Thompson would show them all. Her and Lorcan says and the whole lot of them. He would be a world-famous artist and he would give lots of interviews on television. Where he would tell everyone it was all due to the great love of his life: his dear wife, Róisín. He would smile then at me sitting beside him, eyes downcast modestly to hide my blush. Oh yes, he would tell them, she always saw his genius – even as far back as High Infants. She stood by him in the early days when the rest of the world scorned. Yes, she was indeed the Mystery Lady in his Green Period. The Mona Lisa of the twentieth century. Hers was not an obvious beauty, a gaudy prettiness destined to fade, but a haunting, elusive, and natural grandeur torn from the sheer, craggy magnificence of the very cliffs she walked. (I was reading *Wuthering Heights* around then.)

Truth be told, it wasn't as much the cliffs I was stalking as Church Road away out by the West End where Ben Thompson lived. Most days found me out there with my hair backcombed and lacquered to a frowsy tow, my best clothes on, and the jaundiced orange stockings popular at the time.

I didn't like going on my own, but Fionnuala was away and Bernadette had much bigger fish to fry.

I went to great rounds to ambush Ben Thompson. I learned his habits from dawn to dusk and there I'd be, blocking his path four times a day. It always went the same: he'd be on the bike, he'd blush, smile, and say hello. And he never once as much as slowed down, let alone stopped and got off that bike.

Three months this went on. I can well see how some poor deluded sot spends years pursuing the object of an obsession. I was well on the way myself.

But, of course, there was also something about the climate at home then fertile for obsession. Bride magazines with little swatches of fabric as bookmarks tripped you up at every turn. There were pictures torn from the dentist's waiting room and articles on mud packs for a radiant skin on the big day. There were volumes on every aspect of suggested behaviour, dress, demeanour, and emotion appropriate to the bridal party. And Deirdre was charging down home to Duneen between stints of duty with more magazines and more articles, along with bolts of silk from Thailand, lace from Brussels, and whatnot from Paris.

The house reeked of paint. Mammy was having it done up because Grainne and Jack Comiskey were bound to want to come and meet us all some day.

Harry never came home now if he could help it. No one missed him except me. No one noticed what I did either, as long as I kept my opinions to myself about the latest idea for the dress. Daddy kept his opinions to himself too, working harder than ever at grinds because he knew who would be footing the bills in the end.

In March, there was a change. Our dining room had been sealed off to the dress. In there, Duneen's dressmaker was commissioned to come up with the impossible: a wedding dress which would live up to both Mammy's and Deirdre's expectations. Mrs. Kelly did her best, consenting to work in our house under Mammy's eye and where the room could be given over entirely as a shrine to the dress. But by early March the inevitable was apparent to all: the dress was a holy show. You wouldn't ask a tinker to get married in it.

So the action moved to Dublin and a dressmaker who hadn't two left hands.

Another thing happened that March: Ben Thompson's grandmother died.

All I saw in that poor woman's death was the perfect chance to get inside Ben Thompson's house and somehow closer to him. I was hoping for the kind of Irish wake you read about, but no luck. As a matter of fact I have yet to see one like that. I don't know where they have them, but no one has ever danced me off my feet around a coffin for three days.

Fionnuala Fitzgerald was home from boarding school for the long Saint Patrick's weekend, so I persuaded her to go with me to pay our respects to the dead.

She did not want to go. Her mother might be there, she said. Fionnuala's mother, of course, would be the one to lay out old Mrs. Thompson in the linens of the dead.

"She can't be there all the time," I said. "We'll pick a time we know she's not there and then we'll go in pretending we're looking for her."

I bullied and badgered Fionnuala until she agreed. We awaited Mrs. Fitzgerald's return home the next day and headed for Church Road.

It wouldn't be my first dead body by any means. Most of the corpses in our town were laid out by Mrs. Fitzgerald before removal to the church. It was a matter of great one-upmanship how many you saw.

The Thompsons' was a small squat bungalow, its pebbledash

face black with grime. Neighbours had tried to cut back the brambles in the small front patch for the occasion, but it now looked worse for its wounds. Only a black bow and thumbtacked mortuary card indicated the position of a hall door in the dark recesses of the porch cave.

Inside was dark too, with sombre cold walls and a runner of tintawn the length of the stone hall floor. Small rooms ran off each side of the hall, none bright.

When the old woman who answered the door turned on the hall light, you could see that a long time ago someone had painted the walls green down as far as a black stripe, and brown below.

Although she looked feeble, the old woman grabbed us with two brown-spotted claws: "Come in. Come in. Aren't you the wise girls now, coming to see what life holds in store for you."

It was too late to back out.

The old woman looked enough like Ben's grandmother for us to presume she was a sister. She kept a tight grip on both of us as she shuffle-marched us down the hall and into the last room on the right.

There old Mrs. Thompson lay in her white bed. Candles flickered creamily around her, making her skin softer than in life, her hair fluffier, more white. But gone was her birdlike lightness, her frailty, her look of twisted pain. Just her yellow, waxen shape was left.

There was such calmness and beauty in that room it was impossible to feel afraid. Mrs. Fitzgerald's linens had turned an ugly bed into a perfect altar. Embroidered birds fluttered in the candlelight. Fish, bread, goblets of wine flickered and shone softly. Life itself danced around the draped body and folded hands.

An aged Snow White, she lay there. She wore a dress of blue and white, pinned with the emblems of her prince. It was easy to see how he might have kissed that lightness in her and drawn it up to him.

I felt such a louser. Here I was, with no thought in my head but would I catch sight of Ben Thompson. I said a quiet Act of Contrition as much for myself as for the old lady.

"You don't think this will ever happen to you, do you?" I jumped as my shoulder was gripped. The old lady was back.

"Soon I'll be lying in my own candlelight," she smiled. "No tears now," she said. "No tears. Or if you do cry, cry for the joy of it. She's the lucky one. Come with me."

We followed her into the small kitchen. It too made you want to shiver and hug yourself: stone floor and cupboards of dark green chipped paint. A fruitcake sat on the rotting draining board over a sink yellow as old false teeth. There were tins, packages, biscuits, and bottles everywhere. She put lemonade, shop cake, and biscuits in front of us.

"This is a sad house," she said. "You can see that, can't you?"

I nodded, my mouth full of Kerry Cream. Fionnuala was eating nothing, of course, but I think I would still eat in front of a firing squad.

"But death is not why it is sad. It was life," she said.

She leaned forward, staring into our eyes. She had us now.

"She could never reach her son. No matter how hard she tried." We stared at her.

"And now her grandson." That was Ben she was talking about. What did she mean?

"Death is the best thing in this house. You can see that, can't you?" She looked from Fionnuala to me and then back to Fionnuala. Suddenly she snatched Fionnuala's hand.

"You can see that, I know you can," she said again.

"No," said Fionnuala.

"Yes you can. The other one can't, but you can."

"No," said Fionnuala, nearly shouting now.

"Yes you can. I see it in your eyes."

She was clutching now with both hands, her face close to Fionnuala's.

"You do understand. Admit it," she said.

"Yes," said Fionnuala. "Yes." And she tore herself free and ran out of the house.

"You old witch!" I shouted, spitting Kerry Cream at her. "Just because you have one foot in the grave yourself . . . ."

"That's right, child. You can see more clearly from there."

I ran out after Fionnuala.

Outside, the sun was blinding and the air sweet with hyacinths from neighbours' gardens. Across the road crocuses and first daffodils bloomed. Children played and shrieked.

"I'm sorry, Fionnuala," I said, running after her. "Stop, Fionnuala, stop. She was only a stupid old woman. One foot in the grave herself and she can't bear to see us young. Jealous old witch."

"She's right, can't you see? Right," said Fionnuala.

"What do you mean?"

"You can't get away from death . . . . "

"What are you talking about, Fionnuala. That's nonsense."

"Ben Thompson's father killed himself."

"He did not. It was an accident. Everyone said so."

"That's what everyone was told. Father O'Hehir's orders."

"How do you know?" I asked her.

"Who lays them all out?"

"Your mother never told you that."

"She told my father. I heard them."

"But he's in the graveyard. You can't be buried in consecrated ground," I said.

"No full knowledge. No full consent. Grievous matter, yes."

"Oh, my God. Well don't mind that old biddy. It has nothing to do with you, Fionnuala."

"It's such a tragic house . . . . "

I tried but I couldn't seem to console her no matter what I said. The whole thing seemed to have taken on a shape of its own, far beyond my understanding.

Instead of it frightening me off, I felt worse. I knew I had to save Ben Thompson. From what exactly and how I didn't know. But that didn't stop me trying. By God, how I tried.

However, Ben Thompson didn't seem to want to be saved. This became finally apparent at Bernadette Gibbon's fourteenth birthday party.

It was to be mixed – the very first mixed party in our class. The only reason I could go at all was because Mammy was up in Dublin seeing to the dress.

"Who are you asking, Bernadette?" I wanted to know.

"Well, of course, there'll be Lorcan for me. He says he can't wait. He's got a really smashing present I'm going to love. I don't know who else I'm asking yet. I suppose I'll ask him who he wants –"

"Bernadette, will you ask just one person for me?"

"Who?"

"Ben Thompson."

"Ben Thompson! He'd ruin any party single-handed. Sure that fella has never been known to open his mouth to speak. Not on your life will I ask Ben Thompson."

"Please, Bernadette. I'll do every single thing you want before the party. I'll do all the work . . . . I'll . . . I'll get the loan of Harry's records," I finished rashly.

"What has he got?"

" 'Expresso Bongo,' 'The Twist' – "

"They're ancient, Róisín McGovern. Forget it. Lorcan has better than that."

" 'Halfway to Paradise,' 'Can't Help Falling in Love' – "

"Done," said Bernadette. "You just show me those first and we have a bargain: Ben Thompson comes to the party. God, there's no accounting for taste, is there?"

Daddy said I could go if he collected me himself at eleven and Harry said on the phone I could borrow his records, but if one came back with as much as a hair or a speck of dust on it, I would have to cough up. "Halfway to Paradise" was mine. I saved up the five and ninepence for it. But Harry was the donor for that too: I bought it out of the money he gave me for Christmas.

You'd think it was a Roman orgy we were planning at Gibbons's to listen to Miss McAloon and her cronies in the post office: "They're taking up the carpet and shaking stuff on the floor for dancing. To make it slippy, if you don't mind. And Brendan and Kathleen Gibbons off to the pictures so they won't be in the way of the fun. That's asking for trouble. Begging for it. Did you know

Father O'Hehir offered to drop in and keep an eye on them and he was more or less told mind his own business. Things were very different in our day, I'm glad to say."

The scandalous event arrived at last.

The room was cleared for dancing, and by eight o'clock the girls were peppering with impatience that the boys would never get on with it. They just kept hanging around in corners, no matter what great records of Harry's we put on. Mr. and Mrs. Gibbons would be back on top of us and the whole party over before they'd move.

Bernadette finally had to drag Lorcan out, and after a while the others began to sidle out too.

Ben Thompson came to the party. I didn't think he would until the very minute he shuffled in. He stood in the doorway between the hall and the living room for two solid hours. Even when all the others had long begun to dance, he stood with his shoulder hunched to the doorjamb, his head permanently and apologetically bent.

There was food in the kitchen, records and dancing in the living room. There was no drinking, or anything like that, and only a little bit of smoking. And I kept putting on records I liked, records I'd like Ben Thompson to dance with me:

> I want to be your lover,
> But your friend is all I stay.
> You leave me halfway to paradise,
> So near, yet so far away.

And I wouldn't mind, but that blessed record cost me five and ninepence just for this party and now he wouldn't even ask me to dance.

But Ernest McMahon kept asking me to dance. Home from posh boarding school and only invited because Lorcan licked up to him and his money. He had a fat face and wet lips.

It was Ben Thompson I watched. I watched him just stand there with his eyes on the floor and his hands in his pockets.

I willed him to speak. To move, to smile – anything.

But he paid no more heed to me now than he had in High Infants; *Go and stand with your face to the wall, Róisín McGovern. How many times have I told you not to prompt Ben Thompson?* No, Ben Thompson never would listen to Róisín McGovern's prompting, would he?

It was then Bernadette Gibbons announced her surprise – her parents would be home soon, so hurry up everybody. She was going to turn out the lights for two minutes and every boy was to kiss the girl he most wanted to in the whole world and no one would tell.

There was a minute's sniggering and a lot of shuffling and everyone looking around to see if the way was clear in whatever direction mattered. I perched on the arm of the sofa, near the door to the hallway but not too near. Just close enough so nobody could possibly miss his way getting to me.

Bernadette touched the switch and the room was plunged into giggling blackness.

I sat like a lit squib in the dark. He would. He would. I just knew it. Could he get to me from where he was in the dark? Was that a creak? Was it him? It was someone – someone coming closer and closer. I could feel the warm breath and then the hand on my shoulder. Then I could feel another hand on my cheek and a face very near mine. The kiss missed, touching my jawbone. And then he was gone.

I hugged myself there in the dark; it had to be Ben Thompson at last. I knew it just had to be.

The lights went back on and there was no sign of Ben Thompson anywhere. Bernadette was at the switch, all red and with the dimples showing. Everyone was a bit red, straightening clothes and sitting up properly. Some of the girls had their hands to their throats.

"Where's Ben, Bernadette?" I asked.

"How should I know?"

"Did you see him?"

"He's gone. Took off through the back door like greased lightning when I turned out the lights. He's gone home. Good riddance to bad rubbish."

"Are you sure? Are you absolutely positive?"

"Ah, stop annoying me, Róisín McGovern." Lorcan put his arm around her again and they began to dance.

It was then I saw Ernest McMahon looking at me like a cat at cream. He put on "Halfway to Paradise" and lumbered towards me in time to the music: "I want to be your lover . . . ." Billy Fury and Ernest McMahon sang it, but it was Ernest McMahon who asked me to dance.

"I have to go home" – I heard my own voice, high-pitched and shrill.

"So go, Róisín McGovern," shouted Bernadette across the dance floor. "And good riddance to you too."

I made a plunge at the record player.

"It only lasts a few minutes. Will you leave it alone," said Bernadette.

"It's my record and I'm taking it right now."

"Well, honestly," said Bernadette. "Some people. Would you mind what you're doing to that record player. You'll wreck it. Go easy. God, you'll wreck that needle."

I wrenched off the record and left.

I headed for the sea, running. I threw the record on the ground and stamped on it. It wouldn't break. Bloody unbreakable plastic. I picked it up and ran on.

On and on, over the bridge. I raised my hands and brought them and the record down on a stone jutting up from the bridge wall. The record snapped in two. I hurled the pieces far into the stream. On I ran.

I threw myself on a bench overlooking the sea. All I could hear was my own violent breathing; the pounding of my heart rising and filling up my head.

Then slowly, ever so slowly, the hammering subsided and the sounds of the evening began to creep in: the sea swishing quietly over the stones below. *Wishing . . . whispering.* And then its deeper answer: Ocean, Róisín, Róisín . . . . It was my name . . . the sea was whispering my name . . . calling me back . . . softly bringing me home.

And then I noticed the sky was still there – it hadn't fallen or disappeared – and there was even a moon cutting a glittery slice in the inkiness of the quiet sea. The moon was a D. What was it Daddy used to say? When it's a D, it's a C . . . when it's a C, it's a D . . . decreasing. It was a D now . . . increasing . . . a new moon.

I went quietly back to Bernadette's and when Daddy came for me I was sitting on the steps outside with Harry's records.

Ben Thompson did fail the Inter. Lorcan said and Lorcan was right.

He left school forever then, and he left Duneen for construction work with his brother in Dublin. He went without even saying goodbye.

He went just before I got the Louis-heeled shoes; someone at a party in Deirdre's flat forgot them and she gave them to me. They were a bit tight but gorgeous: black patent leather with three stripes across the toe and beautiful baby high heels.

I rubbed Vaseline into them every day, and I would not even go into a room with a lit fire, in case they might crack. And every night going to sleep I put them up on my dressing table, where I could see them in the moonlight. I looked and looked. And I wondered, if Ben Thompson had only seen me in those, would he have got off the bike.

I read an article about our old school in the Irish Times *last year. I thought of you. But then I hardly ever read, see, or hear anything that I don't think of you. When something moves me – and that is often – I go back and try to feel it again with your senses.*

It spoke of the enlightened and forward-looking attitude of the teachers and remaining nuns; the girls were learning to soak up the history of their own town and seek their own sense of place. They were being encouraged to choose and research their own projects, interview whomever they wanted, and so on. The broader and deeper their perspective, the better.

Towards the end of the article there was a wistful little quote from one of the older nuns. She was regretting that the school was not like this in my day. And for me that was the most hopeful note of all.

Bernadette Gibbons said that Lorcan Burke said that I was ugly. That Róisín McGovern was UGLY; and he, for one, wouldn't be caught dead near her.

The cavalry came in the unlikely shape of Crunchies O'Laughlin.

He was Frank O'Laughlin now and would beat up anyone who reminded him of his baby nickname. He was the answer to no maiden's prayer himself, his own attractions not exactly sighed and moaned over in female huddles. But he had one great attraction as far as I was concerned: he was showing distinct signs of wanting to be where Lorcan Burke said he wouldn't be found dead – in the vicinity of Róisín McGovern and her flawed accoutrements. Frank O'Laughlin didn't seem to mind it being known he fancied ugly Róisín McGovern. And me? Well, I was afraid there would never again be another such blind fool.

There was one great obstacle in the path of true love: Frank O'Laughlin was riff-raff. I already knew where my mother and father stood on this subject regarding girls. I was well aware of the further unsuitability of male riff-raff. And that Crunchies definitely was: he had left school at Inter Cert to work in Doyle's Grocery and Provisions, he lived in the cottages, and his father dug roads for a living. And if that wasn't enough, not even the minutest flaw in Frank O'Laughlin's character was likely to have escaped my father. Because he had had him in his classroom for three fruitless years. Frank O'Laughlin had resisted the Latin declensions one and all, and x was the same unknown quantity on the last day as it had been on the first. For three years he tolerated my father's attempts on his mind, but only until he was old enough to leave school.

No, Frank O'Laughlin would never be a welcome guest at Deirdre's wedding in any capacity, let alone a contender for the ugly sister.

Actually, I had trouble seeing him as contender myself; I was more anxious to have a boyfriend – any boyfriend – than covetous of Crunchies in particular. I wanted to see if all boys were dead set against having anything to do with me, or was it just Ben Thompson. And Lorcan Burke. How many more?

And, of course, there was nothing frightening about Frank O'Laughlin. Not like Barry McCann, for instance. Barry McCann had stories whispered about him which would make your hair curl. I'm not sure exactly how he managed this because no one ever admitted to co-operating with him. But Crunchies had no such stories whispered about him. On the contrary, he was most understanding, most accommodating as to the peculiar hours I managed to steal with him: Sunday afternoons, maybe the odd film when I was meant to be going with Bernadette Gibbons. Certainly no dances. It never once occurred to me that Frank O'Laughlin might be a little pleased to be "going with" the daughter of the master who made his last years in school such a misery.

Actually, my father had very little reason to worry, even if he had known all this. Because, although I was close to brilliant at devising schemes for keeping the illicit company of this threat to my unsullied self, I was quite at a loss as to how to behave when the impossible was managed and I was alone with him once more. Oh, I kissed him and all that, but I don't recall anything very earth-shattering about it. I don't remember any reactions at all to his onslaughts. I don't even remember his first kiss or his last kiss, let alone the ones in between. This may well be due to the fact that we were often double-dating with Bernadette Gibbons and Lorcan. At times like these my most passionate efforts were devoted to trying to show Lorcan what he was missing. Right in flagrante delicto one eye would be over Crunchies' shoulder at Lorcan and Bernadette; willing Lorcan to realize he had the wrong girl.

Oh yes, Lorcan Burke might say he wouldn't be caught dead going with me, but he could tolerate my presence in a foursome all right. Because that was often the only way Bernadette and I could get away to meet them at all. Like a graph in Maths it was: If two cyclists A and B leave point X for point Y at two o'clock travelling at four miles an hour, and two other cyclists C and D leave point Z for point Y at two o'clock at four miles an hour, where will the cyclists meet? Up behind the cliff path beyond the Fairy Bridges, that's where. Every time. It never failed. About half past two.

Even if my father didn't know about this scandalous affair, there were others who suspected. Duneen was a small, self-righteous town in the winter – only its summer visitors were depraved. And Father O'Hehir, with the willing aid of the nuns, was going to see it stayed that way. I was being watched.

The first evidence of my depravity was the discovery during Geography of certain artistic works of what Sister Cecilia could only call a salacious nature:

"Róisín McGovern, what have you got there?"

"Nothing, Sister," I said.

"Don't add lies to your wickedness. I saw what you were doing. Show me at once."

"I have nothing, Sister, honestly."

"Don't *honestly* me, you two-faced girl. You pushed it under your atlas. I saw you. Give it to me this minute. This minute, Róisín McGovern, do you hear?"

I handed it over.

Sister Cecilia's eyes bulged behind her milk-bottle spectacles. She tapped my *World Geography* with agitated fingertips at an alarming speed:

"Just what I'd expect from you, Róisín McGovern. I've heard stories. Oh, I've heard stories. Dirty, impure pictures. No more than I'd expect from you, Miss."

"It's a ballet dancer, Sister," I said in genuine amazement. Dirty? Impure?

"It's impure, I tell you" – the spittle was gathering at the corners of Sister Cecilia's mouth. "Impure, do you hear? Impure. This . . . this . . . person has hardly any clothes on at all. She has . . . pro-tuberances . . . . "

"But, Sister," I said.

"But nothing, Róisín McGovern. Wait until Reverend Mother sees this. Just wait. And turn out your desk at once until I see if you have anymore of this filth."

I did. I had scores of drawings of ice skaters and ballerinas, traced, copied, and otherwise stolen from the pages of schoolgirl magazines: *Stacey Dean, Ballerina for the Queen, Phantom of the Rink*. I was good at drawing dancing and skating figures, and these pages were as close as I was ever going to get to an ice rink or a ballet stage.

The nuns didn't see it that way: Should Father O'Hehir be informed? Her parents? The nuns didn't know what to think of such a thing. They were shocked, disappointed. Saddened beyond belief. To think this was the use to which Mother Thecla's excellent teaching of art was being put.

Maybe just this once they would not upset Róisín McGovern's poor parents. Yes, a warning this time and one more chance. Of course there was no question but that Father O'Hehir must be informed the next time the nuns saw him. Oh yes, he should know exactly what he was dealing with among the youth of this parish. They would keep the evidence.

The second offence was the sighting of Róisín McGovern by the beleaguered warrior against moral turpitude himself, Father O'Hehir, complete with his flashlight.

What my father called the sacerdotal searchlight was a well-known weapon in the fight against evil. Illuminating the high-ways and byways, hedgerows and dance halls, in the quest for lust-driven sinners of the flesh – I used to hear my father laughing with Sergeant Egan. But he wasn't so amused when I was the one caught in the beam.

It was in the back row of Twomey's cinema in the company of a member of the opposite sex: one Francis Xavier O'Laughlin. Father O'Hehir's torch shook with righteousness as he expressed his grave doubts that either party had the faintest notion of what was happening on the screen above them. And this time, Miss Róisín McGovern, there would be no second chances. No, this time parental enlightenment was a necessity for Father O'Hehir's peace of mind and sound sleep. No, he was off right now to see if Master McGovern was home. That poor man doing his level best to shape and enlighten young minds and this was what his own daughter was at.

All this he delivered loudly in the back row in front of everybody. Even as Dirk Bogarde fought his own battle with the clergy in the form of John Mills on the screen.

"He won't tell, Róisín, honestly," said Crunchies. "He was only saying it."

"Shut up, you, it's all your fault. You know damn well he'll tell."

There wasn't much Father O'Hehir could have complained about after that in the back row. The only thing I could do now was brazen it out to the end. To bite my nails as I watched Bogarde die with a lopsided grin and the words "the singer, not the song." He was not converted; it was the priest he liked, not the church. He should have met Father O'Hehir, then he could talk.

I needed Bernadette for cover; I would walk home with her. I made a beeline for her as soon as the film was over.

"No, I will not, Róisín McGovern. Me and Lorcan are going for fish and chips. I have no notion of ruining my night just because you got into trouble."

I turned to Lorcan: he would see the sense in it and not let me down. He would see she had to come with me.

"Are you coming, Lorcan?" said Bernadette.

He looked at the ground, he wiped the sole of his shoe on the pavement, he looked at Crunchies, up the street, anywhere but at me.

"Lorcan?" Bernadette said again.

"Okay, Ber-Ber," he said.

Ber-ber, indeed. I never thought I'd see the day, *Lor-Lor*.

I took off for home, Crunchies trying to grab hold of me. Father O'Hehir was the laughing-stock of the whole town, he said. He was renowned. There wasn't a young person in the parish he hadn't caught somewhere at something and nobody knew that better than my father. The whole thing was only a big laugh, he said.

"It's all your fault," I shouted over my shoulder at Crunchies.

"Would you take it easy," he said. "Don't act so guilty. You were doing nothing. We weren't doing anything."

I turned on him viciously: "No thanks to you we weren't. If we were doing what you wanted, I'd have been rightly caught, wouldn't I?"

"Well, there's never much chance of that, is there?" said Crunchies.

"Whatever there was, there's less now, I can tell you." I was rounding the corner for home. My father was on the doorstep and I knew it was not for the evening air. "Get away from me, Frank O'Laughlin. He'll see you."

"Do you want me to talk to him?"

"Are you mad? Get away from me."

I walked towards home. Slowly. Breathing very deeply.

"Night, Daddy."

"Go to bed, Róisín. Remember, you put your own price on your head."

That was all? All he had to say to me?

In a way, I'd nearly rather he killed me.

Crunchies courted steadily, if not contentedly, from a distance for a while after the surprise extra feature at the cinema. Until the pageant. Everything was forgotten in the excitement of that pageant.

A year of planning and rehearsing had gone into it. More. It was eighteen months now since Ted Kelly of the Chamber of Commerce had been to Austria on his holidays – a little promotion trip aided in part by the Chamber. And he hadn't wasted their money. On his travels he had hit on a place called Oberammergau. This little village was famous for its passion play, said Ted Kelly. We wouldn't believe it, he said. Week in, week out, the whole town re-enacted the Crucifixion of Jesus. And most of the townspeople were doing very well, thank you, selling associated mementoes and generally looking after the many visitors who came to witness this unique event.

Well, well, said Ted Kelly then, but wasn't next year our own town centenary? (Centenary of exactly what was still under dispute.) But next year was definitely the centenary, and what better shot in the arm for the tourist industry than to stage a passion play of our own. Easter would be the time to go for, both religiously speaking, and as a great early start to the season. And Ted Kelly said we'd make a right job of it while we were at it. Yes sir. We'd make the Oberammergau lot look like a bunch of amateurs in from Tubbercurry.

He was on.

For authenticity, he said, it was essential that every man taking part should have long hair and a beard. No bother, there was a year to work on that. Every red-blooded male in the town took it as a personal challenge. All grew as flowing a beard and as lengthy a mane as the year permitted. There was great rivalry among thieves, scribes, and Pharisees in the unspoken contest for the most fertile follicle.

The fever was contagious. Every dogfight wanted in on the act. For a while it looked like there would be two thousand participants and no local audience.

At last the year passed and the pageant had come to fruition. It was a roaring success – much better than a *fleadh ceoil*.

It went well from my point of view also. Bernadette Gibbons and I, among others, had secured positions as raffle ticket sellers for the church roof fund. This job we were holding on to grimly because it carried with it the fringe benefit of free entry to every performance of the pageant throughout its run at the football grounds. I would never have been allowed out every night but for the laudable motive of the roof fund and for the fact that Mammy was still up in Dublin most of the time working on Deirdre's wedding.

The trouble was that Frank O'Laughlin's nose was out of joint at this arrangement. He'd been very patient since the cinema episode. But watching me flirt giddily as I peddled my wares nightly at Douglas Hyde Park was hard on his nerves. Especially from his uncomfortable position atop a tree on the wrong side of the wall. He hung around one night and caught me on my way home.

"Hey, Róisín, I have an idea."

"Oh yeah, you and your ideas got me in enough trouble."

"That's all forgotten. Listen, I can't afford the price they're asking in to the bloody pageant."

"So don't go," I said.

"It's the only chance I have to see you."

"You're seeing me now, aren't you?"

"You know very well what I mean," he said.

"Yes, it's not seeing you're after."

"I've been thinking. Here's what you'll do. You and Bernadette and Angela Whelan get in free with those ticket books, don't you?"

"You know we do."

"Well, tomorrow night, when you get in, take the other girls' books and come out the second gate. Lorcan Burke and I will be waiting. Just give us two books and we're all back in free."

"But our names are on them," I said.

"They'll never look in the crush."

"I don't know. I'll ask Bernadette."

Bernadette was all on because she was fed up with no Lorcan every night. Angela Whelan didn't want to know. Why should she? Why should she put herself out for two boys who wouldn't give her the time of day? But she must have decided in the end that even this dubious contact with the opposite sex was better than nothing, because she finally agreed. Only she would be the one to take out our books to the lads: there was no boy getting his nasty, dirty hands on her book.

It worked beautifully. Miss McAloon was on gate duty and never said a word. Glanced at the lads, they said, then at the books, and waved them through.

Well, to hell with the roof fund tonight, girls. You've done more than your duty all week. It's your night off, girls. Come away here behind the high backstands. Sure we haven't seen you in ages. Lie down there till we talk to you.

And that's where they found us. All comfy. Miss McAloon and Ted Kelly.

"There they are," said Miss McAloon triumphantly. "Merciful hour! Just like I told you they'd be. A disgrace. And thinking they could fool Eilish McAloon. Oh, if only their parents could see them there now."

"A disgrace, all right," said Ted Kelly. "At a passion play, of all things. And not a ticket sold for the roof fund."

My downfall became complete soon afterwards. It was in Geography class again.

I was near the back with a Valentine comic, part of the collection paradoxically called "Cheap Imported British Literature" by Father O'Hehir when speaking "ex catheter," as Harry called it. Valentine (or its sister, Roxy) was always full of curvy girls, alike as twins except for an enormous body of hair which could be either black or white. They hankered after Steves or Marks – alike as twins also, with lantern jaws and leather jackets and great heads of male-length black or white hair. This week Steve had a motor bike, and Linda finally won his heart when he discovered that she not only looked better than his mate both on and off the bike, but was able and willing to grease it on a Saturday before watching "Match of the Day." This week also had a great bonus:

a pin-up of Elvis Presley. I held it up behind Angela Whelan's back for Bernadette Gibbons to see. Obligingly, Elvis leered greasily over at her.

"Whatever are you rustling, Róisín McGovern?" said Sister Cecilia, squinting short-sightedly from her desk.

"Map of Africa, Sister."

"Put it away. We're on South America now."

There were giggles all round. We were emboldened by this proof of Sister Cecilia's ineptitude as custodian of law and order, and the mood heightened.

Bernadette Gibbons and Angela Whelan started passing notes with elaborate don't-let-anybody-see-this kind of faces and moves. "Ah go on show us," I mouthed back over. Bernadette shook her head. I offered Elvis as a swap. She accepted. From desk to desk a sheet of folded paper made its way to me. It was a list of questions. I was to write in the answers. So I did.

Name a boy	Frank O'Laughlin
Do you like chocolate?	Yes
How much?	I love it
What do you take off first when undressing?	My dress
And last?	My underwear
Name a make of car	A Volkswagen
What age would you like to get married?	23

Well, so what, Bernadette Gibbons? What was so great and so funny about that? She passed over another set of questions: "Try these on your answers."

Who do you love?	Frank O'Laughlin
Do you let him touch you?	Yes
Do you like it?	I love it
What does he take off first?	My dress
And last?	My underwear

Where do you do it?   A Volkswagen
How many children will
     you have?   23

"Bernadette, that's awful. Awful." I skidded it back to her along the floor.

"Róisín McGovern, what did you throw to Bernadette Gibbons?"

Oh God. "Nothing, Sister. Just a note. To wait for me after school."

I was trying to play for time, trying to palm her off with the wrong one – the innocent one. No good. She went straight for the one under Bernadette's shoe.

She turned red and then white and then purple. "Never in my life have I been subjected to anything as vile as this. And I've seen some things in my time. You're a wanton, wicked, immoral girl. Words fail me, Róisín McGovern."

But they didn't fail her at all. She kept up a steady stream of them all the way to Reverend Mother's office. Father O'Hehir was called by telephone. "Emergency, Father . . . . Sorry to take you away from your lunch, Father . . . . Oh yes. Immediate action. We think so too, Father. We'll expel her this time."

I was sent out into the schoolyard to meet him. They weren't about to dignify this sordid affair within the walls of a convent, they said.

There were thirty-three buttons down the front of his soutane and he had a spot of egg on his chin. And through the open window of High Infants was sung the news that two and one are three, and two and two are four.

"This is the fourth time you have come under my official notice."

"Yes, Father." Bless me, Father, for I have sinned. I had a terrible urge to giggle and it wasn't funny at all.

"There is something to be said for a girl who falls once and repents her wicked ways . . . . "

"I'm sorry, Father."

"But four times . . . ."

"Yes, Father."

"Of course, your parents will have to be told. Again."

"Yes, Father."

"It'll be a sore trial on them."

"I know, Father."

"Why did you do it then?"

"I didn't know what it was at the time."

"Even so. You should never have been doing anything but geography in Geography class, let alone that filthy scandalous thing."

Back and forth and back and forth it went until I was sent home with the black word *expelled* over my head forever. There was no one at home, so they were sending word to my father over at the Brothers'.

Now Daddy would have to say something. He would have to say something this time.

But he didn't. He had nothing to say except how worried and disappointed he was, how upset my mother would be. And it wasn't as if they hadn't enough worries without this just then.

And he did have one more thing to say. He said he and Mammy had finally made up their minds what to do with me. Even if this hadn't happened. They had given matters much thought and there was really only one solution: they were sending me to boarding school. Luckily Dermot Comiskey had some influence in a very nice convent and because of him they would overlook my bad record. Because of that and the one model student they already had from Duneen – Fionnuala Fitzgerald.

"And what, might I ask, are you in training for?" Harry asked, a few weekends later when he came home. "The next Mata Hari?"

I didn't know who or what this Matt O'Hara was. "What do you mean?"

"Hormones barely in gear and already you're the talk of the town. Expelled from school."

"Have I outdone you or what? Are you jealous? If you had to go to the nuns to school, you'd have been out in the first hour."

Harry laughed. "Well, there's no doubt about it, but you're a terror. Still, I'd lay money on that lot in the boarding school to put a stop to your gallop. They did a good job on Fionnuala Fitzgerald. A right dose of *uisce fuar* there."

"I don't know, Harry McGovern. No educational establishment ever managed to pour cold water on you, that anyone'd notice. And if anyone needed it, you did."

"Well, maybe I did, and maybe I didn't. The point is no one expelled me or had to lock me up for the good of society. Anyway, I'm a lost cause now, thank God. It's you we're concerned with. But you'll be okay. Look at young Fitzgerald. Any cooler and she'd freeze."

He was right.

There was definitely something different about Fionnuala Fitzgerald. I suppose there always had been, but it was just getting more pronounced. Or maybe we were growing up a bit and becoming more observant. And I certainly was, now that I was going to be locked up with her.

I did not know what to make of her. That summer she sometimes did perfectly ordinary things with me, like picnicking or swimming. Other days I spent with Bernadette Gibbons, when she could be torn from Lorcan, usually because he had to work for his mother. His mother always seemed to have jobs for him whenever Bernadette drifted on to the horizon. But even with all Mrs. Burke's determination, she couldn't prise them apart.

Other days, I stole time with Crunchies – against all orders. But no matter how shamelessly I dropped Fionnuala at the last minute for more exciting commitments, she never showed the smallest sign of crossness. I'd have had her guts for garters if it had been the other way around.

But no. Often I hid behind whatever I could find when I'd see her coming back from the island with a book. But I needn't have bothered. She'd have a dreamy half-smile on her face, the book tucked under her arm tight to her body. Even when she passed near us, she mightn't see us. If she did, it was just to smile more widely and walk gracefully on with a hello.

That was another thing that was different about Fionnuala Fitzgerald – the rest of us ran hither and yon in search of excitement, but she seemed to find her own head the best company of all.

And then there were the really strange things about her. That day in Ben Thompson's house, for instance. Well, there was another day sort of like that, only worse: the day we went to the palmist. The fortune teller. They were supposed to be a joke – cross my palm and I'll tell you about the tall, dark stranger about to cross your path. That sort of stuff.

All we were after that day was a bit of fun. Bernadette said I was a worse eejit to let Fionnuala Fitzgerald tag along in the first place, because she was death to any bit of crack.

Bernadette and I had decided a while back we were going. She wanted to see when exactly she was going to marry Lorcan Burke and how many children they might have. I doubted there was anyone in the world who was "all there" and who might still marry me. But I thought maybe it might be better to know in advance for sure that there wasn't. Then it couldn't bother me as much.

Fionnuala Fitzgerald wasn't admitting to wanting to know anything.

We went on one of the last days in August when the visitors were over and done with mostly, but the attractions still half-heartedly open and limping along.

Gypsy Bróna Lee had a little hut all to herself, between the swinging boats and the bumpers. It was wooden, painted pinkish red, with all her titles and claims in big, bold white letters on all its four walls. You couldn't pass it from any angle and miss that she was a palmist, could read cards and tea leaves, and that ten minutes with her were sure to be the most important minutes of your life. I never saw the curtains open even a crack, so you'd have to go right in to see anything inside.

What surprised me was how ordinary she was – take the scarf off her head, the jewellery and shawls, put her in a jumper and skirt, and she could have been anyone's auntie.

She wanted us separately but we didn't want to miss any of the fun. So we all sat around her little table. It was suffocatingly dark, the only light from a dim lamp. Photographs, postcards, and bill-boards cluttered the walls. The eyes of a dwarf bored from one: I CAN READ THE SECRETS OF YOUR MIND. DO YOU DARE ALLOW ME?

She took Bernadette first. We had only enough money for palms.

Bernadette would be a renowned beauty. She would be famous for that beauty. Yes, she could see a husband: dark, handsome. She would be envied for him. Men would vie for Bernadette. No, Gypsy Bróna Lee could see no children. But crowds. Yes, she could see admiring crowds. Applause. Perhaps an actress? A famous, admired actress? Anyway, a long and prosperous life of great fame.

Bernadette was delighted. She wanted to go on and on. But Gypsy Bróna shook her head and reached for my hand.

She said I was as one asleep. I might wake up one day, she could not tell. She could see children. Many, many children.

I asked her would I have a husband and she said yes and no. Yes, I would have a husband and have children, but not like other women.

I asked her what she meant and what was the husband like, but she said that was all she could tell me.

And then she reached for Fionnuala's hand. She looked at it only briefly and put it down.

"No more today," she said. "I am tired."

"Ah, go on," said Bernadette. "That's not fair. We paid you. You can't do that."

"You can have hers back," said Gypsy Bróna. "I said no more."

And nothing we said would shift her from that. As we went out the door, she ran her fingertips lightly down Fionnuala's arm, as if in sorrow. She looked at her and shook her head. She opened her mouth, then shut it. She opened it again.

"You are growing too fast," she said. "Too much, too soon."

"Jesus, Fionnuala Fitzgerald," laughed Bernadette, as we linked along the prom, "but you were always a wet blanket. Even in High Infants. And what about Bernadette Gibbons? Dame Bernadette, please. An actress. A bloody famous actress. Is this an Oscar I see before me . . . ?"

Mammy came home from her wedding preparations to pack me off to boarding school. "I wish those poor nuns well of you, Róisín McGovern. If they can make anything of you, they're better women than I am."

It was the day before my departure. Again she checked the list, the cases, checked each label I had sewn on. One dozen handkerchiefs . . . two dozen pairs of stockings . . . one dressing gown . . . .

At last I escaped. I had some final business.

It was the end of Fair Day in Duneen. All over now, bar the odd raucous shout from the dung- and spittle-fouled square. The pubs, as I passed, were warm and loud with gappy yellow guffaws. Sending out strange strong smells.

I squinted around the square: yes, there he was, over by the courthouse.

I picked my steps carefully and nonchalantly threw my shoulders and the sole of one foot against the courthouse wall.

"Hello, Frank," I said.

"How'ya Róisín. Off in the mornin'? Are you all set for the slaughter then?"

"Don't even say it. I'll go mad."

Frank applied his right shoulder and the sole of his right unpolished shoe to the wall also – about a foot away from mine. He had his hands in his pockets. Lorcan Burke was circling around on his bicycle at a respectful distance.

"Róisín, will you miss me?" said Frank.

"Of course, I will. Didn't I tell you."

"I'll miss you too. Will you write?"

"You know very well I can't. Fionnuala Fitzgerald says the nuns read all the letters coming in, and you have to leave them unsealed going out."

"You won't talk to me at all when you get back."

"Don't be daft, Frank O'Laughlin. Why wouldn't I talk to you?"

"You won't. Wait and see. Fionnuala Fitzgerald was never the same once the nuns there got their hands on her."

"I'm not Fionnuala Fitzgerald. Fionnuala Fitzgerald, indeed. I'll never be a wet blanket like that and don't you dare say I will."

"You wait and see, Róisín."

"Would you shut up. Is this what I broke my neck to see you for?"

"I gave up football practice for you, Róisín."

"Greater love hath no man."

"Why are we fighting?"

"I don't know. You said I'd get drippy like Fionnuala Fitzgerald."

"I'm only afraid you will."

"Well, I won't. Did you bring the Latin grammar?"

"What Latin grammar?"

"Bernadette was to give it to Lorcan, to give it to you, to give it to me."

"Well, she musta forgot."

"That's the only reason I was let out."

"Is that all you're worried about, Róisín? An oul' Latin book? I was fool enough to think you might be here to say goodbye to me."

"Of course, that's why I'm here. I could just have got Bernadette to call at our house with the book, couldn't I?"

"Prove it then. Give us a kiss."

"Are you mad? In the middle of the square, in broad daylight?"

"Go on. There's nobody looking.

So I did.

"Róisín, hey, Róisín, here's your father" – Lorcan Burke wobbled to a skiddy halt in front of us.

Sure enough, there was my father striding across the square. But it was all right, he wasn't even looking this way. He had a big brown envelope under his arm; he was going to catch the evening post. Still, I wasn't taking any chances.

"I have to go, lads."

"Not yet, Róisín," said Frank.

But I was gone. Home like the hammers to change every stitch of clothes, in case the sight of me would change vague notion into certainty for my father. I wasn't reared on the Hardy Boys for nothing.

If my father did see me, true to form, he didn't say. Instead, he covered all my books for me and went downstairs to the parlour for cellotape to mend any weak spines.

At ten o'clock the doorbell rang.

I knew it. I just knew it. It had to be Frank O'Laughlin with the Latin grammar. No one ever rang our doorbell at ten o'clock at night. And my father downstairs between me and the door.

I took three steps at a time to get there first.

Sure enough, there was Frank, hand up with book, mouth open to speak.

My father's head was bobbing towards us.

I grabbed the book, closed the door, and flung myself against it.

My father just looked at me. Out over the bifocals. Sadly.

Mother Elaine, the mistress of schools, felt it better the other children knew nothing of the disgrace surrounding the new arrival. I couldn't have agreed more.

Fionnuala Fitzgerald knew of course, said Mother Elaine. Being from the same town. But she would say nothing, said Mother; she was a dear, obedient, well-mannered girl. Not like me, hung unspoken in the air around us.

"How beautiful the school is, Mother," said Mammy. "More like a stately home. Róisín is a very lucky girl and we're immensely grateful."

My mother was torn between telling them how bad I really was and knowing that if she overdid it she might have me back home in the car with them.

"We have asked Fionnuala Fitzgerald to help Róisín settle," said Mother Elaine.

Fionnuala materialized from nowhere, propelled by a black shadow which immediately disappeared again.

She smiled her goody-goody smile. Not at me. Oh no, first at my father and mother, then at Mother Elaine. All she was missing was the halo. On some kids, shoes never scuff, collars never turn up, stains never land. Fionnuala was one of those. I was one of the others. I hated her polite boarding-school smile on sight. She gave us the benefit of it again.

"Fionnuala will show you everything, dear. Run along now, girls, while I have a little chat with Róisín's parents."

"But her things, Mother . . . ." My mother was not used to someone else actually being seen to accept responsibility for her cross in life.

"All taken care of, Mrs. McGovern. Say goodbye to your parents now, Róisín, dear."

And so it was mercifully over before we knew where we were. I hadn't the nerve to cry.

The first week was the worst.

Up at half past six. Strip the clothes from the bed. Over your chair now, please, and well outside the cubicle. Oh Jesus, through the most pure heart of Mary, I offer you all the prayers, works, and sufferings and joys of this day for all the intentions of thy sacred heart, and particularly for the intentions of our Holy Father, the Pope. Wash well, now, girls.

After mass it was breakfast at half past seven. Not on long wooden trestles I had imagined like the ones in *Oliver Twist*, but smaller tables seating seven and covered in white linen. I was at Fionnuala's because she was from my town and the only person I knew. She broke the rules to whisper to me before grace:

"Tuesdays, Thursdays, and Saturdays we get sausages for breakfast. That's Sister Martha pouring the tea. She's called Sister because she's only a lay sister. That means her family is poor and didn't have much of a dowry for her when she entered. You call her Sister. Sisters do the housework. The rest are all called Mother, which means they had a dowry or education. Mostly they do the teaching and you call them Mother. You stand back to let them pass whenever you meet them. You don't have to do that for the sisters, but I always do because I think it isn't fair . . . ."

I began to like her.

We said grace and started to eat. Mother Elaine stood at the massive sideboard and gave some etiquette reminders, all for the benefit of the newest savages.

"Never eat and drink together; that's disgusting; like making a pudding in your mouth. Cut a slice of bread in half, then in quarters, finally in fingers as you need them. Place a pat of butter on your plate and little marmalade . . . . Now butter each bite . . . . Break a roll, never cut . . . . And never brandish your cutlery about . . . and never hold your knife thus – *that*, girls, is how one goes about writing, not eating. Fork tine down and knife blade out, tips meeting will show any civilized being you have not finished eating . . . . Fork tine up, knife blade in, both straight will signify you have."

It was bedmaking then at eight; the vast dormitory appeared once more with the drawing back of pleated linen walls. It was pleasing: airy and fresh and gay, with many coloured eiderdowns all arranged the same way on white honeycomb counterpanes. The wooden floor shone warmly; a pitcher and basin stood on every oak locker.

Fionnuala had a bed on the window side, a privilege of being in the school longer. We looked out when everyone had gone. Down over the gardens, the tennis and basketball courts farther on, and the three hockey fields on the fringes. All dominated by a tall white statue: the Virgin Mary. We would be crowning the statue queen of the school in May, Fionnuala said.

"You can't be serious. They crown a statue?"

"Yes. We walk around the grounds, singing hymns every Saturday in May, and on the last Saturday the three head girls wear long white dresses and veils, with some little ones as attendants. The girl here the longest crowns the statue with a wreath of flowers."

This was worse than I thought. "Dressing up to crown a statue? Sounds unbelievably childish to me."

"It isn't, honestly. But you'd have to be there. I can still smell the wallflowers and feel the peace if I close my eyes."

Holy Jesus, not only a goody-goody but a religious maniac as well. Let me out of here.

We went back to the study then to collect books for class. My desk was out in the middle of the floor – the bigger desks around the walls were for seniors, and ones at windows for girls who were here longer and daughters of Old Girls.

After class it was games outside and no choice in the matter. According to Miss Dowling, anyone could play hockey, or tennis, or rounders, or basketball; it was just a case of wanting to and trying. Well, she didn't know me, who couldn't master Tig. She had her first exception to the rule. After a week she was glad to let me bring a book and sit on a bench behind goals.

111

It was afternoon tea at four, which sounded much better than it looked: white sliced bread and butter. There was jam on weekends, cake only on feast-days, few and far between.

After tea there was Study until supper at seven. Then optional indoor recreation from half past seven to eight: you could twist with Chubby Checker, or drool about who you'd really like to be dancing with for the slow ones. I remember Brendan Bowyer's smoochy "Love Thee Dearest" best. He was really big in our school because he was famous and yet practically engaged to a friend of one of the Galway girls. We had "Twenty Four Hours from Tulsa" too, but the nuns took it away when they listened to the words and realized it was about adultery.

On the fifth day, there was a letter for me from Daddy. There it was, neatly slit open, when I came in for Study. It didn't say much: "Wear your warm vest so you won't catch cold; you know how your throat can give you trouble. If you have to go out to the dentist and you get lost, be sure to stop and ask a civic guard." Why doesn't he just say a guard . . . or even *gárda síocána*. Who ever calls them civic guards . . . . "The house is flat without you . . . very quiet . . . . " No warning at all and the tears came. There they were, huge patchy splashes like the first drops of a downpour. All dark on my navy cotton desk cover and everybody looking . . . .

I asked to be excused before the deluge hit. But there was nowhere to get away. I was buried under the coats in the blazer dressing room when I felt a hand on me. It was Fionnuala Fitzgerald.

"Go away," I said. "Just go away and leave me alone. Is there any corner in this bloody place where I don't have to have someone looking at me?"

"I'll show you. Come on, Róisín."

I followed her down some stairs, along a few corridors, and into a small music room.

"Is something wrong?" she said.

"Everything's bloody wrong. Mind your own business."

"I only want to help. Are you homesick?"

"Homesick? That's a laugh. They couldn't wait to get rid of me. Why would I be homesick?"

"Well, what is it?"

"Mind your own business. What do you care anyway?"

"I know what it's like to be new. And I'm supposed to be helping you settle in, remember?"

"So that's it. You're afraid I'll get myself into trouble again. Expelled maybe. And your nice perfect record would be all ruined. You were supposed to be minding me."

"That's not it at all." She looked so hurt I had the grace to be sorry.

"Why should you care?" I said a bit less roughly. "I was never exactly a good friend of yours."

"You were never mean. Not like Bernadette and some of the others."

"I wasn't very nice either," I said, guilt jogging my memory and my tongue.

"You know when someone's being mean and rotten and when they're not. And you weren't. You used to remind me – no . . . . "

"You might as well say it," I said. "It won't be any worse than anything I've heard already. What did I remind you of?"

"My dog."

"Jesus, thanks. I needed that. I suppose he was a boxer, was he? Or a Saint Bernard?"

But Fionnuala was laughing: "He was a pup. A Labrador. And he didn't look like you."

"Gee, thanks."

"It was the way he'd sniff off in ten directions at once. You were always like that. Someone would only have to suggest anything for fun and you were on."

"A bloody dog. I've heard everything now. A bloody dog. Woof, woof."

"Don't take it wrong," said Fionnuala. "I only meant you were nice and never mean. No matter what trouble you've got yourself in . . . . "

"I don't know whether to be complimented or to hit you in the mouth. Well, what happened to Woofwoof? Did he grow up a delinquent, too?"

"No, he died. He found poison on the golf links."

I didn't know what to say to that. "I'm sorry he died, Fionnuala."

She shrugged slightly and nodded.

"Are you actually saying you don't not like me, then. You're not just being nice because they told you to?" I said.

"I like you, Róisín. I always have."

Damn it if the bloody tears weren't back. It was so long since anyone said anything nice. Harry used to a little bit, but he was gone. And Daddy used to, but somehow I had lost him along the way – I didn't know where. Nor how to find him again. I let rip and bawled.

It was after that Fionnuala Fitzgerald became my BF.

Having a best friend was life and death in boarding school. You knew her step on the other side of the study hall, her giggle behind you in the ranks, and every shred of the meagre possessions allowed her in school.

You supported one another. If she shone at games, it was her duty to pick you for her team. About sixth or seventh choice; you couldn't expect her to pick you before the real bulldozers, like Frances Corry or Helen McMahon. Fionnuala always picked me for her side the moment before humiliation. She was hot favourite for next year's captaincy of the First Eleven, so her selection of me before less useless dregs was tolerated if not condoned.

Best friends had other duties too: they had to send you endless streams of holy pictures. Mostly these were in rem. of being your BF. They were in remembrance of other things too: from the Christmas holidays being thirty-seven days, six hours and fifty-two minutes away to half-hourly bulletins on the state of your pimples / homework / hunger – to descriptions of the chocolate cake Pidge Mackey got at the parlour. Having visitors was called "going to the parlour." Pidge Mackey was always going to the parlour and always getting chocolate cakes or, my God, biscuit cakes weighing half a ton. The trick was to be at her table or, if not, to lick her boots with such eagerness she might get permission to send you a piece at yours. Lots of people were Pidge Mackey's BF for about three weeks.

Fionnuala had one terrible drawback as a BF: she was a serious student. She spent every minute at homework, but I wasn't so hard up. I'd look longingly over in her direction when Night Rec rolled around. Not a chance. She'd have her head stuck in the Third Punic War, even though Roman History was only worth a lousy five per cent on the Latin paper. Rec was no good at all without her, so, with a sigh, I'd reach for my other friend, Georgette Heyer.

Georgette was sort of like a mistress to me, a kept woman tolerated by a virtuous and somewhat unwilling BF. If Fionnuala would not provide me with her own company, the least she could do was turn a blind eye while I took my pleasure where I might. And Georgette was where I took it. Maybe there were good books in our library, I don't remember; I couldn't see past Georgette.

And so, nightly, it was off to Almanack's, where I was the one with the whitest shoulders, the longest, most graceful neck, and a patch under my glittering eye. Nursing a passion for some titled dandy with naught on his mind but the "demned" speck of mud on his boots and how he might add to his already scandalous reputation. In no time at all I'd be shivering to his promises to lay his "demned" whip by my sides if I didn't behave myself.

But we had to return library books on Monday morning until Friday afternoon, the better to concentrate on Pythagoras and Aeneas and Alfred de Musset. Georgette and her whips weren't anywhere in the reckoning.

And that is where Fionnuala came in: she was librarian. It was her duty to collect all library books on Monday morning for the week. She did, and kept scrupulous records. But she turned a blind eye to her key now and then and to a few gaps in her shelves where I was concerned.

"It's your mind, Róisín," she shuddered fastidiously.

"Hey, Fionnuala, did you hear Anne Fleming is drinking since she went to university?" She was last year's head and president of the Pioneers' Total Abstinence.

"How do you know, Róisín?"

"Pidge Mackey heard it from her brother at the parlour today. He's in her class."

"That doesn't make it true. And what if it is anyway?"

"Did you hear Mary Thompson won't go to sleep at night unless Ida Daly gives her a goodnight kiss?"

"That's just silly gossip," said Fionnuala. "And it's dangerous."

"She cried last night because Ida never came. Rosemary Cassidy heard her. She said she went on and on."

"Róisín McGovern, you'd believe anything. Anything. It's those books you're always stuck in."

I suspected she was right. I had no strength of character at all. My mind wandered constantly and alarmingly and refused to make it through the day without a good slink through sensation. I knew the kind of history never asked on an exam paper: who killed Marat in his bath and why. I could tell you nothing Parnell did for Ireland but everything he did for Kitty O'Shea. And I knew everyone who ever had syphilis and from whom it was probably acquired.

One day I was called to the parlour.

Me? Who on earth would want to see me? I thundered downstairs, hoping it might be Daddy. It wasn't, but it was the next best thing: Harry. Trying to hide a box of Black Magic under his arm.

"They're letting me take you out for a couple of hours," he said gruffly. "What kind of a place is this? They gave me the third degree before they'd believe I'm your brother."

"They have to be on their guard constantly against men," I whispered, in case one of the nuns might still be hanging around. "You wouldn't know where one might be waiting to pounce on you."

I made Harry bring me to the greasiest café we could find. I had bacon, eggs, and double chips. I didn't even notice he was a bit quiet. It wasn't until we were back in the car he let his bomb fall.

"Deirdre's wedding is off. Well, it's not exactly off. She's married already."

"What? Comiskey?"

"Oh yes, it's Comiskey she's married to."

"But why?" Even at that ignorant age I somehow couldn't imagine our Deirdre getting herself *caught* in a moment of passion.

"It's not what you think," said Harry. "What everyone will think."

"Well, what? What is it then?"

"Nothing. Snobbery and viciousness and ignorance and stupidity, that's all."

"Harry, would you just tell me. If you don't, nobody will."

"I know. That's why I came. You have a right to know. Some of it anyway. They might have sent you a letter, if you were lucky. By the way, the wedding's over."

"Would you ever just hurry up and tell me then."

"Well, you knew the Comiskeys were always dead set against it, didn't you? The wedding? Dermot's people? They never thought we were good enough for their white-haired boy."

"Go on. Go on."

"They weren't having anything to do with us if they could help it. Everything they could, they did, to put Dermot off Deirdre. But there was nothing doing; he had it bad. So they sniffed and they sniffed until they got something he couldn't ignore . . . ."

"What?"

Harry sighed. "Mam," he said. "They found out about Mam. About her little trips to her sister's. You really don't have a clue, do you?"

"No," I whispered.

"They found out Mam's little rests were really in a psychiatric hospital. All those visits. All those years. And they couldn't wait to tell Dermot about the taint – the fatal flaw in his jewel. Stop looking like you're about to be murdered, would you. What's wrong with you?" said Harry, as if life were somehow still quite normal.

"But you said she's . . . . Do you think she's – "

"Mam, is it? Mad? There's nothing wrong with Mam a swift . . . " he laughed bitterly. "Look . . . the trouble with Mam is that she was given every single thing she wanted all her life and not one thing she needed," he said. "That's a lot of what's wrong with her."

"You said Deirdre was married?"

"She is. The Comiskeys couldn't put Dermot off her, although God knows they tried hard enough. They threatened to make Mam's history public if he insisted on marrying her. So what did the pair of them do, only off to Rome and got married on the QT. It was easy; they had everything they needed ready – letters of freedom, and so on."

"Did they tell? The Comiskeys, I mean? Did they tell anyone about Mammy?"

"Not on your life. You never saw anything like the clam-up once they were cornered with the wedding cert. The last thing they want is word out, now that it's in the family, so to speak."

"Well, anyway, at least Daddy won't have to pay for the big wedding now."

"Jesus, but I'd keep that bit of consolation to myself if I was you. As a matter of fact, keep it all to yourself. I'm not supposed to know half what's going on, let alone you."

It was time to go back then. I asked could we buy a cake.

"Jesus," said Harry, "I come all the way just to tell her this and all she wants to do is buy a bloody cake."

But Harry didn't know boarding school. News went around you were at the parlour. And the world might well have fallen around your ears there, but you still had to have a cake for your table.

Harry came back after that to see me a few times. Sometimes he brought his girlfriend. Her name was Teresa and she was a nurse. She wasn't really glamorous or beautiful or anything, but I liked her. She was good at listening. And smiling.

I knew somehow, too, that Harry had other girlfriends, but not the kind you'd bring – or would come – to a girls' boarding school.

He always brought a cake after that too.

I told Fionnuala there would be no wedding. And when I saw that not having a great thing like a wedding to bring her to didn't make her like me less, I told her why.

"Did you always think there was something . . . something strange about my mother?" I asked her then. "Did everyone in the town know except me?"

"No," said Fionnuala. "Your mother was just quiet. She kept to herself. There was nothing to know. The whole town wasn't talking behind your back, if that's what you mean. I swear." That was exactly what I meant.

But if they weren't talking before, they sure were now. It was still the be-all and end-all when I got home from school for Hallowe'en. While a big splashy society wedding commanded envious respect, there was something hole-in-the-corner about jumping the gun and running off to Rome. Duneen smelled a story it couldn't quite get its teeth into.

Deirdre and the new husband came down to brazen it out. You could see Miss McAloon's eyes slide to her stomach before jumping brightly back to her face.

Dermot Comiskey did his part by behaving to Deirdre as if she were royalty and letting it be known Duneen was his new cause. He came right out and said so on national television – when he made one of his frequent appearances on "The Late Late Show." We didn't see it, of course, in school but the whole town was watching and still talking about it when I got home. He raved about his wonderful new family and the picturesque charm of Duneen – he made it sound like the French Riviera. The salt of the earth he called its people, and he left Gay Byrne with little choice but to go down into the audience and interview his new bride. Duneen was entranced and the scandal was overshadowed.

I wasn't above enjoying a bit of reflected glory myself, as I walked up Main Street to call for Fionnuala.

"Róisín! Hey, Róisín!"

Frank O'Laughlin came tearing up to me.

"Hello, Róisín. I just thought that was you I saw through the window."

"Hello, Frank." He was wearing a brown shopcoat, Doyle's

Grocery and Provisions emblazoned on the pocket. And Judas Iscariot, if under the overall he wasn't wearing the same green jumper he always wore – Bernadette Gibbons was right: she used to say it grew on him. He had a lock of hair in his eyes and was breathing noisily and heavily.

"You haven't changed, Frank," I said.

"Neither have you, Róisín. You're lookin' very well, if I might say so. I saw you in the uniform. Friday."

"Oh yes?" I did walk up the town in the uniform when I got home – well, it was much nicer than Imelda Harney's from the Ursulines and streets ahead of the local one.

"Yeah. I'd have talked to you then, only Fionnuala Fitzgerald was with you. How long are ya home?"

"Until Tuesday. Only five days. Chronic, isn't it?"

"What? Oh, you haven't much time then."

"No."

"Could I see you sometime?"

"Well, as you said, I haven't much time."

"I'm not workin' this afternoon."

"Can't. Daddy has arranged tennis with the Duggans. They have a daughter who's coming to our school next year. And a son in Highgates – we debate with them sometimes. It's a panic usually, debating. An absolute panic. No, this afternoon's out."

"Tomorrow?"

"No, sorry. Fionnuala Fitzgerald is coming for tea. When she's in our school, too, it's only manners, don't you think?"

"Yeah, I suppose. And you're gone on Tuesday."

"Yes. Absolutely chronic, isn't it?"

"Maybe I could see you when you get back. Send us a card. I suppose there's still no chance of you writing to me from school?"

Here he nearly got me. Because I now knew there was indeed a way. It was a new rule that parents' letters into the school were not opened. Any letter in your parents' handwriting with their name and address on the back escaped Mother Elaine's dagger. And I had already figured it would be dead easy to a master forger like Harry to provide me with a dozen suitable envelopes. It was a matter of great prestige getting letters from boys in this manner. Another way to get them in was rolled up in a newspaper, but that was chancy. Getting replies out was simple with the day girls.

It was tempting. A boy writing to Róisín McGovern? But then Fionnuala would know it was only Crunchies. And sooner or later I'd have to show one to the other girls, just to prove. And I bet he would use ruled paper and he'd have no margins and maybe even bad grammar.

"Oh no, Frank. You know they open all our letters."

"Yeah, I thought so. But it was worth a try."

"Well, it's been awfully nice seeing you again, Frank."

"Yeah."

"I have to go now."

"Well, see you around, Róisín."

"Yes. Yes, of course."

Imagine him thinking I would get snobby and not talk to him. Really.

I walked on.

I'd have died before I let on in school that I didn't count the hours to getting home for holidays but to going back after them.

Our house was still like a morgue; not even Dermot on the "Late Late" worked. Daddy went for two walks with me, all right, but he didn't speak unless I made him; I think he had worn out all his conversation efforts on Mammy. He was always bringing her home flowers or chocolates and trying to press a shopping trip to London on her.

I was glad to get back to school. I couldn't believe it, but there were things about school I loved that I never would have suspected. Rituals and traditions. Even religious rituals. While I still couldn't see traipsing around a garden, in dress-up, to crown a statue as anything but ridiculous, there were other customs I loved instantly.

I loved choir singing, even practices. All the work was well worth it for the peace after the last amen of the *Missa Solemnis*.

And nothing could touch the atmosphere of December the eighth as a holiday. We had Christmas fare in the dining hall that day, the tables laden with fruit and evergreens, and decorated with laurel leaves.

"Inviolata, integra et casta est Maria," we sang all day, the last time sitting on the floor in the darkness around the crib lights in the study. I hummed the Immaculata all day, never once noticing I was praising the very qualities I hated in friends, especially Fionnuala Fitzgerald. It never even struck me as odd that I could so enjoy that day and yet berate Fionnuala for dressing up statues.

And what was so gloriously right about festive tables and so prissy and wrong about pale lifeless statues and flowers on a May altar?

Later in the year, another favourite: Quarant-Ore. Every hour, for forty hours, two replaced two in constant vigil before the Blessed Sacrament in the chapel. Fionnuala and I volunteered from three to four in the morning.

At a quarter to three we were up. Dressed and ready and having milk and biscuits alone in the refectory. Then, for once, we were silent and thoughtful in the dark corridors on the way down to chapel. Both wearing our Sunday uniforms and white Sunday mantillas, and with our shoes polished.

Fionnuala touched my arm at the chapel door.

"Let's pray for our future. That we'll always pick what's right . . . . "

I nodded.

She hesitated, still gripping my arm.

"What is it?"

"Let's never forget those souls farthest from God."

"Okay."

Reverently, for once again, we tiptoed up the polished aisle, side by side. We passed the front row and went right to the gates of the altar. There we went down on both knees and bowed our heads. Behind us, the two girls finishing their vigil slipped out of their places and went through the same ritual. They tiptoed down the aisle as we knelt in the first seats, Fionnuala to the right hand and me to the left.

Three o'clock, four o'clock. Life at its lowest, death at its nearest. Hovering. Harry's Teresa once told me she loses more patients to death at this hour than any other.

Kneeling there in the polished glow I believed her. In that soft island of light in the dark night there was peace. Life and death met in the flame of those candles and in the scents. In light and darkness. Easy to imagine the passage and presence of souls. Gazing sadly on dead statues.

It is so easy to believe at moments like this.

But in what?

I looked at Fionnuala, absorbed as always. For the souls farthest from God.

There was something oddly comforting about that. As if they could indeed come close somehow. If we got it right.

"Just as well you learned in time to behave yourself," said Miss McAloon – I was never sure was it joy or regret in her voice. "A lucky escape, if you ask me. Your father knew what he was doing when he sent you away to school."

Bernadette Gibbons she was talking about. Bernadette everyone was talking about.

Because Bernadette Gibbons had disappeared.

I was in the post office to buy a special Christmas card for Fionnuala. Miss McAloon and Mrs. Grimes were there and all set for an inquisition. But when Mrs. Kathleen Gibbons – Bernadette's mother – walked in behind me, I might have begun to dance naked on the counter and not been noticed.

Kathleen Gibbons caught sight of herself on the front page of the *Champion* on the newsstand by the counter and burst into tears. In the picture she was wearing a look of annihilating suffering, as well as her best fur-collared coat. "LOCAL GIRL MISSING. MASSIVE SEARCH PLANNED." All over page one of the *Champion*, and a good part of pages three and five as well.

"It's always the best that are taken," bawled Mrs. Gibbons to Miss McAloon and Mrs. Grimes. "A better girl to her mother never walked shoe leather." All Mrs. Gibbons asked now was that they find her girl alive or even . . . . Oh God have mercy, dare she say it: dead – so that she, Mrs. Gibbons, a poor widow, would be put out of her misery. She worried in case her beautiful Bernadette, like the sainted Maria Goretti, had given her life in defence of her purity.

Oh well, indeed, and there was very little chance of that, said both Mrs. Grimes and Miss McAloon to her. But they assured her they would not be off their knees for her until her girl was found. They were very generous with little pats and squeezes and leanings forward until Mrs. Gibbons took her sniffling departure.

"The sad thing is you could see it coming," said Miss McAloon, shaking her head as she watched her leave.

But Miss McAloon might have had more than a passing interest in the Gibbons's affairs. For although it was over thirty years since Bernadette Gibbons's father – Brendan – had jilted Eilish McAloon to up and marry her friend Kathleen, no man had come along in the meantime to dim the spinster's memory.

"You know" – she clutched Mrs. Grimes's arm over the post office counter – "I'm only glad that poor man, Brendan Gibbons, didn't live to see this."

"True for you, Eilish. It would have killed him. May the Lord have mercy on his soul."

"Indeed. Or maybe He did have mercy in taking him early. Nothing went right for that man. First the business going wallop and then the heart. There wasn't a reason in the world that business of his should have gone west."

"Do you say that? Ah well, you'd know."

"I would. I might well have gone the same way myself if I didn't see the sense in going into the fancy goods and the bit of whipped ice cream in summer."

"You were always the great businesswoman, Eilish."

"Not bad, not bad. But if things aren't all right at home, how could you keep your mind on your business? Heart attack, indeed. More like a broken heart that man had, if you ask me . . . ."

"Well, if he didn't have the heart attack then, he certainly would have this summer with the carry-on of young Bernadette."

"Did you ever? Not a shoulder to any of her dresses, don't mind a sleeve. And the waist pulled in that tight . . . . Leave me alone with young ones –"

A board creaked under me and I was remembered.

"Lovely bit of weather we're having for this time of year, Mrs. Grimes," said Miss McAloon loudly.

"It is that. Ah, Raymond McGovern's girl. Hello, Róisín. My, my, how fast you young ones grow up. Dreadful about poor Bernadette Gibbons, isn't it? A friend of yours, wasn't she?"

"Not really, Mrs. Grimes," I said, beating down the cock crowing behind me. "Not since we were a lot younger."

"No. Ah no, I suppose not. She hadn't many girlfriends in the end . . . . " There was great emphasis on *girl*. "Still, I think myself people are just encouraging such dreadful conduct by making so much of it. There isn't another thing in the paper this week. It's a pity the town can't find more to interest it."

"Do you think so?" said Miss McAloon, patting the back of her hair, her eyes nowhere in particular. "Ah, you're right, too. Then the story of your husband's retirement and the lovely clock they got him would have made more than a measly paragraph on page seven. In such a dither with the big news, they didn't even spell his name right. I'm sure no one but myself saw it tucked away where it was . . . . Are you all set so, Róisín? That'll be one and six-pence, please. Dreadful price these cards are. Well, bye now." She didn't even wait for me to leave before she and Mrs. Grimes were off on Bernadette: "I always said it, but that girl got not only her mother's beauty but her brains too: best suited to a sparrow . . . . "

Suddenly everyone in the town was an expert on Bernadette Gibbons. Could have foretold the whole story if only asked. Every iota of her past conduct was raked up, clear signposts to her end. Right back to the ten-pound note that wouldn't flush down the school toilet.

What were we then? Nine? Ten? Anyway, of an age where one pound was great wealth. The very sight of the enormous ten-pound note in a school toilet bowl – made more vivid a blue by its unlikely surroundings – drew a huge crowd. We all squashed into *an Leithreas* on top of one another. Stood four at a time on the flanking stalls' fixtures to peer over the partition for a better look. Until the sound of Sister Ursula's beads swishing businesslike along the corridor melted and flattened us back like the Red Sea. Sister Ursula swept in, shuddered an instant, then rolled up her sleeve, adjusted her wimple, and fished the note out.

Dripping, and at full arm's length, the note preceded her down the corridor to her office. Trampling on one another's heels, tumbling and shoving, we crowded after her. She went to put the wet money on her windowsill, changed her mind, and wrinkling her nose and fingers at it, dropped it carefully on to her blotter where she looked at it for a while. It was then she noticed the herds behind her at the door and was galvanized into action.

We were whisked back into our classrooms. All schoolwork was abandoned as the teacher of each class was ordered to keep us in perfect silence so no doctoring of stories could take place. Father O'Hehir was summoned immediately and Sergeant Egan would have been too, only he was in court that day.

One by one we were marched to Sister Ursula's office, and a couple of hours later the story was out. Anne Brown, it turned out, had the most light to shed: having been awarded *cead dul amach* by Sister Breda, she had gone about her legitimate business where she heard four different and successive attempts to flush the next toilet. Fearing someone in need of assistance (the logic here was not examined too thoroughly), Anne Brown had climbed up and peered over the partition. There she saw Bernadette Gibbons. She was positively certain – Bernadette Gibbons.

Faced with this evidence, Bernadette was forced to confess, although she had apparently sailed through her own questioning with a brazenness that had Sister Ursula doubting her well-documented stupidity. She admitted she had taken the money from her mother's purse, thinking it to be one pound. She panicked when Miss McAloon and two other shops refused to change it for her without a note from home and tried to get rid of it down the toilet.

That's when we should have realized it was strictly the big leagues for Bernadette.

She cooled it on the grand-larceny scene for a while and honed her other talents as femme fatale. She continued her dreamy indifferent passage through school, unperturbed whether her bread in Domestic Science class emerged emerald green from too much soda or flat as a brick by its omission. Floating somewhere well above concern over school reports or the attaining of any quantifiable academic standards, she drifted in to school most days. But when she failed the Mock Leaving Cert quite spectacularly, she viewed the nuns' plan to hold her back a year as the last indignity.

So she simply left school to bring her unique talents to Lynch's grocery shop. Never did so much beauty dispense rashers, raisins, and flour, and never with such disdain.

Bernadette's lack of academic background was not a drawback in all areas. Because Bernadette Gibbons was never unattended. She was constantly to be seen dining at the local hotels both in and out of season. Or driving off into the sunset in the passenger seat of some expensive car. Not for long did she entertain Lorcan Burke, and after him there were no other acned and penniless inmates of the Christian Brothers' school for our Ber-Ber. No. Wealthy visitors in season or well-heeled locals any time. Fellows taking over family businesses. Fellows with cars and money to lash around on Bernadette Gibbons.

There was one in particular, an extremely handsome and generous travelling salesman. He wooed her with a smouldering ferocity seen before only on the screen of Twomey's cinema. And then he fulfilled Miss McAloon's darkest prophecies: he dropped Bernadette Gibbons like a hot potato. Into thin air he disappeared, leaving eight shops in the town high and dry for orders.

And it was six weeks after that Bernadette herself disappeared. Leaving Lynch's with not only less to sell, but no one to sell it.

Never was the *Champion* more pillaged for news. One report had Bernadette last seen on the Dublin Road in tight jeans. Another had her on the opposite side of town in a red dress. "Nonsense," said both Mr. Lynch and her mother. "She was wearing her best white suit." "And little did she know where it would lead her when she put it on in all innocence that morning," her tearful mother was quoted, who by all accounts was fit only for the hospital. Meths Muldoon insisted he had seen her getting into Father O'Hehir's car and the pair of them nearly knocked him down where he stood. But it didn't even need mentioning that the last time Meths Muldoon was seen upright unaided was about 1936.

Reports of Bernadette's renowned saintliness followed, a litany by her mother mainly, similar to the one she had given Miss McAloon in the post office. Miss McAloon herself was a little more reserved in her judgements: yes, she had watched Bernadette Gibbons this past month or so and had been nothing but gratified by her conduct. This was as close as Miss McAloon could get in a newspaper to saying her conduct before that was anything but gratifying. As to that, her opinions were so widely known, they didn't have to be actually printed to come through between the lines: the shameless way Bernadette Gibbons did not seem to mind what hour of the night she was seen getting out of that salesman fellow's car. And the windows so steamed up, it's a wonder he could see where he was driving at all. From Castlebar he was. And a poor wife probably waiting there in vain for him. It was also Miss McAloon's private – though equally widely known – opinion that this recent decorous behaviour of Bernadette Gibbons's was proper order for a girl who had thrown herself so shamelessly at a fellow, only to be dropped as the plaything she'd made herself. Because that fellow was gone, all right. No doubt about that. Hadn't shown his cowardly face in the town since. And eight shopkeepers still on their uppers for orders.

There wasn't so much excitement since a cousin of the O'Flahertys' was murdered in England. And you couldn't by rights call that a local story at all. True, the girl's grandmother lived over in the cottages, but she herself had only set foot in the town once at the age of three.

But the disappearance of Bernadette Gibbons – now that was as close as you ever wanted to get. Because only four days ago she was up calmly weighing onions and slicing ham in Lynch's shop. And there wasn't a child in the town who didn't remember her magical first week on the job – when she'd give out a big bag of the best chocolate sweets for threepence worth until someone went and put her wise.

Sergeant Egan licked his pencil and made house-to-house inquiries. Inquiries as to the whereabouts of Duneen's inhabitants at the time of the disappearance.

"Mind, I'm mentioning no names now, Raymond."

"Of course not," said my father.

"Well, I called to a certain house around six yesterday. Missus was just serving up the tea and your man dozin' by the fire. 'Where were you now on the evening of December the seventeenth when one Bernadette Gibbons disappeared from her place of employment?' I says to him. 'When that poor girl was last seen? Say from four o'clock onwards?' 'Out delivering for the Vincent de Paul,' says the wife for him, as she swiped past to put the fry in the oven to keep it warm. 'Is that true?' says I. 'Of course it is,' says she. 'He spends all his time running round in rings for that lot.' 'Is that true now?' I asked him again. 'Oh, it is indeed,' he swears.

"Well, you know, Raymond, I wasn't properly home and in the door of the barracks when your man was in after me. Uneasy he was, to put it mildly. I made him stew for a bit. 'Obstructing the course of justice is a serious offence,' I said. 'But sure I couldn't with the wife there,' he said. 'Couldn't what?' I asked. 'Couldn't tell you,' he said. 'Couldn't tell me what?' I asked. Couldn't tell me where he really was. 'And where was that?' I asked. Do you know where he was, Raymond? Now mentioning no names again, but your man was carrying out the corporal works of mercy all right: consoling the bereaved, you might say. A certain widow with a bit of fire left in her blood . . . . And he wasn't the only one, by any means. Half the town was somewhere it shouldn't that evening . . . . "

"Your mind would be boggled, Raymond," said Sergeant Egan. "You wouldn't believe the wonderful things the people in this town were supposed to be doing. Until the truth came out later."

Days passed and still no news of Bernadette. Frank O'Laughlin had a black eye at midnight mass on Christmas Eve. It was rumoured Lorcan Burke gave it to him for saying it was he set Bernadette Gibbons on her downward path.

Father O'Hehir was at a complete loss when it came to sermons. On the Sunday after Christmas he had nothing to say at all. It was well known some of his very best sermons in the past had been inspired by none other than Bernadette Gibbons herself. And who were we to tell him he might as well keep his breath to cool his porridge? That it was a while since he'd have caught her ear at any mass? No matter which one he picked or how many he tried. Anyway, he was on slippery ground now no matter what he said about her. In the end he said nothing much at all. He could only offer his prayers for the poor girl who was missing and her sorrowing mother. God was indeed hard on mothers, he felt.

It was a subdued crowd that funnelled down Church Street after mass. Suddenly, advancing from the post office to meet it, came Miss McAloon, waving aloft a pale green envelope.

Pale green envelopes like that came around telegrams, which you hoped would say you had won the Sweep, but usually they meant you'd be needing a black suit.

"Telegram for Mrs. Gibbons!" Miss McAloon was fully charged and bristling with energy. "Is she among you, by any chance?"

She was. Word was passed back and Mrs. Gibbons was produced and propelled to the front like a reluctant soprano at a singsong.

"Oh" – Miss McAloon's hand fluttered to the chest she always said was delicate – "I'm glad I found you so quickly, Mrs. Gibbons. I thought this might be important, considering . . . . Oh dear, I hope it's good news . . . . "

"What do you mean you hope it's good news?" demanded Mrs. Gibbons sourly. "You know every last word that's in it."

"That's a lie!" gasped Miss McAloon. "Are you all going to let her say a thing like that to me?" She swept the gathering crowd with an outraged eye. "Every one of you knows I never take a blind bit of notice of any message not meant for my eyes. They might as well be Greek . . . . "

"Thank you so. In that case, I'll take it home and read it privately, like it was meant to be read." Mrs. Gibbons went to stuff the envelope into her pocket.

"You're not doing that to us," shouted Mrs. Grimes, elbowing her way in and snatching the envelope. "Oh no, and us never off our knees this past ten days for that girl of yours. Give me that, Kathleen Gibbons. Anyone can see you're not yourself. Here, I'll read it to you . . . . "

Mrs. Grimes tore at the envelope with plump but amazingly quick fingers: "Sorry, Ma. Stop. Married Jim. Stop. Will write. Stop. Love Bernadette."

Miss McAloon's eyes bulged. "That's the salesman fellow. Meths Muldoon was right after all – your man's car was the dead spit of Father O'Hehir's. We should have put two and two together long ago."

Mrs. Grimes was looking at the wire and envelope. She turned them upside down and inside out. "It's postmarked England – London, no less. How well the pair of them knew the right country to go to with that class of behaviour . . . ."

But Mrs. Gibbons's eyes were on Miss McAloon. Someone was holding her back. "You kept it, y'oul' harpy. You frustrated old sourpuss . . . . You kept it and watched for your moment, didn't you, instead of delivering it quietly like any decent Christian. I bet you got that wire yesterday, but you just had to have your satisfaction . . . ."

"I'll have you know that as a government employee I don't have to take that raving from the likes of you." The whites of Miss McAloon's eyes were fluttering alarmingly. "That is all the thanks I get for personally delivering what I in my innocence thought might be good news for you. You can't blame us, you know, if you raised a heathen. A branch is only as good as the tree it comes from – "

"You dried-up old hag," screamed Mrs. Gibbons. "You've no right to be in charge of decent people's business. You couldn't get a man yourself, although, God knows, it was never from want of trying. You tried hard enough for mine in your time. Well, if you only knew the number of times he said he was well shut of you . . . . It's no wonder you have nothing to do but stick your nose in other people's private business. You're in the right job, aren't you?"

"You make an accusation like that again, Kathleen Gibbons, and you'll be in real trouble. I'll let it pass this time on account of the distraught state you have every right to be in. Because I bet that's one wedding never got the blessings of the clergy, and I didn't see it! If I was you, do you know what I'd do now? I'd be away home to start knitting: bootees, matinée coats, and the like.

You mightn't have as much time to finish them as you'd want . . . . "

Sergeant Egan arrived then and the fun was over. Mrs. Gibbons was borne off by her cronies, still struggling; Miss McAloon was induced to bring her delicate chest back into the post office.

"Let that be an end to that," said Sergeant Egan. But it wasn't. Mrs. Grimes was heard to say that although she was never gospel-greedy, she had felt the need to go back to twelve o'clock mass to give thanks for the girl's safety. "Well," she said, "you would not believe Father O'Hehir was the same man as read the ten o'clock." It was doubtful if the pulpit would take much more of the treatment he gave it when talking about the evil done by shameless women. You could hear the congregation sighing with relief to be back on the old ground.

But there was never a need for the bootees and matinée coats. None that we heard of anyway. Bernadette had gone into the modelling business and her husband was an actor on television, Mrs. Gibbons said. How she knew all this was a mystery to Miss McAloon, because she certainly was not run off her feet at the post office with the weight of communications between mother and daughter.

The next news we got of her didn't come for a while. And when it did, it wasn't through the post office it came. Not through letter, telegram, or telephone.

It came in the English newspapers, and not the respected ones either: SEX SCANDAL ROCKS THE HOUSE OF LORDS.

Well – orgies, duplicity, complicity. Not to mention leaks in security. And at the centre of it all, Lord Friday and beautiful playgirl Isolde Meredith. That was the name but the pictures showed Bernadette Gibbons.

Talk about a whole town nearly speechless with shock – almost united. There were record-breaking sales of English newspapers and throngs in Miss McAloon's post office. There were shaken heads, and "it only goes to show" and "I don't like to say this but I always knew," and "for God's sake, whatever we do, don't let any of us say anything to poor Kathleen Gibbons. Especially the bits about the black leather . . . . "

133

While Bernadette Gibbons was bringing down the British government single-handed, Fionnuala Fitzgerald and I studied for our Leaving Certificate. Her Irish was shaky, so she wanted to get to Irish College the summer before to brush up. Not only was it a compulsory subject, but any examination paper answered through Irish was worth an extra five per cent.

I went too. There was no way she was getting away without me.

We were billeted in a huge farm house outside the Gaeltacht village. Radharc na Mara it was called, but we renamed it Boladh na mBó instantly because the smell of the cows was much more impressive than the view of the sea.

There were classes every day in the village school, as well as picnics and hikes. And, of course, the nightly highlight: the *céilí*. We had to dance with one another mostly because although the group was mixed, there were three girls to every multicoveted boy.

"Hey, Róisín," said Fionnuala one afternoon we were extremely busy sucking some grass stems on the cliffs overlooking the sea.

"What?"

"Not that you'll be able to see anything, goodness knows" – Fionnuala was shading her eyes with her hand, peering off into the distance – "but two fellows have just headed into the tennis courts."

"You're saying all the right things there. Who are they?"

"I don't know. I never saw them before, as far as I can make out. I don't think they're our lot."

"Better and better. You and I are going to play a nice game of tennis now. Come on."

"Róisín McGovern, you know you have not only two left hands, but two left feet for games."

"I know that. But it's not really the tennis anyone'll be interested in. Come on."

"Well, all right, but not that way. We better have our racquets first, what do you think? Even you would not attempt to play tennis without a racquet."

"I might. I'd probably do just as well."

"We have to at least look the part."

"I suppose. Okay, Boladh na mBó first."

Once at the court we stationed ourselves elaborately and elegantly in playing position. We completely ignored the thwacking and pounding of the two lithe bodies at the next net. Fionnuala lobbed me some really easy ones and I even managed to hit one or two back. One I hit with an almighty wallop and it banged off Fionnuala's knee, sending her to the ground. She grasped it, rocking in pain.

"Are you okay there?" Two solicitous bodies in shorts arrived immediately to offer succour. One blond, about eighteen, okay. The other, dark, hairy, and very old. Must have been at least twenty-two. And gorgeous.

The hairy one knelt and fixed his black eyes on Fionnuala, long manipulating fingers around her knee.

"Ow," yelped Fionnuala. "It really hurts."

"I'm sorry," said Gorgeous. "Listen, if it's that sore, we'd better give you a hand home."

We made a bit of a protest. Just enough to look good. And then we gratefully accepted. The two chair-sat Fionnuala, one of her arms around each hard shoulder. Róisín got to carry four racquets, all the balls, and assorted clothing.

The introductions were made: the dark one was Hywel Griffith and the younger blond one Barry Evans. They were part of a Welsh cycling group passing through the village on a tour of Ireland. They were staying overnight, and all were student teachers, except for Hywel who was qualified and their leader.

They deposited us at our house. By carelessly surrendered, seemingly irrelevant scraps of conversation it was established – that there was a *céilí*, when and where, that the Welshmen would be there, and so would we. Barring earthquakes and wild horses and things like that. But, of course, we didn't say that.

"Judas, Fionnuala, but you laid it on a bit thick about your knee. It was a great idea for a start – "

"It really is sore, Róisín. I wasn't pretending at all."

"Ah, go on out of that, I didn't hit you that hard. We could have had a great afternoon's crack up at the courts instead of being dumped back here."

"I'm sorry, Róisín."

Fionnuala's knee remained sore and she wanted to rest it up for the *céilí* that evening. That suited me fine, really, because I had about a hundred and two combinations of clothes I wanted to try on. We didn't tell the other girls in the house about the Welsh invasion until we were good and ready because that would have put an awful run on the meagre water supply and the one rusty bath.

Fionnuala had oodles of clothes, being an only child. She lent me a gorgeous cream and mauve dress. The best thing about it was a low neck gathered across bosom giving 34B the look of 36C. Skin tight to the waist and then flared. Hair lightened by sunlight and lemon juice and Inecto Hint of a Tint. And last, a goodly layer of that pale mauvy lipstick, Bean an Tí, called gleester. It was not gleestery; it was pouty, like Brigitte Bardot.

I looked not bad, but Fionnuala was downright beautiful in red, with her creamy skin and veil of shiny dark hair.

We arrived at the *céilí* and found the Welshmen out in force. We could hear them before we got near the hall at all. They were giving an impromptu concert: "We'll Keep a Welcome" and "All Through the Night" harmonized in the minor keys. Hywel Griffith was there and he never took his black eyes off me while they were singing. I was giddy with relief; I was afraid it would be Fionnuala he'd go for.

Word had got around the parish that the Welsh were there and about to put us to shame with their music. "We'll see about that," said Dan Pat Geoghagan, the organist and choirmaster, as he sent out the one semihighway and the many byways for every voice and instrument in the parish to drown out the Welsh.

So, the *céilí* was packed and throbbing before we got there, though the dancing hadn't even started. Finally it did and Hywel Griffith strode over. He took hold of me and he didn't let go for the rest of the evening. Ten minutes and he had learned most of the steps and contemptuously thrown out the "regulation" swing. There are two ways to swing your partner in *céilí* dancing: you can hold hands like arm wrestlers and catch your partner's elbow with your other hand and off you go, or you can put your arm tight across your partner's chest and grip around the waist, no nonsense.

Hywel Griffith was having none of this hands and elbows only regulation swing. We swung at breakneck speed, one hairy arm tight across my breast where it had no right to be. Yes, and getting there and back by even more forbidden routes. Merciful hour.

Other nights the *céilí* was just a *céilí*. Maybe a chance to touch and hold briefly what was forbidden at other times and fraught with God knows what mysteries.

But tonight – Georgette Heyer and Almanack's were only trotting after it.

One, two, three, four, five, six, seven. One, two, three. One, two, three. I tried to concentrate on simple steps. Anything but think of what I was doing. Or look at those eyes.

One and two and three, and a one, two, three. Strong arms encircled and shocked. "Swing fast," he said. Tighter. Harder. "Swing faster." "Can't hear you," I said, but I'd want to be blind, deaf, and numb. Hearts beating – Welsh, Irish, Indian. Call of a crossroads millennia ago. Faster the Uilleann pipes, fiddle, tin whistle. Whack the taut skin of an animal drum. Flight of the flute – rhythm, ritual, memory. Clacket of spoons, rattle of bones.

The dancing stopped for old Mr. Kavanagh to *n-yaaa* his way through all forty-six verses of "An Ciarraíoch Mallaithe." And all the time Hywel Griffith sat perched on the edge of a table, his arm around my waist, clamping me against him. Blowing in my ear and through the back of my hair on my neck. Whispering things I didn't dare listen to. When the singing was finally over Hywel Griffith said he had this awful headache, which only a walk in the night air would clear. With me. No, later, I said as the dancing resumed.

If I thought of Fionnuala at all that night, it certainly wasn't for more than two seconds at a time. Maybe a vague fleeting wish that she was enjoying herself somewhere half as much as I was. I did actually give a half-hearted look around for her when time came to go home. No sign of her anywhere. Ah well, all the better; that gave me carte blanche to take off with your man for the dangerous but delightful journey home.

We were headed for the door when out of nowhere came the head teacher, Tomas O'Flatharda, followed by a limping Fionnuala, nearly in tears.

"*Róisín Ní Shamhráin, níl cead agat dul as an halla seo leis an fear sin agus maith an fhios agat freisin.*"

"What's he saying?" hissed Hywel Griffith in my ear, his grip on my elbow vice-tight.

I couldn't move, couldn't answer him. I was frozen to the spot looking from O'Flatharda's purple face to Fionnuala's frightened one.

O'Flatharda fixed Hywel Griffith with a glare: "I am saying this girl has no permission to leave this hall with you. Or with anyone else, for that matter. College regulations."

The humiliation of it. How would I ever get out of there? Fionnuala took my arm, and for an awful minute it looked as if I were the meat in a ham sandwich and no way out of a tug of war between her and Hywel Griffith. At last he dropped my arm.

We were nearly out of the hall before I heard the shouts: "Untouchable virgins. Untouchable little Irish virgins. Why didn't you tell us? Who are you saving yourselves for? The priests?" He had a lot more to say besides – in his own language this time, thank God.

I almost ran home, Fionnuala limping along with her arm still in mine until I shook her off.

I got ready for bed in raging silence – she was supposed to be a friend of mine. Never one for a cold war, I burst out at last:

"You went and got O'Flatharda, didn't you? He never goes to a *céilí*. Where did you dig him out of? The pub? You told on me. Why?"

"Róisín, I'm sorry. I'm really sorry. I just couldn't let you go off with . . . with him . . . ."

I pulled the clothes off her side of the bed viciously. We had to share a tiny double bed that sagged like a boat in the middle. No matter what we did, we'd end up in a tangle of elbows in the middle of the night and fight, tugging at the skimpy blankets in temper until the whole thing came adrift. After three nights' pitched battle we had finally made a pact: it was nobody's fault and there was nothing we could do about it. Anything said by either of us to the other between the hours of eleven and seven was not to be taken down and used in evidence the next day.

Tonight we lay in stony silence.

"Róisín?" Fionnuala's voice came in a whisper from the wall. "Róisín? I said I was sorry."

"Why did you do it?"

"He was horrible. You couldn't see the way he was looking at you. He was taking the clothes off you all night with his eyes."

"Don't be ridiculous. I wasn't going to . . . to do anything."

"I know you weren't. But your man sure was. And from the look in his eye it would have been rape or murder."

"Ah, go to hell, Fionnuala Fitzgerald. I'm supposed to be the one with the imagination around here."

"It's all very well for you, but what would I have told your family? That I just stood back and let you get yourself raped?"

"Ah, go on, you're worse than Miss McAloon in your opinion of men. But do you know something, Fionnuala?" I said. "I never realized until tonight just how dead the Irish language is."

"And what on earth has that got to do with anything?"

"If I wanted to shout back at your man's Welsh, I hadn't one word I could use."

"They're not words you find in the *foclóir* right enough," said Fionnuala. "But they must exist."

"Of course they exist. But they're not about to put them in the Leaving Cert syllabus. They'd let a language die in the name of holy purity."

"Well, it certainly wasn't the litany your man was shouting at you. Welsh must be alive and kicking. God knows what he'd be whispering in your ear right now. I'm not a bit sorry for what I did . . . . "

"I'll forgive you this time," I said. "Because it just so happens I didn't fancy him anyway."

"Liar!" said Fionnuala as loudly as she dared, considering it was after lights-out in Boladh na mBó. "You've been foaming at the mouth since the first minute you saw him."

When we got home from Irish College, Fionnuala's leg was still stiff. She told me her mother was bringing her to the doctor just in case she might need an x-ray.

"Judas, Fionnuala, I never realized I was that strong. I think I'll go in for the pentathlon."

"Well, you might laugh, Róisín McGovern, but if there's anything wrong with my leg, I'll sue you for permanent damages."

"Are you insured?"

"No – all the more reason to sue you."

"Those legs should be insured – where would the First Eleven be without them? Did you hear Elizabeth Taylor insured her legs for a million pounds?"

"Go on, she did not."

"She did so. And between them she made a fortune."

We still had a few weeks before going back to school, and I intended to make full use of them. Because if Fionnuala was a serious student before, she'd be unbearable this year between the First Eleven and the Leaving Cert. I knew I'd be seeing a lot more of Georgette Heyer than of her once we got back.

Then what did she do, with three measly weeks left to enjoy, but play the meanest, lousiest trick on me. She took off with her family on a holiday and never so much as told me she was going, much less where. She left me to discover it for myself when I found the bakery closed with a note in the window. And not as much as a bloody postcard did she send. Not even as much as a scrape of a line to say where they were.

Well, see if I care, Fionnuala Fitzgerald.

But I passed the bakery more times than I had to. Three days later it opened up but with the assistant, Denny Armstrong, in charge. He was looking after things for Mr. Fitzgerald, he said. No, he didn't know where they were or when they'd be back. None of his business, he said.

Mr. Fitzgerald had never left the bakery before. The staff, under Denny Armstrong, was mustering along somehow, but the place hadn't the track of Mr. Fitzgerald's dapper little hand. The displays were haphazard, gobs of cream and glaze bulging any old how out of oddly shaped buns. Crumbs weren't being wiped away as often as they used to, and Betty McIntyre behind the counter grew more pasty and untidy herself by the minute. Ugh. Fitzgerald's Bakery had lost all its magic. Good enough for you, Fionnuala Fitzgerald, for going off and leaving me like that. Just good enough. Serves you right.

And then, just as suddenly as she had left, Fionnuala returned. I spotted the car going down Main Street, and before I knew it I was at home looking at the telephone. There was absolutely nothing else to do that day, otherwise I'd have had more respect for myself than to hang around the phone just in case she might ring. Which she did, not ten minutes later. She asked me to come over to her house. I said yes. Not that she deserved it, but there was absolutely nothing else to do.

I strolled up Main Street. No hurry. Not after her going off like that for so long without as much as a word. I took my sweet time going to Fitzgeralds'.

It was five o'clock now and the bakery had subsided to a faint yeasty cool – in the mornings it's hot and steamy, and the smell closer to a brewery's. Betty McIntyre was still behind the counter. There were chocolate tarts still left; they were usually gone by three o'clock. And there were oodles of lemon puffs and cream horns. Must have been a bad day for business. Serve the Fitzgeralds right.

Were they upstairs or down? Fitzgeralds' was a tall, narrow

141

building with the shop on the main floor. Downstairs to the back were the bakery kitchens. The Fitzgeralds were always down there, but I couldn't hear any sound today. I clattered down anyway.

Mr. and Mrs. Fitzgerald were sitting at one of the tables. They didn't even look around when I spoke. Honestly, how rude can you get. I tried again.

"Hello, Mr. Fitz, Mrs. Fitz. Fionnuala phoned me to come over. Where is she?"

"In her room, I suppose." Mrs. Fitz didn't even look up. Good God, she was sitting in her coat and there were dirty dishes around. And there was brandy or whiskey or something on the table. At this hour of the day. This wouldn't need to get back to school . . . .

"I'll go up and see Fionnuala, if that's all right . . . . "

There was no answer. Be rude. Suit yourselves.

I went up to the shop level. Up past it and on up to the living rooms. Up past the wedding picture of the Fitzgeralds on the landing. Already Mrs. Fitz dwarfed him in it; could have made two of him. And a suit, for God's sake – why was she wearing a suit? You only get married the once. Why not a wedding dress? Of course, because she was as old as a bush. Why did I never think of that before? That was why Fionnuala was the one and only. On up the spindly stairs I went. On up to the top of the house and Fion-nuala's room.

I threw myself down on Fionnuala's bed with a deeply wounded sigh. I'm here, Fionnuala Fitzgerald, it said. Although I shouldn't bother. No sir, not after the way you've treated me. Going off like that as if I didn't exist.

"Hello, Róisín."

"Hello."

That's all? After all this?

She was even quieter than usual. Sitting in the old wicker chair she had since she was eight. Everything looked the same, but there was something different. What was it? The room was the same. Yes, all her things exactly as they always were. She was a great one for little things of her own; she guarded them as if they were treasures. From being an only child, I supposed.

She was hugging that bloody old rag doll of hers; her two arms tight around it, clutching it to her chest.

Suddenly I was afraid. I didn't know why on earth I should be, but I was.

"Well, well" – I heard my own voice – "the dead arose and appeared to many. Where were you, Fionnuala Fitzgerald?"

"In Dublin."

"Dublin, no less. Thanks for all the cards."

"We went to the doctor."

"Sure that was ages ago."

"My leg got worse."

"What? God, you're not on about that still?"

"Yes."

"What do you mean, yes."

"It's worse."

"What do you mean, worse? How could it be worse?"

"The doctors in Dublin said there was some sort of a growth."

"A growth? What sort of growth?"

"I don't know. They just said a growth."

"Is it like a cyst, or an abscess, or something like that?"

"I suppose."

"Well, that's not so bad."

"The pain was terrible."

"Is it better now?"

"A bit. They have me on pills all the time for it."

"Oh God, I'm sorry Fionnuala. It's my fault. I hit you with that tennis ball."

"Oh no, Róisín, no. That had nothing to do with it. The doctor said I would have felt the pain there soon anyway. The ball just made us notice it a bit sooner, that's all. Don't worry – they all said it has nothing whatsoever to do with the ball."

"Well, I'm glad about that, but I'm still awful sorry, Fionnuala. I thought you were only off on a holiday. When will it be better?"

"I don't know."

"It'll be better by school time surely." I said.

"I don't know. I don't think so."

"Fionnuala, you're frightening me. I don't want to go back without you. They must have told you something. They must have given you some idea when you'd be better . . . . "

"No."

"Sure it's only your knee? I mean it's not as if you were sick or anything. You could easily manage at school with a sore knee . . . . I'll help you any time it gets sore . . . . I'll help you get around . . . . You'd just have to give up the old games for a while, that's all."

"Maybe."

"You know I'm sure it was those blasted games did you in, in the first place . . . . You must have done something to yourself. Athletes are always wrecking their knees, or their ankles, or something . . . . " I smiled at her, a feeble attempt. "Maybe now you'll listen to me and take up Georgette Heyer . . . . She'd be a lot easier on you."

"Róisín, I'm going back into hospital tomorrow."

"For what? Sure you're only back . . . . "

"I don't know. More tests maybe."

"For how long?"

"I don't know."

"Jesus, now you're really scaring me."

"I'm scared stiff myself . . . . "

"Oh, Fionnuala!"

Down went her head and she wouldn't look at me at all. Down on her old rag doll. She clutched it even tighter. "I heard my mother on the phone . . . . " It was barely a whisper and I nearly missed it altogether.

"What? What did you say?"

"Nothing."

"You did, Fionnuala, tell me."

"I heard my mother on the phone. They might –"

"What? They might what? Tell me, for God's sake."

"They might have to –"

"What? Jesus, Fionnuala, will you tell me!"

"They might have to take off my leg."

"What?"

144

"They might have to cut off my leg. Above the knee."

"What? Oh, Jesus Christ, will you stop saying those awful things, Fionnuala. It isn't funny. Stop!"

"It's true, Róisín."

I shot up. I clapped my hand over my mouth and lunged for the door.

"Where are you going? Don't go, Róisín . . . . "

"I'm going to get your mother for you. Jesus, Fionnuala, I don't know what to say to you . . . . I'll get your mother. Don't ask me, Fionnuala. I don't know what to say . . . . "

"Do you think I do? Or my mother does?"

"Oh God, Fionnuala . . . . "

Christ let me out of here. What do I do? What do I say? I couldn't tear my eyes from hers.

"It could be a mistake, Fionnuala. Doctors can be wrong."

"No mistake. That's why I was away so long. No, they're sure, all right."

I couldn't stand it. I couldn't move. Couldn't do anything. There she was with her rag doll, the girl in the storybooks with the long brown hair and the straw hat tied with crimson . . . .

Suddenly I knew what to do. I rushed over to her and covered her with kisses . . . any part I could get at . . . her eyes, her neck, her hair, her lips . . . .

"I love you, Fionnuala. I love you."

Her tears began at last. She wept from somewhere bottomless and hidden that tore at me. I remembered the music room at school and I held on and rocked her and held on until she dropped the rag doll and clung to me instead.

"Help me, Róisín. Help me to bear it . . . . "

"I will, Fionnuala, love. Oh, I will, yes, yes, I will."

We cried together then until we were too exhausted to cry anymore. It took a long time to calm down. When it was finally over, I washed her beautiful face and combed the tangles of nearly a week out of her long hair.

"I'm staying with you tonight, Fionnuala."

"It's okay now. I'm all right, honestly. You've helped a lot. Thanks, Róisín. I'm all right now.

"I'm staying."

Downstairs Mrs. Fitzgerald was still sitting at the table, her coat still on and the dishes strewn around her exactly as they had been when I came in.

"I'm staying with Fionnuala tonight, Mrs. Fitzgerald, if that's all right with you." I was staying whether it was or it wasn't.

"What?" She looked at me as if I was a long distance away.

"Tonight," I said. "I'm staying with Fionnuala."

"But . . . oh, all right, I suppose. How is she now?"

"She's okay. She's been crying a lot."

"Thanks be to God for that. She needed it. Not a tear all day . . . all week . . . it wasn't natural. God help us all, Róisín, but what are we going to do?"

"Anyway, that's settled," I said quickly. "I'm staying the night."

"All right. You can have the spare room. We're airing it for Fionnuala's Aunty Peg anyway. She's coming to help out for . . . for the while she's in the hospital . . . . I'll send Fionnuala's daddy up to tell your people. To get your nightie and toothbrush and things. God knows, it will give him something to do . . . . "

"Thanks, Mrs. Fitzgerald."

"Good girl, Róisín. Thank you, dear. It will be a hard time for all of us. God knows. Would you tell Fionnuala she'll have to have a bath before going to the hospital?"

I started to shake terribly. I had to grab hold of the table or I'd have pitched and fallen. Tell Fionnuala to have a bath. The ordinariness of it caught me unawares. I wanted to scream but I didn't know the right words. So I said nothing at all but held on to the table until the shaking stopped.

Then I went back up to Fionnuala. Together we prepared her beautiful young body. Heartbreakingly perfect. I washed her long

146

legs, both of them: long, curving, brown and smooth after their summer in the Gaeltacht sun.

I ignored Fionnuala's mother's suggestion of Aunty Peg's bed in the spare room. Instead, when bedtime came, I curled myself right around Fionnuala in her dainty little girl's bed. My nostrils filled up with Loxene shampoo and fresh talcum powder and toothpaste.

"Róisín?" whispered Fionnuala.

"Yes."

"Do you believe in God?"

Already the doubts were starting that any god could allow such a thing to happen, but I knew somehow this was not the right place for them.

"Yes, Fionnuala, of course I do."

"I mean, do you *really* believe?"

"I don't know, Fionnuala. But if it was all easy to believe, there would be no such thing as faith, sure there wouldn't."

"Róisín, I'm so frightened. I know I'm going to die. I feel it already . . . . "

"Hush, love, that's nonsense. You're not going to die. That's nonsense."

"Maybe it is. Róisín, do you think this is wrong?"

"What?"

"You holding me . . . kissing me . . . . Is it wrong to love another girl?"

"Of course it isn't wrong. Saint John himself said in the Gospel that he was the disciple Jesus loved."

"I don't think it's the same thing."

"How do you know? How could it ever be wrong to love someone? And John always called himself the apostle Jesus loved. Jesus loved everybody. So what was so different about John?"

That quietened us both for a bit. Then, "Róisín?"

"Yes."

"What will I do if I die and it is wrong? If I find out it was wrong? What will I say?"

"Fionnuala Fitzgerald, you blame it all on me. You tell Jesus Christ I just didn't know any other way."

They took Fionnuala Fitzgerald away the next morning and I never really had her to myself after that. Her only request was that she be sent to the hospital nearest our school, so I could be with her. She never got home from the hospital again the thing was so fast-growing.

There wasn't much I could do for her except be there whenever I could and love her with everything I had. And not let on that her hair was grey and that she looked like a shrunken old woman with a cage in the bed where her leg should have been. And I could comb her hair and put on a little makeup – never so much that she just looked worse. I painted her nails pink to hide the blackness underneath.

And, somehow, reading about Georgette Heyer's kind of love didn't work anymore. Because the person I loved most in the world would never go to that ball. She would never stand on the stairs – toast of the season for creamy shoulders, chestnut hair tumbling in waves to her waist. Her fiery dark eyes breaking hearts all around her.

I tried to hide my terror as I watched her disintegrate, as I watched her tenuous hold on life loosen. No – life's tenuous hold on her.

"I'm just going early, that's all," she said.

"Why, Fionnuala, why?"

"Who knows?"

"Can you let me know somehow?"

"Afterwards? No. That much I know – no bargains ever."

"How can you bear it?"

But Fionnuala would only look at me helplessly, as if she knew I could never understand but would love it if I did. Sometimes she'd look at me like a teacher trying to coax out an answer I should know.

"You've left already, haven't you?" I accused once, suddenly, bitterly. "You're happier with them in your own head now."

"What else can I do, Róisín? I can't stay. I love you, but I have to go."

"What's it like?" I could barely whisper it. "What's it really like?"

"Remember when we prayed at Quarant-Ore to choose what is right? Always what is right?"

"Yes. Yes, of course. But –"

"No matter what, Róisín? Remember? No matter what?"

"Yes," I whispered miserably. "I do. But I never meant something like this. Did you? You didn't, did you, Fionnuala?"

"No, but you can't say no matter what and then take it back if you don't like what . . . . It's okay, Róisín, really. It's just saying yes. Yes, I'll trust you, God, who or whatever you are. Yes, I'll walk the water. Yes, I'll leap the unknown. It's like saying yes, yes, until I can't stop – for all the times people say no."

"I'm frightened, Fionnuala."

"So was I, but I'm not anymore."

"I'm bloody terrified, Fionnuala. Jesus, oh hell . . . I'm sorry. See, I'm even afraid to curse in front of you now."

"I love you, Róisín."

"I'm supposed to be the one comforting you."

"You are."

"What? With all this whining and moaning and fear? Sure I'm only making things worse for you."

"No. You are exactly what I need. You do comfort me."

She saw that I couldn't understand. So she stopped, with a sad, small smile. Came back to the world of nurses and injections and cups of tea and how's the pain. Not too bad, Doctor.

But sometimes after that I used to see Fionnuala look at me as if wondering whether to speak. She would hold my hand, her eyes willing me to do something.

"What, Fionnuala, love, what is it?"

But she only shook her head. "I don't know. I just don't know."

As the first shoots of spring burst from the earth, we laid her beneath them. And down with her went the last part of me that believed this world might be any comfortable place to live in.

I passed Fitzgerald's Bakery on the way home from the funeral. Ghosts of childish voices:

> *Fitzgerald's bread would kill a man dead,*
> *Especially a man with a baldy head.*

After Fionnuala's death nothing was ever the same. I began to wake up. To watch the play from a better seat.

I couldn't open a book at school without a holy picture tumbling out: *In rem. of you being my* BF.

Why her and not me? Why should I survive? Or had she achieved something the rest of us were light-years from meriting? If so, that was one we'd all gladly fail. Fionnuala, too, at the start.

I dreamed of her funeral a great deal – but it had become my own. I was always laid out in her coffin in the school chapel. A grown dead baby in a pram. From the cold white satin surrounds, and in the modest lacy blue Child of Mary dress, I watched the faces circling morosely around me. Looming heavily, each with the weight of some wrong done me that could never now be put right. Like fairy godmothers with the wrong gifts for Sleeping Beauty. Faces I knew well as my own in the dream, but could not later name or remember.

The other girls never talked of Fionnuala. Certainly not to me. I wished they would. I wouldn't have minded what they said if only they had included me in talk of her. They did talk, I know that. I'd see the whispering off in the distance – the tilted heads, the half-glances – the switch to loud hockey or homework talk as I approached.

All the time she was sick they removed her farther and farther. She became a freak, an accident, not normal. Her death was almost a charm. Seventeen-year-old girls don't die. But Fionnuala did. It was like winning the Sweep, marrying a prince; it wasn't going to happen to you. But it did happen to Fionnuala Fitzgerald and that removed the rest twice as far from death. Lightning was not going to strike twice.

"Whom the gods love die young," said Miss Hester, the Latin teacher.

"Don't be too good, girls," giggled Breege Finnerty. "You could be next."

"And that explains," said Evelyn Doyle, "why such an ancient oul' rip as Mother Carmel is still with us. No gods would call her anywhere next, nigh, or near them one minute before they had to."

"A saint, that child," said Mother Perpetua. "I'm not a saint, girls; I haven't suffered enough. Although that is not for want of your trying."

"God fits the back to the burden," Evelyn Doyle would finish from under her breath.

A pity Mr. and Mrs. Fitz didn't know that. From what I heard from Harry, not only were their backs not up to the tragedy, but their hearts were broken too.

But Mother Hilda took the biscuit: "Fionnuala Fitzgerald is the lucky one, girls," she said. "Died before she could offend God. Who knows what evil she avoided. He took her because He can see down the road."

That I couldn't swallow. Fionnuala, with ten times the integrity I'd ever have. My fingers shook on my social science book in the desire to throw it at the shiny pink barrel of her face. She, the diseased one, the whites of her eyes a permanent yellow, her breath the most stinking I ever remember.

I could not keep quiet.

"Why doesn't God take all potentially evil people so, Mother?" I asked. "Why Fionnuala Fitzgerald and not Hitler?"

"How dare you speak with such impertinence, Róisín McGovern. Thirty minutes' detention."

I didn't say a word ever again. I put my head down and studied for the Leaving Certificate and escape.

"Look at this, Róisín," said Breege Finnerty one day. "Look at Evelyn Doyle's *Hamlet*. In our school edition, Hamlet says to his mother: "Go, but go not to my uncle." In hers it says: "Go, but go not to my uncle's bed.""

"Are you surprised, Breege? They've probably rewritten our

152

history books too. The Bible. We'd probably fall down with amazement if we knew half of what they've removed from our nice, sanitized education. They're only throwing us a few pieces of the jigsaw. And even those they skelp here and there to make them fit their own picture."

"I didn't ask for a lecture, Róisín McGovern. Judas, it was only one little word. You used to be a bit of fun at least. Now you'd take the nose off anyone. You'd go through them for a shortcut. It was only because Fionnuala Fitzgerald was so nice she had any time for you."

If I didn't murder then, I never will. The anger rose up and surged down until it possessed every hair, every toenail. One person in my whole life had loved me – one. That this might have been because she was nice, and would have liked the Abominable Snowman, nearly dismantled me. I wanted to pull and shred every thread and frizzy curl on Breege Finnerty. My hands itched and my teeth bared. But something outside me saw the tittering gallery gathering. Don't give them the satisfaction, Róisín.

But still this anger possessed me. Up it would rear at the most unlikely moments. Indeed, I never knew when a tide of the most inappropriate emotion was going to engulf me. Like the day Mother Margaret Mary was berating Triona Byrne about the ladders in her stockings.

Triona Byrne was about six feet two, and M-Cubed was four feet ten any way you looked at her. So the ladders were nearly at eye level. Triona stood in the door-frame of the classroom, trying to angle herself smaller. Pulling down the sides of her cardigan to match her mouth, bending her knees, as if to lower herself to a more respectful height to receive the onslaught. No good. M-Cubed still addressed the grubby tails of her tie, furled inside out.

Huge squawks of laughter erupted from somewhere. Heads turned. Mine turned too, but I noticed then they were all looking at me. Great gusts of laughs, like demented hiccoughs, worse than farts, were coming from me. The class stood frozen, mouths gaping in disbelief.

153

But M-Cubed was not forty years a teacher for nothing.

"Hysterics," she said, and in three paces had whacked my face and was assigning the class a page of algebra equations, her pudgy warm fingers closed around my wrist like a handcuff.

"This will take five minutes," she said. "If you are slow starting, I'll give you extra homework. Now begin."

She brought me to her office. I thought I was in terrible trouble again, but no.

"I lost a few friends myself along the way," she said, just as she'd say: Open your algebras now, girls, at page eighty-seven. She was rooting in her bookshelves.

The laughs had subsided to real hiccoughs now. The exhausted kind you get after abandoned crying.

"It helps if you think of her world and ours somehow connected," she said less gruffly. "You'll be surprised. It really does help."

She smoothed a story from Lady Gregory's *Gods and Fighting Men* in front of me and also indicated two poems.

"Read these for your lesson today," she said, and was gone, bouncing along on tiny strides like one of those inflatable clowns you can never push over no matter how you try.

"And don't think for a minute this gets you off your homework. Breege Finnerty will have it for you" – just in case I thought she might have lost the run of herself completely. Or that this might work again.

I started to read only because I was afraid M-Cubed would question me and I might be in real trouble.

The first poem was Yeats's "Stolen Child." The words sort of washed over me, but the refrain at the end of every stanza seemed part of me already. As if the words came from inside me, as well as from the book. I knew them for somewhere:

> *Come away, O human child!*
> *To the waters and the wild*
> *With a faery, hand in hand,*
> *For the world's more full of weeping*
> *than you can understand.*

Next was the story "The Children of Lir." I half knew it. Probably in one ear and out the other in some junior class. And yet it had remained somewhere, half-remembered, like a dream.

Fionnuala and her three brothers lost their mother, Aobh, in the birth of the youngest. Lir, their father, later married her sister Aoife. She was jealous of Lir's love for them. She changed them into swans and banished them for nine hundred years. Three hundred here, three hundred there, three hundred elsewhere, each destination more frozen and barren than the last.

Aoife almost regretted then what she had done, but it was too late. So she promised the curse would be over when the Man of the North joined the Woman of the South and a thin bell was heard. Also, she told them their music would enchant all who heard it. They would fall asleep instantly and be happy.

Lir was bereft. But all he could do was come with their people – the Tuatha Dé Danann – to listen to the swans' music. The Tuatha were happy for the first three hundred years. Until the swans had to move and they could hear them no more.

The swans were more desolate than ever, banished farther to the frozen wastes of the Moyle. They barely managed to stay alive and together. Fionnuala watched for them constantly, sleeping at night, warming one brother under each wingspan and the third before her under the feathers of her breast.

Nine hundred years passed, with Fionnuala leading and sheltering her brothers. She led them to each new place of exile and when the time was up, back towards Lir's country.

There they waited, and one day she heard a solitary bell. She rejoiced with her brothers. She led them to the bell, and the hermit saint Mochaomog.

He was there because he had heard of the plight of the swans and had travelled to the wildest and farthest islands to wait for the children of Lir. Mochaomog was the first human to hear again their beautiful, eerie swan songs. Joyfully he prayed for guidance as to their deliverance.

Then he gently approached the swans and offered them his care and protection. Wearily they accepted.

Meanwhile, Deoch of Munster had married Lairgnen, King of Connaught, and this was taken to be the joining of the Man from the North and the Woman from the South. Deoch heard of the swans and wanted them.

But Mochaomog refused both Lairgnen and Deoch the swans. Lairgnen tried to take them by force, but when he touched them their feathers fell away leaving four nine-hundred-year-old humans.

"Baptize us," said Fionnuala to Mochaomog, "before we die." And she asked that they be buried with her brother Aodh under her right arm, Fiachra under her left, and Conn ahead of her. Just as she had sheltered them all the years of their exile under the feathers of her wings and breast.

Little things about the story got to me: Why are all stepmothers wicked? And her name was Eve while their real mother's was Aobh, nearly the same, yet close to the Irish word for beauty, *aoibhneas*.

But what made me cry was Fionnuala's burial wish for herself and her brothers. To me, they were clearly in battle formation. To come back again and again. To regroup and arise until that day when the Man of the North truly joined the Woman of the South.

I don't really know why that made me cry. M-Cubed stuck her head around the door and caught me.

"Good girl, yourself," she said. "Tears are wonderful things, Róisín. Aren't they lovely stories?"

"The swans' time – the curse – that was long before Christ, Mother?" I asked her.

"Long, long," she said. "Time of the goddess Dana. Tuatha Dé Danann. They were defeated later and taken over by the Celts."

Bloody tears again in spite of me.

"Don't you be too worried about them, Róisín. Sure the Tuatha are probably still laughing."

"Why, Mother, if they were defeated?"

"Because it is said the Celts won everything above ground, everything you can see. But the Tuatha got everything else. The Celts thought they won, but they only got the tip of the iceberg. The Tuatha are still laughing."

She went back to class then, still chuckling herself. I was left with Moore's "Song of Fionnuala."

> *Silent, O Moyle, be the roar of thy water,*
> *Break not, ye breezes, your chain of repose,*
> *While, murmuring mournfully, Lir's lonely daughter*
> *Tells to the night-star her tale of woes.*
> *When shall the swan, her death-note singing,*
> *Sleep, with wings in darkness furl'd?*
> *When will heaven, its sweet bells ringing,*
> *Call my spirit from this stormy world?*

I read them all again then, a sad kind of peace settling upon me. I had somewhere to go when the world got too much. The possibilities were endless. I could think and I could wonder.

Everything I had believed to be so cut and dried and worked out – opened up again. Maybe there were countless points of view where I had believed only one.

If Fionnuala could wait, regroup, and arise, so could I. It made eminent sense to me that some otherworld had stolen Fionnuala. If I'd had half a chance, I would have stolen her myself.

Breege Finnerty sat opposite me for Quarant-Ore that year. But if she did, Fionnuala was there too.

It was here Fionnuala lay overnight before burial, her coffin one with the light golden oak of the chapel woodwork. Like the offering. The missing last piece in a puzzle. The ark.

Now at two o'clock in the morning, the chapel was again unearthly. A hospice, respite for the pilgrim. Nurses tiptoeing, guarding the sick. Soundless feet, dim searchlight shining, checking the sleeping.

Always it reminds me of nursing and dying. Fionnuala old as the mother of sorrow. Haggard as a crone at the crossroads. Looking at me with eyes that have already left. Have already joined the conspiracy of silence. Seeing after, rolling upwards and sideways towards their new orbit – gone.

I am the Lord, Thy God.

Fionnuala! is that you?

Only you could interrupt the first commandment: Thou shalt not have strange gods before me.

I know that, Fionnuala. Everyone knows that.

Really? You can't see anyone worshipping golden cows, so everything is all right?

No, it's money and fame and things now, isn't it?

They're just the easy ones. The obvious.

What do you mean, Fionnuala?

Think. Figure it out. You who'd spend half the night on a corollary in geometry.

I smiled. It was Fionnuala, all right. Only she would know I always had to get QED or die in the attempt. No French done, no Wordsworth learned, the Boer War in the wrong century – but by Theorem 1, Theorem 16, Theorem 35, or, by God, QE would have to be bloody well D.

What are you saying, Fionnuala? Give me a hint.

Silence.

Fionnuala!

Silence.

You always were stuck in the Pyrrhic Wars when I wanted to talk to you.

Better that than Georgette Heyer.

She was gone then. Stuck in some homework, as usual.

"God," said Breege Finnerty as we were leaving the chapel, "but this is a terrible bore. I don't know why they make us do it. I slept me way through most of it. Did you?"

"Oh yes," I agreed.

I went to university, but only just.

I was to go on the grounds I could stay with Deirdre in Foxrock and babysit her two little girls sometimes in return for my keep. But Dermot Comiskey was transferred to Brussels and I was out of luck. Three years' college fees plus maintenance costs were out of the question, my mother said. I could have a one-year secretarial course and that was that.

Harry, of all people, came to the rescue. No one should be denied the chance of a university education, he said. That he had personally tried two and found both wanting was no reason for other people to dismiss them.

He offered me a poky little room in his flat in Northumberland Road on the strict understanding that he could and would go ahead with whatever he wanted to do with his time without any comments, advice, or suggestions from me. I was there on sufferance. I could go to my lectures and live the rest of my life in Harry's pad, provided I did nothing to remind him of his foolish generosity in allowing such a circumstance. This suited me fine.

Harry's room was actually a butler's pantry in other days. Long and narrow to start, it was all the more passagelike because of floor-to-ceiling shelves along both side walls. Teresa – the one human out of Harry's girl-doll collection – helped me to rip out the shelves on one side. She found me a nice table down the quays for the end window and a narrow bed. We bought two pairs of red and green tweed curtains at a jumble sale, one set for the window, the other to cover part of the remaining shelves. Of these, we removed some, raised and lowered others, to accommodate clothes. The remainder we left bare for books and knick-knacks.

Two chairs, a gallon of white paint, and one oriental carpet runner later and I wanted to tell *Ideal Homes* all about it.

Harry's pad was great when Teresa was there: lazy hours at the kitchenette table with endless cuppas. Harry happily sprawled with his feet up, watching sports or the "Late Late" on TV. To size up a guest's mood with whom he would have a meeting lined up later. "How to Handle a Woman," he'd hum to himself, making notes and phone calls and plans.

It wasn't too good with Hilary or Rosemary there. They were Harry's other two main girlfriends. They were not much interested in cuppas, in staying in, or indeed in sisters. They were interested in TV all right, but only if they were the ones on the screen. They both fancied a career in the "arts" and saw Harry as a shortcut. Through him they smiled regularly out of the social columns in newspapers and magazines, secured parts in plays, interviews, and advertisement work. I'm not sure what Harry got out of all this beyond the obvious.

After a while I wouldn't leave my room if it was Hilary or Rosemary out there. Most of all, I hated the hours I lay awake waiting for Harry to come home safe. By the stinking fumes in his room after a night with one of that pair I knew there was always serious drinking done. I knew, too, that Harry drove afterwards – from Wicklow or God-knows-where – and I didn't like it. I was petrified he would kill himself or someone else. But I knew better than to open my mouth about this to Harry.

There wasn't even Deirdre for diversion when either Hilary or Rosemary was in favour. I would have enjoyed babysitting my two little nieces, Sarah and Eithne, but the Comiskeys were well settled in Brussels by then, the big house off Brighton Road in Foxrock rented out to a colleague of Dermot's, another diplomat.

Teresa started asking me to her little flat in Raglan Road. I wouldn't go, couldn't go, knowing Harry was painting the town polka dot just up the road with one of his floozies. But Teresa told me not to be daft; she had known Harry for years now and understood his ways. And could she not just like me for my own company now and then? And anyway, since when was I responsible for the behaviour of my big stupid lout of a brother? We laughed over that and over the floozies, and Teresa told me it was a strange old-fashioned word for a young one like me and I should think of something more "with it."

If, indeed, I wasn't with it, it was not Teresa's fault. She took me in hand. She was a lovely dark redhead herself, the kind with creamy skin and dark-fringed hazel eyes. She suited her crisp white nurse clothes, with her capable arms and cool, tender fingers. I thought of her as a natural beauty but unfortunately Harry was more partial to what he called "a bit of oomph in a bird." He used to say Teresa was a nurse all right: more the kind of girl to check your temperature and pulse than to raise them for you.

But what Harry didn't even notice was how Teresa managed him when she was around. She had no bother wheedling money out of him for clothes and a haircut for me. Everyone was trailing around in long coats and laced-up boots that year – after Lara in *Doctor Zhivago*. Teresa soon saw to it that I was trailing too. Then back she came from a week in London with a white fur hat and cravat for me. The only snag now was the hedgehog hair that would not entertain this or any hat.

"No problem." said Teresa. "If we're doing this at all, we do it right." So she negotiated more of Harry's money into my hand and then pushed me into Dublin's best hair salon.

The Lion's Den was the best because Michel there could both cut and insult better than any hairdresser in the city. He told me I was a disgrace and a crime, and such a hairdo should be illegal and punishable by banishment to Mayo. In a frenzy of self-righteousness he clipped and sliced and snipped and complained until nine-tenths of my hair lay on the floor at his feet. The remainder clung terrified to my skull in tiny wisps, not even enough spirit left to curl.

When I got over the shock, I had to admit it wasn't all bad. My head, and somehow my whole body, looked about two tons lighter. And I seemed to have acquired a more definite face.

"Come back on Thursday and I'll shape your eyebrows," said Michel, waving me to the cash desk. "Maybe then you will be fit

161

to appear in public. I'll do it for nothing in the interests of aesthetics. And do try and wear some clothes, dear, not those orphan ragbags. Thursday at sevenish."

Teresa liked it. Harry guffawed and asked where were the tar and feathers.

But what I didn't tell them about was "Thursday at sevenish" and the free eyebrows. Because I knew that was a strange arrangement for a hairdresser's appointment and I didn't want them to stop me or Teresa to come.

I read an article about Michel in *Woman's Way*: he was really Mick Ryan; he was thirty-four and had a wife and three children in Templeogue. But that didn't stop me either.

There were only a few clients left in the Lion's Den, and that few thinning fast.

Michel was still not ready for me. My cheeks flamed as one by one everyone left, the girl stylists with smirks and knowing looks among themselves.

By now I would have left if there was any way I could without looking a complete fool. Well, almost, because I also wanted to stay. A dangerous game but, oh, such an exciting one.

At last we were alone. He washed his hands with a great flourish and then advanced towards me with a shoe box full of makeup.

"Come and stand here in the light where I can see you," he ordered, waving tweezers to the spot. I stood there and he began to pluck. He was shorter than I, if anything, and very good-looking in a glamorous sort of way. The kind you'd see in magazine pictures, but almost never in the street and certainly not at dances. His hair was reddish brown, exactly the same colour as his eyes, and his skin was a few tones lighter. His shirt was reddish brown and so were his pants. There was no colour on him anywhere that wasn't a tone of copper. And very little of this arrangement the Almighty's.

"Hold still. How can I do it if you keep moving?" And how could I keep still with him pressing against me like that? So I kept backing away and he kept pressing after me until I was half-nelsoned firmly in a corner. Well and truly wedged from the hips down.

There he ordered me to close and open my eyes and look left and right and up and down while he worked with his head critically on one side, as if he were painting the *Mona Lisa*.

When he was satisfied he put down the box and we didn't even have that between us anymore. Then, as if it was the most natural question in the world, he asked me if anyone had ever sucked my nipple. I assured him no one had and no one was about to. He assured me I'd love it. He proceeded to show me and I proceeded to panic.

God knows what I babbled then, because I have no wish to remember. And what made him finally decide to throw in the towel and go home to the wife and three kids in Templeogue, only God knows too. But what I do remember is how glad I was to be standing at a bus stop, peering into the gloom for a 7A or 8 out to Harry's.

After a bit I forgot my fright. Well, actually, it was embarrassment that overcame it. Because I couldn't miss the way everyone was staring at me on the bus.

But it wasn't until I was safely back at Harry's I realized why. Thank God Harry was out as usual, because when I looked in the mirror, what a sight looked back – eyebrows up like the bridges of Paris, but nothing compared to the makeup under them. Elizabeth Taylor in full regalia as Cleopatra was Blessed Imelda compared to that face. Every harlot and Jezebel I ever heard of or read about looked back from my own mirror.

The awful thing is I was pleased. How did my eyes get to look like a film star's in a magazine? The whites almost pale blue around so much flashing colour: turquoise, green, yellow. Centred and ringed with black, like exotic twin planets.

I always saw my eyes as plain pale blue. Found in books on ugly people. Old men and spinsters. Watery eyes. With the words rheumy, bland, cold, weak, and bloodshot tacked on.

Wrong. I hugged myself tight. Thank you Michel of the Lion's

Den, Mick of Templeogue. I felt a bit sorry for the wife then. For all Thursdays at sevenish. He must have more success usually than with me or he wouldn't waste his talent.

Or maybe he just likes it that way. Frightening the wits out of gauche lumps like Róisín McGovern. But showing even this most unlikely raw material, when it comes to femmes fatales, they haven't been completely and forever left out.

"Well, the hair and the eyebrows are not going to be wasted," said Teresa. She and Harry were going to her hospital's dress dance, and I was coming along or Teresa would die in the attempt.

She borrowed an armload of dresses in the larger sizes from her heftier pals. The only one that would both zip up and come near the ground was a silver one you'd need sunglasses just to look at. In the middle of the bosom a pink rose, sad and crushed from too many passionate waltzes. Harry said I looked like the inside of a tea chest, but Teresa and I knew I was lovely.

I might have the dress now, said Harry, but there was the small matter of a partner. He was drawing the line there. Hair and wardrobe by Harry McGovern, he said, not to mention tickets. There was no way he was providing the stuffing for a monkey suit as well. He valued his friends. He was sorry, but I'd have to come up with my own man.

I told them Lorcan Burke was in First Arts too.

"Who is this creature?" said Teresa.

"From altar boy to sex scandal," said Harry. "His last girlfriend overthrew the British cabinet."

"You told me that story," said Teresa, "but you never mentioned this Burke."

"That's because he had nothing to do with it," I said. "It was long over before Bernadette got going. Anyway, he's more interested in other things now than going out with girls."

"Proper order too," said Harry. "After igniting a set of fireworks like Bernadette Gibbons's."

"He didn't."

"How she leaps to his defence," said Harry. "And how do you know?"

"I just do. He's not interested."

"Maybe that's why," said Harry. "Burned to a cinder the first time out." Sudden recollection flooded his face. "But it was not his first time out, was it? I remember the playing doctor. The groping and pawing behind my back in the cinema. Yes – "

"If you say anything to him about that . . . . " I blushed furiously.

"Can't wait to see this fella," said Teresa.

I first had to ask Lorcan. It wasn't easy, remembering what he said. When someone says you're ugly and he wouldn't be seen dead with you, it's not a thing you easily forget.

"Will you come to a dress dance with me?" I did finally ask him one day, after knocking forty-two chairs to get to him between lectures.

"What?" he said warily, as if I'd asked him for one of his vital organs.

"Harry has some tickets for a dress dance, so I have to find someone to go with and I don't know anyone. But you don't have to . . . ."

"I'd like to," said Lorcan. "I'd like to see Harry again."

"That's great," I said. Wonderful. Maybe he and Harry could dance the night away.

But at least he agreed. And something else happened: Lorcan Burke started to speak to me again. We re-embarked on what I thought at the time was called a "plutonic" relationship. Which really meant he allowed me to join his entourage.

Jimmy Lavelle was first in this. He had followed Lorcan Burke faithfully since High Infants and was still there behind him. Next was Dermot Enright, from Athlone, who shared Lorcan's room in the men's residence.

Firmly attached to Dermot Enright were Breffni Dunne and Jacinta Feore. Breffni streaked her hair ash, wore capes, and puffed through a cigarette holder. Five years in posh boarding school, finishing school in Switzerland, and holidays all over Europe with Daddy the Diplomat and Mummy the Solicitor. Jacinta Feore: from some little place in Kerry near six other little places, none of which we knew. Five years in the Convent of Mercy and holidays all over Ballybunion with Daddy the Artificial Inseminator and Mam the Treasurer of the Irish Countrywomen's Association. Heavy-lidded eyes like a sleepy gnome and a tongue that would blister paint.

On the fringes was a contingent from the North, attending National because they would not attend the Protestant Queen's in Belfast. Streets ahead of us in politics and very useful in the students' union.

Lorcan Burke was always talking to them or somebody. If it wasn't the students union, it was the literary and historic. On and on about apartheid, or campus unrest in California, or Maoist sit-ins in the Aula Max. Long discussions as to whether Hugh Feeney was machine or anti-machine. I think that meant was he a yes man in an organization or not. I couldn't swear. Because I would be looking at Lorcan. Trying to see him as others might. It didn't matter what a fellow looked like to you – it was what he looked like to your friends that counted.

He wasn't bad at all. An eight and a half, Teresa whispered in my ear when she did finally meet him. But she would have been biased because she knew I was interested. He was thin and pale, with black straight hair forever falling over deep blue eyes.

"Alain Delon," sighed Breffni Dunne under her breath and over a chicken croquette in Bewley's. There were nine of us in for lunch together, a typical Lorcan audience. "Just watch his face," she said, as he was expounding on the Apprentice Boys' march with one of the lads from the north. "It's the intensity that makes you watch it."

Breffni Dunne always went for odd things about fellows: their gestures, the way they sat, crossed their legs, a hand on a steering wheel. Came from reading too much F. Scott Fitzgerald.

"That bunch from the north" – Breffni gestured to where Gerry Donegan was arguing with Lorcan – "they're very articulate."

"Taught to stand up, open their mouths, and speak out, instead of sit down, stay quiet, be good," I said.

"They say things are coming to a head up there."

"Don't mind them. My uncle's been saying that as long as I can remember."

"Does he live there?"

"Yes. Teaches in Belfast. We used to go on holidays there," I said.

"What was it like?"

"A great place for cheap comics, trolley buses, free amusements in the parks. Oh – and Mars bars, Bounty bars, Opal Fruits, and Spangles."

"Very comprehensive picture, that," Breffni said.

"I was seven. What do you expect? What else now . . . there was a lot of red-brick housing. I went to school with my uncle one day and I taught them Irish. Colours and counting. They got free orange juice and milk . . . . I wanted to move there immediately."

"Those eyes," said Breffni.

"Pardon?"

"Burke's eyes. Look how they glow when he's excited. And those hands . . . ."

Even I knew what she meant there. Lorcan had long slender fingers. They gently ran over books, glass rims, pens, people's arms. If they were still, they were resting almost caressingly on something.

"Now, if I had to have hands run over me," said Breffni, "I'd like it to be those. I bet Scott Fitzgerald had hands like that."

Probably the very one who'd go screaming for Mummy the Solicitor if anyone did run his hands over her. Not that we all wouldn't maybe, but the rest of us knew if anyone did it was more likely to be a P.J. O'Reilly than an F. Scott Fitzgerald. P.J. would run his hands over anything under ninety any time. You could get yourself a reputation just for letting him stand behind you a second time in a lineup for the cafeteria or the bus. There was no seat safe from him at lunch; he was under the table, around the table, over the table.

167

But there was no sign of Lorcan wanting to run those hands over Breffni. Or any girl. And I suppose he only agreed to go to the dance with me because I was Róisín McGovern. One of the lads. I probably didn't count as a girl. Or a woman, as we were now called. That's Dunleavy's woman. Over there, with Higgins's woman. Has Byrne got a woman for Saturday night?

On the day of the dress dance, a slag heap toppled and fell on a school in Wales, killing one hundred and fifty children and their teachers – only two hours before they were due to go home for their midterm break. All over the evening newspapers and nonstop on television were pictures of distraught parents and relatives numbly watching the hopeless digging in the grey mountain of mud.

Lorcan arrived in his monkey suit with a face on him like the chief undertaker's at a funeral.

"Cheer up," said Harry, slapping him on the back. "It's just for tonight. You don't have to marry her."

"It's those little Welsh kids," said Lorcan.

"I know. I can't look at it," said Teresa.

But we did. We couldn't stop. We stood around the television, ridiculous, traitorous statues in evening dress.

"Come on," said Harry eventually. "We can't do anything by standing here gaping."

At the hotel the Welsh tragedy was all but forgotten. Apart from the odd "isn't it terrible" and "you never know, do you," the evening had taken over again.

But not for me. The further into the dance we got, the more miserable I became. And angry.

You put your right leg in, you put your right leg out. Grown men with grinning red, shiny faces. Tipsy girls overbalancing. Jostling, grabbing, shouting, laughing.

Dancing with Lorcan Burke was everything I had imagined. The floor was alive with people he just had to see: "Hello there, how did the meeting on Tuesday go?" "There you are, Ger. See you after this dance. Is Robinson here tonight?"

He might as well have been holding a laundry bag. While he scanned the floor, I had nothing to do but look over his shoulder at all the other couples. There were some other blind or convenience dates like ours. They were the ones that weren't glued together, oblivious of everything except the length of body pressed close. Silly grins on their faces, like kids having a nice dream.

There was great stamping and hooting as the debutantes were presented in their white dresses. Whistles and wolf calls for the pretty ones, a jeer for one whose escort had the same name. This old wagon could only come up with a brother or cousin to bring her.

Dinner started with soup – corn flour and powder soup, although it was called Crème du Barry. A wedge of stringy chicken flanked by a straggle of peas and soapy canned potatoes followed. Vanilla ice cream, tinned fruit, and half a wafer, under the title of Peach Melba, completed the blandishments.

"Never again," said Harry. "Every time I say it, but this time I mean it."

The dancing resumed. Brown bags appeared discreetly, and not so discreetly, from inside pockets and under tables. No sense in paying the price this kip was asking for booze.

A student was dangled by his feet from the balcony.

"Chattanooga Choo-Choo" got under way. Everyone grabbed someone else's waist and the human train gambolled and teetered over all obstacles. Spectators shot peas through napkin shooters.

"What's wrong?" said Lorcan. "You've a face on that would stop a clock."

He noticed. My face might have stopped every watch and clock in the dance hall for all he'd have noticed before. Maybe I'm due some charity work.

"Nothing wrong," I said. "I hate this, that's all."

"So do I," said Lorcan. "I could have told you that when you asked me to go."

"Sorry, but I like to find out things for myself."

"You hate it. I hate it. Why don't we leave?"

"Harry will be angry after all the money it cost."

"Harry hates it too. You heard him."

169

"Does anyone like this?" I asked.

"I don't think anyone does."

"I know what your problem is," said Lorcan, after a short silence. "It's the letdown, isn't it? You were imagining a lovely evening with Strauss waltzes; you, a glamorous debutante, with some Omar Sharif. White dress, orchid, romantic banquet. And what do you get? Grade five institutional menu, the hokey-pokey, Lorcan Burke, and borrowed plumes that neither fit nor suit. A big sham. And one hundred and fifty kids die on the day. Just to rub it in."

He was partly right. But it was Fionnuala Fitzgerald I wanted more than Omar Sharif. I wouldn't know where to begin with Omar Sharif. Lorcan Burke – although I didn't tell him – was infinitely more welcome there. But Lorcan Burke, or Omar Sharif, or whomever, Fionnuala Fitzgerald was to be right beside me no matter what. Promised on the back of countless holy pictures and even in Quarant-Ore. The partner was always hazy, interchangeable. But she was constant. She was to be right beside me for all the big moments: debutante, bridesmaid, bride, mother, godmother. She was what was missing most.

One of the prettiest debutantes lurched past us towards the Ladies, her dress showered with brown stains. The makeup was clownish now, a child dressed up. She saw nothing, nobody – intent on getting to the bathroom, hand to mouth. She didn't quite make it.

"That's life," said Lorcan softly. "So much for the dreams."

But the dance was worth it if for nothing else than being friends with Lorcan again. Not that college life was any more the anticipated ideal than the debs' ball. Cambridge it wasn't. The only leisurely punting done in Earlsfort Terrace was on horses and dogs. No quads, no lawns, no cobbled paths, no musty residences full of the ghosts of literary history. There wasn't even a place to congregate. You could hold up the notice-boards in the bleak hall, and some students spent entire days on the impressive entrance steps. But an entrance was all National had.

170

"You should go to Trinity," said Harry to Lorcan. "You wouldn't even be excommunicated. No more to hell or to National."

"I like National," said Lorcan. "It reflects Ireland, not Anglo-Ireland."

"Even the name," said Harry. "National sounds cheap. Low standard. Like National Health, National Welfare, National school, National parks. The lowest common denominator."

"Wait until you see Belfield," said Lorcan.

"Supermarket education," said Harry. "I'm sure the great academic seats of Europe are terrified. All the world beating a path to this modern erection in a field in suburban Dublin."

"He's only teasing you," said Teresa. "Stop that, Harry."

"But he's so irresistible," said Harry. "So deadly, deadly serious."

"I don't think your brother is very highly principled," said Lorcan, later, when we were out for a walk. I didn't like the "your brother." Smelled of guilt by association.

"Don't take him so seriously. He's a bit touchy because he dropped out himself. Anyway, can't you ever have a laugh now and then?"

"I'm sorry, but I don't see anything very humorous there. I'm the first to laugh at a joke if it's funny."

Oh no you're not, I realized with a sudden shock. Lorcan Burke had changed, somehow. Not moody exactly, but unpredictable. Touchy sometimes. Not in a million years now could I imagine myself reminding him of the joy of our island.

But, sense of humour or not, I liked Lorcan Burke for the way he treated other people. I had had more than enough of what passed for wit from the other fellows. Lounging near the noticeboards, eyes flaw-detecting all over the hall. I knew my own litany: You'd need a stepladder there. Could eat hay off a loft. Too hefty. Child-bearing hips, how are you, sure those could bear a regiment. And the legs. The backside. Jesus, a wagon.

Not that I am one to be hurling stones. I, who marked fellows in Grafton Street out of ten with Teresa. Three and a half shouted giddily before the involuntary candidate even passed out of earshot. Mea culpa.

171

Lorcan Burke might not have you in stitches laughing but he had none of those petty cruelties either. And it wasn't for hinting and fishing and rooting on my part to expose signs of them.

"Jacinta Feore is an awful wagon, Dermot Enright says," I tried once.

"Just about the kind of juvenile opinion he would have," said Lorcan. "What surprises me is that you would repeat it."

Oh, I would repeat it. Definitely. How else would I find out what Lorcan Burke's juvenile, or otherwise, opinion might be. In case it was only I who was exempt from his findings. Less than a bird, worse than a wagon. Meriting no opinion at all. And when someone has started out saying you're ugly and he wouldn't be seen dead near you, you're doubly cautious. Although the more I saw of him, the less likely it seemed. Either he had changed a lot or Bernadette had fibbed. I could just have asked him straight out, but that would have required honesty and openness. You'd die before showing those kinds of weaknesses to a fellow.

Also, I knew whatever was bothering Lorcan, it was not lack of humour that made him serious. I knew better of old and I also knew one person who could make him laugh, even now.

"What do you think of the Fly?" I asked him once on our way to the one lecture we shared – hers.

"Isn't that a nun sequitur?" asked Lorcan. Yes, the Fly made even Lorcan Burke giddy. "I think she's great," he continued. "But I think she wouldn't get away with half of what she says, only for the habit."

He was always smiling around the Fly, but then I suppose we all were. She was indeed a far cry from our nuns at school. Not so on the face of it – here were Lorcan Burke and I again under the tutelage of a five-foot twig of a nun. But there it ended – the Fly might be skinny as a park railing, but she had a voice and a bearing that would have galvanized a regiment.

One day, for instance, she held up a picture of three spirals in triangular position carved on a rock. Then a poster of a huge shamrock, and finally she wrote "Leopold" on the blackboard, then "Molly," and underneath each she wrote "Bloom." She centred the o of Molly over the oo of Bloom, and the o of Leopold over the oo of Bloom.

"What have these got in common?" she asked us.

"Curves!"

"Circles!"

"Three!"

"Triangle!"

The answers flew. "Great," the Fly said, brushing off the chalk dust. "But I set them up for you. I made the connections, then showed them to you. Would you please remember that education is all about making your own connections and discoveries."

"How do you know they are connected, Sister?"

"I don't. But my imagination, or something, insists they must be. Take these spirals – carved on the wall of a grave built into a hill before the Pyramids of Egypt. Similar to ancient carvings half a world away of the same time. Christ still three and a half thousand years into the future, mind."

There was an electrified silence.

"A bird's-eye view of the grave shows a long, narrow passage and three chambers with round basin fonts," the Fly continued. She held up the picture, then the echoing image of the shamrock.

"Patrick lit his Pascal fires on Tara, only a stone's throw from that grave," she went on. "How many thousand years later? You were told he picked up a shamrock and taught the heathens about the mystery of Trinity. Now look again at those spirals, the stem passage of the grave, and the three rounded chambers, and tell me the shamrock was a new image for these people."

There was dead silence. "The shamrock might just be the greatest Irish joke of all time," she said softly, impish emphasis on *sham*.

"And what has Joyce to do with all that, Sister?" someone asked eventually.

"I don't know, I really don't. Maybe nothing. But something put it in my head and I always respect that. Maybe it's something, maybe not – I always keep the lines open. I think Joyce was more of an engineer than anything else, but I might be all wrong. Anyway, he loved the letter o. Remember 'Moocow' which opened *Portrait*? And what has that to do with spirals and New-grange and shamrocks? I don't know. Yet – will you remember that? Everything we know now was first unknown to the people before us . . . . I put Joyce in so you might remember that."

"Why do you like Yeats and not Joyce, Sister?"

"I don't know that either."

"Is that because Joyce is . . . is on the Index, Sister?" came one of the brave male voices always hiding at the back of the lecture hall.

"Look at this – " The Fly pounced on a dog-eared paperback in her desk. She held up *Ulysses*. She flicked it and let the pages fall open. "I wonder why it falls open there? And there. And there. And why it is mauled and thumbed black?" There was an eruption of desk banging and laughter.

"And I'd bet there's a *Chatterley* around in the same condition." There was more laughter.

She held the book up again. "The so-called modern giants. Don't you think they have failed somewhere if they are only read in snippets for dirt value?"

"But I haven't read any of Yeats at all, Sister," came the same voice from the back, and the laughter and banging became uproarious.

"We could argue this for the whole year and no one be right," said the Fly. "You have to learn to think for yourself. What can I say? Only to beg you to read them all. Try every one of them. As wide as you can, from all corners of the earth." She herself had set us a course that was as flexible as she could make it.

"You shouldn't have to read a book you don't like," she said. "Books are like best friends – either they grab you by the very heart or don't bother – life is too short. O'Faolain, that was. And why do I love Yeats? Because I agree with young Heaney: To read Yeats is to be a child standing too close to live wires in a field.

"Anyway, if a book doesn't do that for you, there is something wrong. Put it down, and try another. Ride all the best coattails. But never forget – the journey is your own. If I teach you nothing else, remember that."

It was a far cry from what I knew of education until now. My chair was nearly on fire. We galloped from Stone Age to Bronze Age to Space Age with dizzying speed. From the Fianna rising to the lost hunting horn, to the hosting on the Last Day to Louis Armstrong singing "When the Saints Go Marching In."

"Ah, when the saints go marching in, indeed –" the Fly leaning over her desk – "I don't know, but when they do, I think maybe we're all in for a big surprise . . . . "

"I had never thought how irrelevant two thousand years is to infinity," I said to Lorcan Burke one day we were reeling out of her class. "An interlude. Our Pre-Christian Era is as relevant as tomorrow's Space Age."

"There's enough living in the past in this country already, Róisín, without you at it."

"Not the glorious past. The Fly makes it feel like everything is connected. She throws a bridge to the heavens."

"It's Fionnuala Fitzgerald again, isn't it. You can't let her go."

He was partly right. It was the old stories brought her alive. Dancing silver sandalled on the sea. Fionnuala the swan, murmuring mournfully. Singing to the night star her song of woe.

"Go and read somebody worldly," said Lorcan. "Somebody concrete, for balance."

But I couldn't. I was hooked. And the more I read, the more I was hooked.

"Yeats had a dream," I tried again.

"Isn't that a bit of an understatement," said Lorcan.

"No, no, not like his work. I mean a cause. He wanted to found a new kind of branch of a medieval order based on the Rosicrucians. The Rose and Cross."

"'Who is she that cometh forth as the morning rises? Fair as the moon, bright as the sun, terrible as an army set in battle array?'"

"Yes! See? I knew you'd be good at this sort of thing."

"Listen, I don't know anything. But I do know those Rose poems were his early ones. And very pretentious. He got some sense later."

"Rubbish," I shouted. "He said her hem always trailed over his pen. Read him before you condemn him."

"Okay. Give me what you've got. I still think, Róisín, you are carrying this nonsense too far."

I knew I was. But part of me belonged to this dark half-world now. World of faeries and spirits. Of Fionnuala.

I dreamed of her sometimes. In the blackness of the sky she glided shimmering. She smiled at me and held out her straw hat, its two crimson ribbons rippling towards me. On her own head now a helmet of stars. Then she always stood still and her naked body bloomed: blue, yellow, blue-green – peacock, stained glass.

Then, as she turned her back, the colours bruised and slowly rotted. Turned brown and obscene.

I think the Fly would have understood that dream.

"Either piss or get off the pot," said Jacinta Feore. "Give a real woman a chance with Lorcan Burke."

"If Mummy and Daddy knew the language I put up with every day," said Breffni Dunne. "Not that she isn't right, Róisín McGovern. Four months and he hasn't even kissed you."

"We're friends. He has no interest in girls that way," I said. "Honestly, you could dance naked."

"Did you?"

"Don't be ridiculous, Breffni."

We were upstairs in Horan's. Horan's pub in Leeson Street was digs for Breffni and Jacinta. There was great smirking about the name because the odd fellow could be sneaked upstairs in spite of Mrs. Horan's renowned vigilance. "I can't be everywhere at once," the poor woman said to Pauline Frayne's parents when she got into trouble and named Horan's as the location for the iniquity. "If a girl is going to do that sort of thing, she'll find a place. It's not my rooms put the idea in her head."

"She could say that again. More orphanage than boudoir," said Jacinta. Spartan and shabby as Mrs. Horan herself, the lino, paint-work, and walls all faded to the duns of her own twinsets and tweeds. "Earth colours," said Mrs. Horan stoutly. "Yes," said Jacinta, "Belmullet at dusk on a wet Monday."

Breffni and Jacinta now had the room. We all imagined where, how, and when it happened.

"You get swept away," said Breffni. "My mother said that. Your whole life ruined for one unguarded moment. One unguarded moment of passion."

"Mummy the Solicitor said that?" interrupted Jacinta. "You got the doctoral course. My mother told me I would bleed. End of story. And she only told me that because no one told her, and she thought she was bleeding to death. 'Impurities in the blood that must pass away,' she said. I swear. True as God."

"It's going to be wonderful," continued Breffni, ignoring.

"Maybe that's why my father took to artificial insemination," said Jacinta.

"Someone like Pasternak's Zhivago," said Breffni. She had deserted F. Scott for Boris. Admired the cinematic interpretation of his beautiful fictional character. The rest of us just fancied Omar Sharif, she said, and there was the world of difference.

"Imagine sitting opposite those eyes in Bewley's?"

"I've seen eyes like his," said Jacinta, "but there were four legs under them and a fur coat."

"Or the Metropole's café," said Breffni, not even hesitating.

"You could bring him upstairs to dance. As long as you got him back in time for the matinée."

Omar was still appearing daily at the Metropole. Upstairs was dancing for over thirty-fives. Known unofficially as the Garden of Remembrance.

"I was approached by a Sapphist last night," said Breffni grandly.

"A what?"

"A Sapphist. Follower of Sappho."

"Sounds like a clown. Who is he?"

"She was a Greek poetess of the sixth century BC."

And she has followers in Dublin? Come off it."

"She was a lesbian also. You two philistines do know what that is?"

"What do you take us for?" said Jacinta. "Of course we do. Lez be friends. There are some things you don't have to go to Switzerland to learn."

"You didn't meet one, did you Breffni?" I asked.

"I certainly did. She told me I looked most desirable in my choker."

We were all wearing cameos on velvet chokers then, like Lara in the scene where she was "swept away." Although, how she could consider being swept away by tubby old Steiger when Sharif was around melting the very snow off the walls was beyond us.

"How did you know she was a lesbian?" I said. "I'm sure they don't rush up and tell you."

"It was in the Ladies at the party last night," said Breffni. "There I was, minding my own business, adjusting my tights. By the way – Dermot Enright says tights have ruined passion as the world knows it. Courting will never be the same without the soft flesh gap between stocking and . . . and . . . ."

"Shove Dermot Enright," said Jacinta. "Go back to the lesbian."

"Well, as I said, I was adjusting my tights. They were slipping. 'Can I help?' came this voice behind me. I turned around, as far as you can when you are tied up in your tights. 'No thanks,' I said. I was laughing. I thought she was joking. She wasn't. She was deadly serious."

"What was she like?"

"Beautiful. In a Grace Kelly sort of way."

"Did she make a go for you?"

"Must you always be so crude, Jacinta Feore? Of course she didn't. She had class."

"Then how did you know?"

"One does. Don't you know when a man fancies you?"

"Doesn't happen very often," said Jacinta. "But I know what P.J. O'Reilly is like."

"Not like that," said Breffni. "He's an animal. No, she wanted to talk. She would have talked as long as I let her. Everyday things: family, holidays, school, friends."

"How did you know so?"

"Just before we left she said my choker was crooked and slipping. She caressed my neck as she did it up and said I looked very desirable. It was then I knew for sure."

"What did you say?"

"Nothing. Got out fast and back to the party. She didn't dance. She was always talking to some other girl."

"How awful," I said. "How lonely."

"She works in Switzer's," said Breffni.

"What? She told you?"

"Yes. Switzer's perfume counter."

"Come on," said Jacinta Feore. "I want to see her."

"No," I said. "That's awful."

"You're the very one who told us the first time you saw a black man, you followed him around to get a better look."

That was true. Halfway around the Green from the College of Surgeons.

And so we clumped our way through the green and down Grafton Street to Switzer's. Three abreast in our ridiculous Russian attire, left, right, to see the aberration.

Up one aisle we marched, gaping from near, and down the other, gaping from afar. She was lovely, far more beautiful than any of us could hope to be. She didn't have horns and she didn't look like she might turn into a man any minute. And she was managing not to molest the assistant near her.

"Come on," I said, ashamed.

But not ashamed enough. Not so ashamed I didn't point her out to others now and again. And if you asked me for points of interest around Trinity, I'd have thought of her long before *The Book of Kells*.

"Were you ever approached by a homosexual?" I asked Lorcan Burke. We were lagging Jacinta and Breffni, Dermot Enright and Jimmy Lavelle down Mount Street.

"Of course. Everyone is at some point."

I might have known. He was always the same – if you had a cold, he had the flu. If you had an uncle a bishop, he'd produce a cardinal.

"It was at the beach at home," he said.

"Duneen?"

"Don't be so shocked. He was a married man too. His wife had the kids over on the swinging boats."

Here Lorcan had to step off the pavement because a skinny woman blocked his path. Her dress was as high as a dress could go, her coat almost to the ground. It hung open revealing white boots and black fishnet tights. She swung her handbag and the wind ruffled the black roots of her yellow hair.

"Good evening," said Lorcan.

"Good evening," she mimicked. "All polite and la-di-da. You students is all the same: all prick and no money."

Lorcan Burke blushed like a kid and he didn't know what to say or where to look.

"Where's the man of the world now? Don't be shocked, Lorcan Burke," I said.

"Did you forget to pay her, Burke?" shouted Dermot Enright, laughing. "Now we know."

"Take it easy, Lorcan," said Jimmy Lavelle, as Lorcan rounded on Dermot furiously. "It's nothing."

Lorcan shrugged up the collar of his coat, dug his hands in the pockets, and walked on.

There had been other signs that Lorcan Burke was at war with himself. It was nothing for him to spend a week in raptures over some symphony concert he was treating me to, only on the day to announce instead we were off to hear the Greenbeats playing Chuck Berry, Jerry Lee Lewis, and the Beatles. And we mightn't even make it to that, because Lorcan had this habit of bumping into troubled friends with broken hearts, broken spirits, broken dreams. Acute discomfort from overindulgence of one sort or another. Then it was into some greasy spoon for two hours while Lorcan would administer therapy, punctuated by rounds of foul coffee and limp fat chips.

And there was the time he tried to survey the students' attitudes to religion and morals.

We made out what Lorcan felt was a searching, appropriate, timely, and deeply significant questionnaire. He knew someone who knew someone who would do the printing.

The forms went out; some even filtered erratically back, but, alas, threw no great illuminating beam on the questions of our time. Would you be a party to the pill? Where's the party? Do you condone sex before marriage? Only on Saturday nights.

"Do you?" I asked Lorcan, suddenly, as I talked about the survey to change the subject from the prostitute. The others had distanced themselves well by now from Lorcan's mood. But I liked it. I sensed a rare crack open.

"Do I what?"

"Condone sex before marriage?"

"No. Leads to nothing but trouble."

"Do you like girls at all?"

"Of course. Why do you ask?"

"Did you love Bernadette Gibbons?"

"How can a fourteen-year-old know that?"

"I did. I never felt as strongly since, as I did for Ben Thompson."

"What?"

"The misery . . . I'll never forget it."

"Yes – I did love Bernadette Gibbons."

"Hurts, doesn't it?"

"I thought I'd never get through it."

"Romeo and Juliet were that age."

"She just dumped me. Told me drop dead and climbed into James Percy's Riley."

"At least you know what happened to her; I often wonder what happened to Ben Thompson."

"I never knew you loved him."

"All through ages five and fourteen. Unrequitedly."

"That better or worse?"

"Much, much worse."

"Poor Róisín. No – poor Ben."

"Bernadette Gibbons said that you said I was ugly. That you wouldn't be seen dead with me."

"She what?"

"That's what she said: 'Lorcan Burke says you're ugly and he wouldn't be seen dead with you.' "

"You know what? I think I just got over her. Thanks."

"My pleasure."

"All lies, by the way."

"Thanks."

"My pleasure."

It seemed quite natural then to slip my hand through the arm dug in the pocket. Equally natural for him to squeeze it gently to his side with his elbow.

Quite contentedly we watched our shoes carry us down Nassau Street. Close as we had ever got to the island.

Our shoes carried us all over Dublin then. Lorcan showed me Saint Michan's, with its crypt full of leathery old mummies. We went to Dublin Castle, Saint Patrick's, the Liberties, and the Huguenot Cemetery. And we often took the train to Blackrock or Dun Laoghaire. Or walked Killiney Hill.

The Fly was with us every step even though she never knew it. Neither of us would ever see the world the same way again because of her.

An afternoon with Swift in Saint Patrick's or Handel in Fishamble Street was just as immediate as a night in the pub. For all anybody knew we were probably sitting on the laps of illustrious ghosts there too.

A pint of Guinness and a white lemonade? Three and sixpence, please. Ah, there's Lorcan and the bird. How's it goin'? You weren't at the match today? No? Ah, great. Furey made a right ass of himself. Couldn't score if they all went off the pitch. Did ya hear Cooney creamed the old man's car last night? Yeah, no joke. Leaving a bird home from Wanderer's. Wrapped it around that pole on Rock Road. You know that corner coming into Blackrock? That pole has something wrapped around it every Sunday morning. That's the one. The very one. Couldn't make it. I'm not surprised. Tires on that thing you wouldn't have on a baby's pram. Totalled it. Creamed. Nobody hurt but the car fuckin' totalled. Sorry about that, Róisín. Oh, there's Kearns. Hey Kearns, how's it goin'.

Everything seemed so cosy, but not quite. Especially when we were alone. Try as I might, I could never get more of that easy honesty touched on the night of the prostitute. If I tried, Lorcan ducked and avoided, armed with steely good manners.

"Has he kissed you yet?" asked Jacinta.

"No," I said. "And I told you he won't."

"I can't make that man out at all," said Breffni. She always called them men instead of fellows. In hopes that if they were called men, they might behave like them. Some hope.

"No," said Jacinta. "I don't know one who isn't trying to get the knickers off you after three sentences."

"Most of them would probably die of fright if you said yes," I said. "They probably feel it's their duty to storm the ramparts."

"That's easy for you to say," said Breffni. "From your seat at the symphony. Your box at the theatre. And if you do go to a film, I bet you get to see it. What would you know?"

"I do know what it's like," I said. "Being groped by some drunken first engineer who doesn't know your name? Of course I do. Keeps calling you Sheila or Betsy. Telling you what a wonderful bird she is. I remember."

"Yes, and then giving out yards because you won't co-operate," nodded Jacinta. "Because you're frigid, of course. How else could you resist him?"

"I don't know much," I said, "but this I do know – being swept away is something I want to smile about when I'm an old lady. And a squalid party in Ranelagh with some creep I don't like, let alone love, isn't it."

"McGovern's speech from the dock," said Jacinta. "Let no man write her – what's wrong with you?"

Breffni Dunne was bawling. Not loudly as Jacinta or I would have done. Genteelly. But bawling.

It took about fourteen tissues to find out what was wrong. After all the hopes of F. Scott or Pasternak, Breffni feared she had lost her virginity to Dermot Enright under just such tawdry circumstances as I had described. She seemed even more upset about where, how, and with whom, than that it was gone. She had lost it without realizing, she said.

"Without realizing?" said Jacinta. "You eejit. Without realizing, my eye. Not a chance. Aren't you the girl that screamed the place down with your first Tampax?"

184

"That's right," I added. "Half an hour in the loo and we had to slip you the map from the box under the door."

"You're fine," said Jacinta.

"Virgo very nearly intacta," I said.

"Don't joke," said Breffni, but she looked a lot happier.

"How big was it anyway?" asked Jacinta.

"Honestly, I didn't bring a ruler."

"I'll lend you one next time."

"It reached past his navel," said Breffni thoughtfully.

"It's only when it reaches past your navel you start to worry," said Jacinta. "You watch it next time. No more of this."

"Won't you come into my parlour?" said the Fly.

When am I going to stop blushing to the ears like a ten-year-old. She was greatly amused.

My paper lay on her table; I recognized the awful handwriting even upside-down – product of trying to copy six different styles in the formative years.

"It's good," she said. "Stop worrying." Harry says I have a face that reads like a ham actor's. I stood over her, the Leaning Tower of Pisa.

"Sit down while I pour some tea."

I did, trying to tiptoe through the tiny cluttered office without knocking something over. An ugly office, partitioned and walled from a bigger space. I wiggled the chair to make sure it was designed for bigger than the Fly.

She poured us a cup of tea from paraphernalia on a shelf. The mugs were sensible, no dainty convent china. She sat at one side of an old oak desk, I at the other. Every available inch of wall space was taken up by books.

"Why 'The Lady of Shalott'?" she asked suddenly.

In haste to answer I burned my lips on the hot tea. I set down the mug.

"Would you relax," she said. "You're bigger than I am. I should be afraid of you."

185

She had a lovely smile. Up close she was younger-looking than she appeared in class. She had freckles I never saw before and inquisitive brown eyes that were almost impish. Somebody had knit the fluffy mohair cardigan she wore; it softened the newly short cream habit. Her mini, she called it. Only her veil was black and she had almost an embarrassment – to me, if not to her – of wavy auburn hair showing under it. A far cry from the wimples, beads, straps, and stout shoes I grew up with.

"Even as an Inter Cert I loved 'The Lady of Shalott.' Because it was more like a story than a poem. I didn't know why that was back then. No one told us. But I used to wish she did as she was told and never left her loom."

"But not now?" said the Fly.

"No. I would not love her or her story if she didn't."

"You have a lot of other ideas here about women in literature that are quite unconventional."

"I'm sorry."

"Don't say something silly like that. Of course, you're not sorry. Why should you be?"

"No. I suppose."

"It's not exactly a crime, you know." She was smiling. "The worst that could happen is that you might submit work to a professor who does not appreciate such ideas . . . ."

"But I wouldn't submit –"

"Ahh" – she waved my paper – "only to the Fly. Why is it you believe," she continued softly, "that you must not think for yourself?"

"I've always been told what to think. What is right, what is wrong, what books are bad. Someone always knew better. The answers were all there for me. I was not to question and think, I was to listen and learn."

"I got a dose of that too," said the Fly. "Only more so."

"But you are a nun," I said, unable to stop myself. "You, of all people, must listen and obey."

"I do. And first I listen to God."

I was right out of my depth now and it must have showed.

"Don't look so horrified," said the Fly. "We are all supposed to

186

be listening to God. But why is it as soon as you actually admit to hearing anything, you're crazy. Ah, God help her, the poor thing – a screw loose. Not the full shilling. Why do you suppose all woman saints are mystics? No other channels open, Róisín."

"But you're a nun. You have vows."

"I am and I have. But the motto of my order is Truth: a scarce thing, and a lot of it buried."

"What do you mean, Sister."

"Everyday things, Róisín. Simple things. *Pagans* and *peasants* are both the same word in Irish – *pagánaigh*. And their pagan feasts Bealtaine and Samhain?"

"That's May and November in Irish."

"Simple, isn't it?"

"Are you never tempted to leave?" I blurted out, astounded at my own boldness.

"Would it help if I left the church? Threw down my weapons and became a secular academic? Would I achieve anything in the area closest my heart?"

"No," I said. The bleakness of her prospects if she did, and ours as her students, made me shiver. "No. You mustn't."

"It's our church too, Róisín. The church is its people, not Rome. We have not only the right but the duty to transform her.

"No," she continued, "this lady is staying at the loom. I'm working for the time when the curse will not come upon us. Too many ladies running too soon."

I gaped at her. I had never heard or thought of anything like this before.

"And where are they, Róisín?" she smiled wryly. "All those ladies? Floating, dead, under the mildly curious gaze of Sir Lancelot."

We sipped more tea then, I with a lovely little feeling growing: were there others like her? Maybe other flies in the religious ointment?

"The stone that was rejected by the builder became the corner-stone," said the Fly, with what looked awfully like a wink. "Right after the parable of the vineyard. Remember where the owner was

187

so unhappy with his stewards for producing a bad harvest?"

"Yes. Yes, I do."

"Well. And can you think of anyone more rejected by the builder, Róisín, than us women?"

I hardly remember what she said about the English in my English paper. I said yes and no and talked about metaphors and gerunds, but they were tame stuff after what I'd heard. My heart wasn't in it. I'm sure she knew that. I don't think hers was either.

"Well, that's enough for you for one day," said the Fly. "Run along now and have lots of unconventional ideas. More the merrier. We need all of those we can get."

I was being dismissed. But I was also being embraced. As part of something new and exciting. And yet a quiet, age-old revolution.

"It took a lot of courage to write that paper," said the Fly, handing it back. "Such courage must be met with courage," she smiled. It was as close as she would come to reminding me she had put her own reputation in my care.

"I'm only beginning to wake up," I said. "I want to make up for lost time."

"Here are some books that might interest you. And one thing: watch out. There's an awful lot of lip service out there. Beware."

I went off at a skip. It was spring outside. There were students planning protests and sit-ins and demonstrations. For the first time I said no without guilt, however good the cause.

Because I knew what she meant about lip service. I was never going to sell tickets again. Collect for a cause. March for an end or a beginning. Instead, I was going to bank the effort. Physically deposit it against the marathon. No more blowing that precious emotion, energy.

I yearned to give, and I would. But I would give where it counted most.

Because someone had stirred my bones. Bones thousands of years old. Bones not to be strengthened tending wounds that were symptoms.

A messy little nuisance, the fly. You never know where it has been and it can get into the smallest spaces. Straight from the cow dung and on to your banquet. Hard to catch and very embarrassing in front of guests.

Carries disease. Dis-ease. Unease. Discomfort. A good thing sometimes. Pesky little fly. Enough of them and you'd have a plague on your hands.

I smiled at nothing all the way down Leeson Street.

First year was gone before we noticed. Lorcan went to England with Jimmy Lavelle for the summer. So also did Breffni with Jacinta, but to different parts. I returned all the Fly's books but she told me to hang on to them, she was going to Harlem for the holidays. I was only too happy to hug back the bag of books – dynamic evidence there were not only many flies but even termites in the church. Priests as well as nuns, all cultures and backgrounds.

I still had Teresa at home and she got me a job with Coleman Catering through a patient. I was to replace cashiers on holidays in their canteens throughout the city. One week I'd be totalling the charge for Brown Windsor soup, plaice and chips, and fruit salad in a genteel insurance office in College Green, the next feeding a vending machine with prepacked meals and plastic time coupons for microwave heating by truckers at all hours of the day and night in a decrepit oil depot down the docks.

That was the summer everyone was busy being psychedelic. When they weren't being a whiter shade of pale, they were going off to San Francisco with flowers in their hair. Or at least to the *fleadh ceoil* in Clones.

Very hard to have a happening when you are the only one to make it happen. I was glad to see them all back at the start of term.

Flush with the wealth of a summer measuring the tenderness of peas for Birds Eye on a tenderometer, Lorcan Burke offered to take me to a film.

He was even more quiet than usual, surprisingly so, considering we had not seen each other for four months. I didn't notice at first, spewing out all the gossip I had saved. Only when I had nearly given myself laryngitis did I notice he was saying nothing.

Not a thing. Although I poked and prodded about *Ulysses* and other uncensored films, bookshops, and Soho and Chelsea, I ended up as wise as I started.

So I gave up, thinking he was now odder than ever. I turned my spurned attention to the film: *Far from the Madding Crowd*. Just as I was wondering whom I would have – Peter Finch or Terence Stamp or Alan Bates – Lorcan Burke floored me completely. Without hint or warning, he suddenly took hold of my right hand. Not only did he take possession of it, but he proceeded during the second part of the film to feather the fingers against his lips. Gently he massaged each fingertip between parted labia, leaving out the poor thumb.

Never in my vast experience had I ever come across such errant and deviant behaviour. I was at a complete loss. I could hardly say, Cease and desist, you are deflowering me. Even the Catholic church could have naught to frown on here. And yet . . . .

Lorcan was silent and inactive on the journey home.

The next surprise came when we were on one of our customary walks on Killiney Hill. It was a sunny Saturday in October, the leaves bristling underfoot, an earthy undertone in the brackish air. We leaned on the wall looking down over Dun Laoghaire, its two stone arms outflung, curved and peacefully asleep in the sea. Yachts bobbed glistening in the embrace and the huge mail boat made ready for its evening departure to England.

"Come on up to the castle," I said.

"All right," said Lorcan, "but it's not a castle."

"God, but you're cussed since you came home from England."

"I met my father there."

"Oh?"

"I stayed with him. He lives alone. Has a nice little flat. Neighbours, friends. He was okay."

"Oh," I said again, not knowing what on earth else to say.

"He asked my mother to come over. Lots of times. I never knew that."

"So it wasn't all his fault as Duneen always believed."

"No."

We got to the castle. Of course it wasn't a castle, but everyone called it that. A keep, I suppose really.

There were two tombs of rooms inside, the walls rising darkly – higher, higher, only a few slits for light. The back room was even darker, black stone walls closing heavily down. In one corner a handbag lay, open, its contents scattered around. Makeup, envelopes, papers, keys. And a ransacked wallet. Someone's life.

"Please," I said. "I don't like it here."

We walked for a long time in silence, thinking. We were still silent as we completed the circle and leaned on the wall looking over Dun Laoghaire again.

"Róisín?"

"Mmm, yes."

"Do you know you have grown up lovely?"

"Course I do. That's why I'm going in for Miss Ireland next week."

"Don't laugh. I think you're turning out lovely – "

"What? Me a swan? Ah, go on . . . . "

To my amazement Lorcan Burke had flushed purple. "Don't laugh when a fellow pays you a compliment."

"But you're not a fellow; you're Lorcan Burke."

"Don't do that."

God, he was gone all peculiar on me. "I'm sorry," I said. "I wasn't laughing at you, honestly. If you must know, I never got a compliment before in my life and I don't know what to do with it."

"Well, whether you like it or not, I think you are beautiful."

"I'm the blind one around here, remember?"

"Would you take it with a little grace and elegance and stop throwing it back at me," he said.

"Sorry. Thank you. Even if you're only saying it . . . ."

"For the love of – look, may I kiss you or do you need a solicitor's letter?"

"You may."

He was a kisser. I suspected he might be, but you never know until they kiss you. Some back up a kiss with all their weight as if they were trying to put you through a wall. Others think a good kiss is one which explores the deepest recesses of your lungs.

But Lorcan Burke was a natural kisser. He asked questions with his half of the kiss; lingered softly for answers. A deeper question then, another answer. A duet of a kiss.

"But don't say I'm beautiful when I know I'm not," I said.

"Look, am I in the habit of saying things like that?"

"No."

"Well, you are beautiful. Not pretty – beautiful. It's not really your looks. It's everything."

"Were you into the LSD in London or what?"

"You're making this very difficult. Another fellow would have given up long ago. I did do some thinking in London, as a matter of fact. There were a few girls there."

"No! Girls? How awful. Imagine."

"This is serious."

"Sorry. Had their wicked way with you?"

"I didn't like it."

"I always thought that sort of thing takes two."

"Afterwards."

"Oh."

"Anyway, it only made me think how different you are and that I love you."

"I don't know whether that's a compliment or an insult."

"You are a completely exasperating girl."

"Now that's true. That I believe."

Lorcan Burke is finally, after all these years, going with Róisín McGovern. Pass it on. I think I'll put it in the *Irish Times*.

If anyone told me I would not be permanently ecstatic over a declaration of love from the man of my heart, I would have told them they were nuts. Nuts. A declaration of love would set the whole world right. Pimples would clear up, hair would de-frizz, eyes shine, and bulges shrink in the age-old radiance of it all.

Not so. I never realized a declaration of love has a shelf-life – unless it is repeated every five minutes, you think you are back on the shelf. If Robbie Burns had written "My love is like a red, red rose" for me, I'd have thought, Yeah, yeah, Robbie, withered tomorrow.

I couldn't understand it. I should be rapturous. I wasn't. But I kept my mouth shut. Awful it might be, but none of it was anyone else's business. I kept quiet because I hated the way girls went on about boyfriends. Whole chunks of days evaporated into the question of whether he would ring or not. If he didn't, well, you just knew he wouldn't anyway. If he did, his mumbles and monosyllables were analysed and decoded for you by a panel of expert non-witnesses.

I don't know what exactly was wrong. It wasn't as if Lorcan gave any indication of regret for his outburst. And it wasn't as if he never said it again.

He did say it the odd time – once was on the anniversary of the dress dance. "I love you, Róisín McGovern. Remember that. And I always will. No conditions, no strings."

But even then I was chilled instead of glowing. I held on wordlessly. No strings. No ties. But no violins either. I remember the traitorous tear that stole down my cheek.

"Hey, what's wrong? I just told you I love you."

"Yeah, me and how many? Some girls I know fancy you a lot."

I knew I had hurt him.

"That has nothing to do with love," he flushed angrily. "All the complications and strings and none of the good things. That's what I had in England. No thanks."

"I'm sorry. I didn't mean that. It's not just girls who like you," I teased, to make amends and to get out of this awkward corner. "Do you know what Harry calls you?"

"I can't wait."

"Don Quixote."

"I can't see Harry reading Cervantes."

"No. He's trying to sell someone a musical – *Man of La Mancha*."

"Now that fits. Are you Dulcinea then?

"No. Actually he calls me Roisinante."

"That is vicious. I hope you don't think it's funny."

"It doesn't bother me; I'm used to him. Come on. I want to get you actually inside this hall tonight."

Being more romantically entangled didn't change our dates. I was still never absolutely sure of getting anywhere I thought I was going. We were on our way to meet Jimmy Lavelle, Dermot Enright, Jacinta, and Breffni at the Tramps Ball. Lorcan was going as a blind harper of old. That he could see and was harpless didn't stop him for an instant.

But we were still troubled somehow. I tried to shake it off. I took his arm and hugged it. "Everyone will know instantly who you are," I said. "Couldn't miss."

"Harry and Teresa guessed you were the Statue of Liberty," said Lorcan, picking up at last. "So don't you talk."

"I've more than enough huddled masses of my own." I was Mise Éire. "If words were wealth, I'd be in business. Every mediocre poet and musician pouring forth. But I do like that nice Mr. Yeats. Even if he is a Protestant."

"'Mediocre musician.' Is it me, O'Carolan, you slander?" said Lorcan. I was glad to see him smiling again.

"No, your music is worthy of any son of mine. Too fond of the bottle though . . . ."

A figure came lurching towards us from the shadows. A fuzzy halo of matted curls shone in the yellow of the streetlight over greasy gabardine shoulders. A butt was shaking in his hand. I stepped off the path to avoid him. It was one thing to pretend to be a tramp for an evening, quite another to hob-nob with the reality.

"Gerry!" said Lorcan. "Gerry Murphy!"

The wobbling and shaking body abruptly ceased its attempt at forward motion but continued on the spot, on legs splayed for ballast.

"Gerry," said Lorcan again, more gently.

"I dunno . . . . Whazzat?"

"Good to see you, Ger, good to see you back. Your ma told me you were staying on in London."

"Wha? Me ma? Oh Jaysus, me ma . . . ."

"Come on, Gerry, old son. Come on for a coffee."

"Have ya drink?"

"No, Ger, I haven't. Sorry. Coffee it'll have to be."

"Have ya match?"

"That I haven't, Ger, but come on with us and we'll get you one. Come on now."

That was the end of the dance; it was back to the greasy spoon for more foul coffee and more greasy chips and more Burke therapy. They should have installed a couch in that place for Lorcan's clients.

It was a good three cups of coffee later and several trips to the Gents before Gerry Murphy could talk at all. First he got weepy and then aggressive, and I don't know which was worse. Some bird in London had gone off on him. Just gone off, he kept repeating.

"And I wouldn't mind, but he wasn't even anything. Some stupid sod from a factory in bleedin' Hayes. Out for her body. And a lovely body too. Oh God . . . ." Gerry thumped the table suddenly, staring at me as if he had just now spotted me. He leaned unsteadily over the table to me, half standing in his efforts to make his point.

"Jaysus. Birds. Yiz are all the same. All the bloody same. 'In Algeria there is a town called Tit.' "

"Gerry, leave Róisín alone. It's not her fault."

"All the bleedin' same. Bitch. See? Well read I am an' all like she wants. And what does she do? Goes off with some sod from some factory who probably can't spell his own name. Yiz are all the bloody cryin' same. Bitches every one." His voice was rising.

"Better go home, Róisín. I'll ring you tomorrow."

I got up to go, and the last thing I heard was Gerry shouting after me that I was a bitch and that he knew his was bigger than most.

It was cold waiting for the bus back to Harry's. A good fifteen minutes I waited. Tears stung my eyes, but it was only the cold and because I felt such a fool in my Mise Éire rags. I huddled the big traily Zhivago coat around me to cover as much as I could.

The bus came and I sat on the long seat at the back out of habit. The television seat – you can watch everyone getting on and off.

Sitting there was a big mistake: there was a pub at the next stop and it was half an hour past closing. The bus filled up with dark damp coats and the smells of drink, sweat, cigarettes, and feet. Four lurching bodies swayed over me. One fell on top of me and leaned heavily on me to get up. He patted my knee elaborately in apology. "Ah, the demon drink," he said. "Sorry, Miss."

They collapsed heavily into the seats around me. On either side they sat and across from me, raw red sausages of fingers on their knees, or holding smouldering butts cupped in nicotined palms. They began to sing solemnly to the roof of the bus, their eyes closed. Four oily heads thrown back, spittle dribbling from the corners of their lips. "When I first said I loved only you, Nora, and you said you loved only me." The shiny pink faces blubbered from side to side keeping time. "The violets were scenting the hill, Nora . . . ."

One of them remembered me: "Isn't she lovely, lads? All on her own-ee-o."

"Leave her alone there, Jim. Should be ashamed of yourself – father of seven chisellers, Miss. Don't mind him. Don't you mind him."

They sang just for me then. Breathed their foul fumes all over me. Touched my knees and thighs with great hams of paws.

Why did that Gerry Murphy say such awful things to me? And why do I feel somehow it's my fault – I deserved it? Girls aren't like that. We aren't. I'm not.

One day near Christmas Lorcan and I were walking among the shoppers in Henry Street. I was clutching my note folders to my chest, tipping them off my chin as I went and kicking the heels of my boots off the pavement to hear the ting of the new protectors.

It was lovely just walking in the dusk with Lorcan, the atmosphere building every day now. People rushing to buy something for the tea or for Christmas. Busy. Jostling. Conspiratorial. One man shouting over the din about the full house they'd have with Peter's family over from Leeds and Peggy's up from Mullingar. His friend off to see the daughter in New York on an Aer Lingus charter. Down getting a bit of smoked salmon. The devil for smoked salmon, these Yanks.

I didn't tell Lorcan how happy I was. I knew what he'd say: Not everyone here was going to have a good Christmas. There were hungry people in this crowd. Pickpockets, homeless, alcoholics. Lorcan always remembered things like that.

"Five for a shillin' the wrappin' paper. Five for a shillin', Miss. Two shillings, the cheeky Charlies. Get your balloowins . . . ." The smell of fish and celery wafted from Moore Street, as well as good-natured shouts from the stalls: "Giblets ya want is it, Missus? Would ya look a' her? No wonder she has the fur coat buyin' the giblets instead of the turkey. Mind your purse now, Missus. Ah no fear there – sure them ones was never known to open the same purses. Well, may God forgive ya! D'ya hear that? Sayin' I gave her rotten ones from the back! Is it the oranges you want there, Missus? Would ya just look at her feelin' the celery. Ah, don't mind her – sure that one has nothing else to feel."

I bought some of the bread in the Kylemore Harry loved and then we continued up Henry Street and rounded the corner at the

GPO. There was some commotion there: a crowd had gathered around something under the front pillars. We pushed forward, curious as the rest.

Two policemen were holding someone down: that manky pavement artist who was usually outside the Bank of Ireland in College Green. They were holding him down as his arms and legs and whole body jerked.

His dull dark hair was halfway down his back, tied back in rubber bands. He wore an old gabardine coat over another old coat, both tied with twine and stiff with dirt. He and the guards scuffled on a blurry landscape of his lurid chalk drawings.

"Come on, Róisín, let's go," said Lorcan.

Suddenly the writhing figure flew into spasm. His arms went rigid, and his legs. The crowd murmured and stumbled back a bit. Then just as suddenly he regained control and caught the two guards off balance. He shook free and hurled himself at the crowd. He landed spread-eagled against a fat man near us. He was gasping and gulping for air. The eyes swivelled over us and then flashed back, burning into Lorcan.

"Burke! Get them off me! Get me out of here!"

"You are all right now. Easy does it," Lorcan said. "Quiet now. I'm here and I won't let anyone get you. You're all right now."

The dirty figure crumpled into Lorcan's arms. Lorcan held him, soothing softly all the time, oblivious of the gathering crowd.

Tears welled up in my own eyes. Tears of longing, then shame for being so selfish. Because in the middle of this, all I wanted was for Lorcan to hold me and look at me with half of that tenderness.

It wasn't exactly jealousy. I hope it wasn't. I don't think it was. More of an unutterable sense of loss.

I had seen Lorcan Burke like this only once before. It was on the beach with the loony.

"I'll see you later, Róisín, okay?" said Lorcan. "Maybe I can help here."

"Who is he, Lorcan?" I dug into his arm with my nails.

"Just someone I know. I try to help now and then but it's a losing battle."

Something in his manner made me persist. He was always a lousy liar. "Who is he, Lorcan?"

"I have to go, Róisín, I'm sorry." The guards asked us all to leave and as they led Lorcan and the man away, we did.

I walked on up O'Connell Street, and headed across the bridge through the heavy, noisy blur of a wettening dark rush hour. Red and then green with the little white man and we're off. It was starting to rain heavily. I quickened my step, an idea forming.

I reached the Bank of Ireland. Sure enough, there in the dark stone rainy evening the remnants of coloured chalkings were washing away. Under the papers, pigeon droppings and rheumy spits of old men. Far in, under the protection of the pillared portico, some pictures were still discernible. Protected from rain they might be, but not from the people for long. Because while the artist or even the light was there, no one would walk on his life. They would pick steps around him, pitying, as I did so many times myself. But he was gone now and soon the rain and the quick steps in the night would obliterate him.

There was talent in those pictures.

I had to remember. Past the bony skinniness, past the filthy matted hair. What colour would it be if it were only clean? Must be dark red or auburn. And the skin? Deathly white. But it was the eyes I was avoiding remembering. Remembering one evening when those Christ-hurt eyes bored into mine from the cross-legged skeleton behind the chalking as I threw down the pennies.

Then he had scored and slashed and seared that pavement before my eyes: a man with the body and ears of a horse, an angel on his back. Flames sparked from the hooves, one crippled and lame. A banner whipped unread in the wind as they galloped towards infinity through a crack in the cement.

"Eve!" he had shouted with sudden terrible hatred. "Eve. Evil! Whore!"

That was no chance acquaintance of Lorcan Burke's. He was no stranger. He was Ben Thompson.

There was never a day better named than Boxing Day, Teresa always said. And not for the traditional reasons of boxing left-overs for the poor either. No, but because on no other day of the year was she ever as busy tending in Casualty and Emergency as on this feast of the maimed. Stitching up the frayed peace and goodwill. The gaping wounds and festering schisms that inched their way out under the festive reunions of the city's happy Christmas families. Feast of Stephen, the first martyr maybe but hardly the last.

There were no physical casualties in McGoverns' that day, but I knew exactly what she was talking about all the same.

It started when we arrived. Deirdre and Mammy weren't talking because Deirdre said she didn't really like the new carpet. Mammy said she had "done" the whole house just to make Christmas a more memorable one for her family and this was the thanks she got for her trouble. Deirdre said that Mammy had whipped off perfectly good and, to Deirdre's mind, much nicer almost new carpet to satisfy her own whim and, thank you very much, not to pretend it was anything to do with us. Mammy asked Deirdre then if she didn't think Sarah was getting spoiled, and, really, did Deirdre not worry that Eithne was not even crawling. There was only a month between her and Bernie Moore's granddaughter, and that child had been walking since the first of October. And don't tell her that was another biscuit Sarah was taking; Deirdre would have to be careful or the child would end up another Róisín.

And that was the first half-hour on Christmas Eve.

Daddy had arranged we have most of our meals at the Imperial Hotel so Mammy would not have so much to do. Of course the food had "gone down" a lot since Mammy's last visit, she said. She and Deirdre took turns seeing who could make the waiter feel smaller with all the cold, over-salted, dried-up food they had been asked to tolerate, and at Christmas of all times which was supposed to be memorable and special.

When the waiter escaped they turned their attention to their absent fellow humans. Deirdre renounced all the career women in Brussels who left their children with strangers for rearing. And how Bernard Lenihan stayed with that frumpy drudge of a wife of his she did not know: chicken, if you don't mind, her idea of a main course at a dinner party for an ambassador. Of course, Liam O'Flaherty's wife was worse: she loaded your plate down with grease and carbohydrate which would sit in a cramp in your stomach for a week. Betty McCarthy went the other way and Deirdre didn't know which was worse: ground all her own grains and sprouted beans. And had children to show for it like something out of Biafra. As for the O'Briens – deadly, you'd be ashamed they were Irish.

Mammy said she was lucky to live in a civilized city and was not stuck for life in the back of beyond. How easy to be a perfect wife, mother, and hostess in such privileged conditions. Where were all the poor mothers of these glamorous women? That's what she would like to know.

Dermot Comiskey gave Deirdre a beautiful antique opal and pearl brooch for Christmas. Deirdre barely thanked him, and said to Mammy afterwards it was ugly and she hated opals because they brought bad luck. Mammy said it was far too good for her, and if her own husband had always showered her with such lovely gifts, she would have been a very happy woman indeed.

There wasn't even cooking to be done at home to take everyone's mind off what to do next. Mammy said she had turned herself inside out looking forward to this visit and preparing for it, and what did she have – only a morose, sulky son, two ungrateful daughters, two screaming brats of grandchildren, and a husband who cared nothing that she had given her life up to this. Only her son-in-law appreciated her. He had brought her a mink tie and beautiful flowers, and the pity was that it was not he who had the rearing and disciplining of those two little girls. Then they would not scream every time their poor grandmother looked crooked at them.

Harry and Daddy and I escaped up the cliff path for a walk.

"It's just the crowd here she's not used to," said Daddy, as close as he would get to an apology for Mammy's outbursts. "I wish Deirdre would understand that and have a little more consideration."

"They're too alike," said Harry.

"I suppose," said Daddy. "But Deirdre's young, and she should have more respect for her mother. Your mammy is fine when she's here with me."

Of course she is, Harry and I didn't say. Sure she's okay when you dance attendance on her every whim. When you spend most of your life working to pay for expensive carpets to replace equally expensive ones barely laid.

"I didn't say it at home for obvious reasons," said Harry to me on the way back to Dublin in the car, "but I'm thinking of getting married."

"Teresa?" I said foolishly, as if I might direct this. "Teresa?"

"No," he hemmed and hawed. "Rosemary, actually."

"Oh no, Harry," I whispered.

"Well, that's very nice now, isn't it? I'll thank you to keep your joy to yourself when you see her."

An awful weight settled on my chest then and neither of us spoke through the small towns and villages of the Midlands. I knew there was something I should say, something that might make some difference if only I got it right.

"I would have thought you at least might be pleased for me and wish me luck," said Harry after a while, in a lost sort of voice that wasn't a bit like his usual bluff.

"You know I wish you all the luck in the world, and everything that's good, Harry McGovern. I can't help it if I don't feel that's Rosemary."

202

"She makes me feel good. I have fun. She's great crack. I don't want some bloody nun for a wife."

"Teresa's no nun, and you know in your heart how unfair that is. No, she's no sport – if sport is drunken parties, you're lucky you don't kill someone coming home . . . . No, she's no sport if you want to dazzle your buddies with the bombshell tart on your arm. But neither would she be sport for those same buddies behind your back. Are you sure your Rosemary wouldn't go off on the arm of some director on the promise of just a little more than you can give?"

"You're only a kid," Harry shouted. "What do you know? I can't marry some bird because my bloody sister likes her . . . . "

"You like her too, if you weren't so intent on blinding yourself, Harry McGovern. I see you hanging around with all of them and Teresa is the only one you are yourself with. The others you trot around after like a pet Pekinese. You relax when Teresa's around; you don't have to say anything or do anything or be anything. The weekend doesn't stand or fall on whether you managed to get her an audition."

It was silence then for another few miles.

"You can move out if that's what you think of Rosemary," said Harry finally. "I'm not having you breathing down our necks thinking that and then smiling like a bloody hypocrite."

"If that's the way you want it, okay, Harry McGovern. But I never did breathe down your neck and you know I didn't. If I'm out of a place to stay and Mammy and Daddy kick up about the cost, I'm sure Teresa will help. She won't see me stuck."

"Bloody Saint Teresa. Who wants to live with a saint?"

"I'd want to live with her. A darn sight more than I'd want to be at the mercy of the Queen of Tarts."

"Then you marry her!" shouted Harry. "And don't you speak about Rosemary like that. Just because she's good-looking and you will never be."

"Go on, Harry. Blame it all on me. It's all my jealousy. Rosemary is gorgeous and I want to tie you to an old hag like Teresa for my own peculiar satisfaction."

"Teresa is not a hag. I never said she was."

"No, I got it all wrong, so. You called her a nun and a saint, which is worse. I'd rather be called a hag by the fellow I loved any day."

"I can't marry someone just because she's nice."

"I can't think of a better reason. Why are you marrying Rosemary? Because she's not nice?"

"No. Because she's . . . she's – "

"She's attractive?" I let him off the hook.

"Yes."

"Because she's fun?"

"Yes."

"Because everyone else can see she's gorgeous, fun, and attractive, and will envy Harry McGovern such a bird?"

"No."

"No? Harry, do you want to have children?"

"What do you mean, do I want to have children? Of course I'll have children."

"Does Rosemary know that?"

"No. Why should she? It's understood."

"Is it indeed? Can you imagine Rosemary's view of the damage to the body and the career babies will mean?

"She'll change as she gets older."

"Maybe she will. Okay then, picture yourself with three children: do you want to come home to a house where they are with Rosemary or Teresa?"

"Shut up," said Harry. "That's ridiculous. How can you imagine something like that?"

"How can you not, Harry McGovern? You could do worse than remember this Christmas. Are you, too, going to spend your life running around after Rosemary, assuring her she's the fairest of them all, only no matter what you say and no matter what you buy her, it will never be enough?"

"Shut up, shut up. You're only a stupid kid doesn't know her arse from her elbow and never did. What do you know?"

"Nothing. Only enough to beg you think. Do what you like if you don't want kids. But if you want children, for God's sake, think of who you are giving them for a mother."

I had a feeling he would be all right; it was no accident he had spoken after Boxing Day in Duneen.

"Aren't we the pair?" said Teresa, licking the inside of a Chocolate Mary from Bewley's off her fingers. "Fellas off elsewhere on New Year's Eve."

I nodded, a knot of doubt and fear I couldn't name gnawing at me. Lorcan Burke had not come home to Duneen for Christmas and had not told me where he was going.

His mother was no enlightenment. She was missing too, the shop all closed up and silent. Maybe they had gone to his father in England. But surely he would have told me.

It was not a complete surprise; he had half let me know he would not be home for Christmas. Told me in a card left at Harry's, with a beautiful gold watch. At first I was delighted, with Teresa hugging the daylights out of me and reminding me the ring came after the watch.

But as Christmas passed and Duneen was so desolate without him, I got more and more uneasy. It was only when Lorcan Burke was missing I realized how much I thought of him as part of my life.

"Do you think Lorcan has someone else?" I asked Teresa. I hadn't told her about Harry and Rosemary. Because I hoped so much it would never be true.

"I don't think it's someone else," said Teresa. "That fella is so honest he'd make you sick; he'd tell you if there was. But there's something . . . ."

"You feel it too?" I said, my heart sinking. "We were supposed to love without strings and complications."

"And now you want every string in the orchestra."

"Every complication. Every last implication," I said miserably.

"To hell with them," said Teresa. "Try on the bargains."

The floor of Harry's hall was knee-deep in bags from Arnott's and Switzer's and Colette Modes.

"Leave them," I said. "We might be desperate for something to do later."

The phone rang. Teresa went to answer it and then called me.

"Saved," she said, her hand over the mouthpiece, "it's a Mr. Lorcan Burke. I'd say it's complications he wants."

He wanted to come over later. I said Teresa would be here. She began to wave frantically, shaking her head. She threatened me with her finger, and then drew it across her throat to show what she would do to me if I wouldn't co-operate.

"He's been trying to get you all day," she said when he had hung up. "I said you were studying in the library, not out picking up German, Asian, and Hong Kong flu in the stampede for bargains."

Harry did put in an appearance too, but only to put on his monkey suit. He had the nerve to ask Teresa to find his studs.

"Here you are, Harry," said Teresa. "I hope they bite you. I hope you break your ankle dancing, and I hope you get the year you deserve in the company you deserve. And a happy Auld Lang Syne to you."

Harry looked daggers at me every time he got a chance for having her there at all. But if she didn't mind, I didn't. She was my friend too.

Teresa insisted on leaving before Lorcan arrived. But before she did she ransacked the bargains. This would be either the first and last new year with Lorcan Burke, or the first of many, she said. And the making of the first option into the second called for ten changes of clothes. A black linen suit with pleated skirt and frilly white blouse was finally chosen and lay on top of the mound on the bed. Teresa spent ages making me up and I ended up somewhere close to pretty.

I had the fire on, steaks at room temperature, and red wine breathing. The Slaves' Chorus played softly in the background – Lorcan loved choruses. In the dim glow of the fire and the one soft lamp, the room invited. Sophisticated bachelor, Teresa had said when she helped Harry choose grey and rust. "I should have made it a horror story," she said to me, banging the cushions when we were giving it the once-over for Lorcan. "Too good for Harry." She had painted the flat a soft peach and lined its walls with books, plants, and prints – mostly framed posters of plays, concerts, and musicals Harry had been instrumental in bringing to Dublin.

Now the Nuns' Chorus softly filled the corners of the little room as 1968 came in. Lorcan and I wished one another a happy new year.

We sat on the floor after the meal, backs wedged against an armchair, and nursed the last of the wine in the firelight. I put my head on his shoulder and sighed and asked him where he had been.

He froze. I could feel him tightening up as if to gather strength.

"What is it?" I asked. I knew this was it. "Just tell me."

"Róisín, love, there is no easy way to tell you this. No right way. I'm going on for the priesthood . . . Róisín? Yes, I went to see the order over Christmas. I'm sorry – "

"Jesus, Mary, and Joseph! Now he tells me!" I said, sitting up and spilling the wine all over the new skirt.

"Here, let me get a cloth," said Lorcan.

"Damn the cloth, Lorcan Burke. Clothes can be fixed. Or thrown out even. But not people."

"I'm sorry, Róisín, truly I am."

"You can't mean it, Lorcan Burke! This isn't funny; you better not be joking." I pounded his chest hoping he was, spilling his wine now.

"I'm really sorry, Róisín."

"You're sorry! Jesus, he says he's sorry! You spend over a year working me into this state about you and then you sit there and tell me you're going on for the priesthood?"

"I'm sorry, Róisín. I don't know how else to tell you."

"Jesus, you're like a bloody broken record with your 'I'm sorry, Róisín.' Will you stop saying that or I'll scream! It's those bloody witch-doctor poems of your mother's, isn't it?" I mimicked again as viciously as I could: " ' 'Twas he who said the mass in black the morning that she died . . . .' Well she has well and truly won this one, hasn't she? She must be laughing tonight. Or saying the rosary. Jesus, will we ever get over Irish mothers! Can't handle their husbands so they start in on their sons. Oh Jesus, it's just the same bloody old story all over again!"

"Róisín, it's not really you talking like that."

"Oh, by God, it is me, Lorcan Burke!" I poked him in the chest. "It is so me! These are probably the first real things I've ever said to you. So much for nice. Nice can go to hell. This is Róisín and this is what I think. Your bloody mother and her novenas and her ninety-nine Fridays have got you. She has you feeling so bad your father deserted her that you are giving yourself to make it up to her. I never had a chance, did I, Lorcan Burke. Bloody fool that I was to trust you."

"Róisín, please."

"Oh, shut up! Jesus, going on for the priesthood!"

"I still love you, Róisín, I always will."

"That's not allowed, Father Burke, or don't you know the rules yet? Jesus, going on for the priesthood. Nobody goes on for the priesthood anymore. Nobody."

"I know. And I didn't want to either. I fought really hard."

"Well, you certainly fought me. That's another thing, Father Burke, take a bow and a canonization for the admirable way you fought me off. Were you afraid if you made love to me you might change your mind? Jesus, just once you might have lost that battle!"

"I couldn't do that, Róisín."

"Why?"

"Because . . . because I couldn't . . . ."

"Well, how do you know you're for real so, Father Burke? How do you know unless you put yourself to the test?"

"I have," said Lorcan.

It was then I let fly with the slap across his face as hard as I could.

"In bloody England, of course. I forgot. With some girl you didn't even care about. Or were there a few? What did they do to persuade you where I failed?"

"Do you think I didn't want to?" He didn't move, and I could see the beginning of an angry red weal on his cheek already. His poor lovely cheek.

"I'm sorry," I whispered.

Still there was no response.

"Oh Jesus, Lorcan Burke, would you go away and leave me alone. I'm sick to death of you and your martyred face. Jesus, will you answer me! Will you scream or shout or fight back or something! Sure, I nearly forgot – you're joining the other-cheek brigade. You're doing well on your first big test, Father Burke. You can tell them all you passed with flying colours. A hard one it was too, tell them – because we all know what hell hath no fury like!"

A single tear rolled down his cheek.

"How can I stand it?" I said. "Just tell me that, Father Burke. How can I ever stand it? How is it everything I ever loved is taken away from me?"

He put his arms around me then and the two of us cried until we were exhausted. Again and again, he said he never loved anyone else and he never would. And he'd change it all in a minute if only there was a way he could, but he'd tried and he couldn't.

And then at last Lorcan Burke made love to me.

It started out right. With that lovely sweet excitement I had barely tasted before. Tantalizing hint of what could be. I had always imagined it would grow and blossom into ecstasy. But it didn't. No, instead it faded and then disappeared altogether into discomfort.

But not for him. For him it did grow. I could feel it in the wild beating of his heart. But his heart was somehow all I held. Because now when he was as close as he ever could be, paradoxically he had also left me alone. Running ahead somewhere for the top of the hill, just like when we were kids. Me left behind, crying, Come back, wait for me, wait for me.

Afterwards the pain in his eyes frightened me. I couldn't let him go without one little try: "Remember, your church grew from one woman's yes to God."

He didn't answer.

"I know," I finished for him, whispering. "Made necessary by another woman's yes to a serpent."

And I knew, too, I had just crossed from one side to the other.

Lorcan wouldn't let it go at that. Next day he wouldn't get off the phone.

"Just give me twenty minutes, Róisín. Fifteen?"

"I'm not making it any easier for you to humiliate me, Lorcan Burke."

"Please, Róisín. We can't part like this. Not like this. Look, say what you like to me. Blame me, swear at me, only where can we talk?"

"Here, I suppose. Harry's not here."

"No!" Lorcan fairly snapped it out.

"I'm not planning to seduce you . . . you – " I couldn't think of an appropriate word. "Coward!" I screamed and smashed down the phone.

I was still shaking when he arrived on the doorstep. He looked awful.

"You start, Róisín. Anything I say now is going to be wrong."

"You might at least try," I said.

"There's only one thing I could say that might help," he said. "And I can't say that. I just can't."

I was past caring how awful I looked or whether I had anything left to lose.

"Then why are you here torturing me anymore? You think we can be friends? What do you want? That I fall on my knees for your blessing? Well, think again. There's no room at the inn for the whore, is there, Father Burke?"

"Róisín, stop please. You'll drive us both crazy. Let's not waste our precious time. We haven't much."

"I have, Lorcan Burke. I have too bloody much." But I led him to the kitchen table.

"Róisín, there's nothing you can say I haven't said to myself a hundred times over. But one thing – even before this – could you have really seen us together for life?

I couldn't. I could imagine it, but not so I could believe. Not in fifty years, not in a million.

"Would it have been so bad?" I whispered.

"Bad? Bad? It would have been heaven," Lorcan said. "But I know it's not for us. And so do you. It's written all over your face."

"All right. But why annoy the heart and soul out of me before you decided you have a vocation? Why didn't you do what your mother wanted in the first place? Why didn't you just swallow your vocation like a good boy with your vitamins? 'Twas he who said . . . .' "

"I hated when my mother did that," Lorcan said. "Hated it. God, I can feel the blood up to my ears even yet. Anything but that. Shut her up, someone. Shut her up. And I used to say that if I could save the whole world ever, by being a priest, just for that I wouldn't.".

"So what packed you off in the end? My charms?"

"Stop doing that, Róisín. You know you are the one reason I almost stayed. If you believe nothing else, will you believe that?"

"Yeah, this is Róisín, remember? The girl you climbed over to get to Bernadette Gibbons."

"That was completely different. What has she got to do with this?"

I was wondering myself. With the world collapsing around me, not one but two cataclysmic events in twenty-four hours, I was going on about Bernadette Gibbons and five years ago.

"I don't know. Jealousy maybe. You loved her too. Yes, you told me. You were miserable when she left you."

"There is no comparison, Róisín." He was genuinely flabber-gasted. "I was a kid. That was jus – "

"Just what?"

"In a word – sex."

"You never told me that."

"I never told anyone . . . . "

"Well, tell me now. I think her reputation is sort of shot at this stage."

"What can I say. Once we started we didn't stop. There isn't a nook or cranny in Duneen that couldn't tell tales."

"Lorcan Burke!"

"Well, you asked."

"And this was when I was thinking french kisses were only for fast girls and wondering if she let you touch her breast."

A thought struck me. "You're not going out of guilt over what happened to Bernadette afterwards?"

"No. She outgrew me in about three weeks."

"But it took you years to get over her."

"Róisín, this is ridiculous."

"To you, maybe. But I'm the girl you wouldn't touch with a forty-foot pole. How do you think I should feel? Maybe if I had a bit more charm I could recruit for the Foreign Legion?"

"It doesn't seem to matter how many times I tell you the opposite. If you must know, I have to practically tie my hands behind my back any time I'm with you."

"You'll be some priest."

"What do you think priests are made of, Róisín?"

"I don't know. Maybe they're just not interested. Like Ben Thompson."

"You think his feelings were any different? Ben Thompson's heart nearly burst for you and he wouldn't even speak to you."

"I kind of knew it," I whispered. "I could feel it."

"And what was wrong there?" Lorcan asked. "So wrong it messed up a whole life? I sure don't know, do you? But Ben will never be okay. He'll kill himself inch by inch. All that talent and love, and yet he'll never know a minute's peace. Explain that to me."

"You know I can't."

"What about my parents?" Lorcan went on. "What a travesty of love. Then look at your own parents. No offence, Róisín, but you know what I mean."

"There are some lovely lifelong relationships," I said, fiercely.

"I know, Róisín. And I do think we had a chance – you and I."

"Then why, Lorcan?"

"Róisín, I've asked myself nothing else for a year. I don't know. Maybe it was the island."

So he did remember. "Damn that island. First Fionnuala and now you. Yes, I will walk the water. Why does it have to be so all or nothing?"

Lorcan whispered softly:

> "They thought she was asleep,
> But she was dead with sorrow."

"I remember Bridget too," I said.

"She is gone, Róisín. We have lost her. No wonder relationships are hobbled. We've lost half the source . . . ."

" 'Who is she that cometh forth . . . .' "

"Yes." Lorcan took out a notebook from his pocket. It was filled with his own neat script: quotes, poems, references. "See, Róisín, I did read all the Fly's books, and more."

I felt a stab of something worse than the jealousy over Bernadette and his other girls. Girls I could compete with, but this – no. I knew I hadn't a chance. I knew the Fly's books and what they could do.

"I read them too," I said. "But they did not send me into the nunnery. Far from it."

"No, Róisín, but you admitted you'd be devastated if the Fly left. That she'd accomplish nothing as a lay person. It's the same for me. How much more can I do from the inside?"

"There is one small, slight difference . . . . "

"Oh, I know. Last night proved that . . . ."

"So why you, Lorcan Burke? Why me and why you?"

"I don't know."

But of course I did know. The very qualities that always marked Lorcan Burke as different were claiming him. The tears over the bloated body on the beach and the shadow that was Ben Thompson, the refusal to blame and judge, all these were drawing him resolutely on. On, past me and away.

And I had pushed him on the path myself. Thinking that books would bind him to me. That he would be moved as I was, feel them as I did and be changed too.

He was all those things and more. Only he moved in another direction altogether.

"There's nothing more, so, Lorcan. You may as well go."

"Is that all you have to say, Róisín? Is there any reason in the world you could see for me to go? You have no idea of the difference that would make."

But I did. And I knew I would have many lonely nights if I didn't dredge it up from somewhere and say it.

"I could let you go, if it was important. No, not exactly important – necessary. If when I die, I'll be glad that I did. If I know then it was necessary I did. For that I could let you go."

"Then I have your blessing, Róisín. Because we want the same thing. You are central to my heart and my life. And I did read your beloved Yeats." He touched the notebook gently.

"I thought he'd be for lovers, if anyone would. I had such notions of him and his ideas. For us, Lorcan. Together."

"You were right. You are right. This is religion, Róisín, never forget." He held my face and kissed it at last with the tenderness I always knew was there.

"So why, Lorcan? I can see so much, but not that."

He kissed me again, and then spoke:

> "He who measures gain and loss,
> When he gave to thee the Rose,
> Gave to me alone the Cross;
> Where the blood-red blossom blows
> In a wood of dew and moss,
> There thy wandering pathway goes,
> Mine where waters brood and toss;
> Yet one joy have I, hid close,
> He who measures pain and loss,
> When he gave to thee the Rose,
> Gave to me alone the Cross."

With that, Lorcan Burke was gone.

And so Lorcan Burke went to Rome. Not before dispatching his old friend Jimmy Lavelle to "look after things" for him. Me. I told Jimmy Lavelle what I thought of him and his efforts and his bloody friend in Rome, but he just said nothing and hung around anyway.

We watched Lorcan go at the airport. From a distance. One must always attend the funeral to know there has been a death. Jimmy could have and should have been part of the send-off group but he stayed with me. I suppose he was under orders. Slightly behind me he stood, earnest, hands in his pockets. He exuded discomfort.

"Only a few more minutes to boarding," he said, brilliantly perceptive.

"Yeah," I said, rising to the occasion. "It's a good day for a flight."

"I thought myself there was going to be fog last night."

He thought himself. Imagine. And who does most of your thinking for you? "Well, there still could be at Shannon."

"It's a direct flight," he said. The other way, he didn't add.

"Of course, I forgot."

Lorcan's mother was fussing around him, brushing his shoulders, her mouth going nineteen to the dozen. Jimmy Lavelle actually smiled a little at the fuss she was making and, what do you know, it didn't crack his face. He even brushed my arm awkwardly with his hand. "I'm sure she's telling Lorcan how poor Charlie would be so proud of him if he could see him now," he said.

I had to smile a little in spite of myself. "Yes. Poor Charlie. You'd think he was only gone to a football match, wouldn't

215

you?" Poor Charlie might have departed for England when Lorcan was about a year old, but she still registered her interpretation of his every reaction. You'd think it was kidnapped for the Foreign Missions by God Himself he'd been, Miss McAloon used to say, instead of deserting his family for filthy lucre in pagan England.

And now Lorcan was saying something to his mother; she was peering up at him, her head to one side, her eyes and lips puckered up tight as if she was already weighing his every word as quotable gospel.

A man from the group sidled up and shamefacedly waved a newspaper towards Lorcan. Lorcan took it and thanked him.

"Who's that, Jimmy?" I asked.

"His uncle. His Uncle Vincent. His father's brother. I met him at – I just met him the once."

"Go on, Jimmy. You can say it. You met him at the farewell do for Lorcan." No one asked Róisín, needless to say, and rightly so. And this, Uncle Vincent, is Róisín – Lorcan's dearly beloved girl-friend. Inseparable they were. No, that wouldn't do at all, would it?

"I bet she did that recitation. Did she, Jimmy?"

"Pardon?"

"At the farewell. Lorcan's mother. I bet she did."

"Well . . . ah . . . she did, actually, now you mention it."

"And I'll bet there wasn't a dry eye in the house."

"No."

Lorcan's flight was called.

There was no unseemly hanging about. Quick hugs all around and he was gone, gin-bottle shoulders bobbing through Gate Twenty-two. Never once looking back.

No last-minute reprieve for the condemned. The severance was complete. Airports are such desolate lonely places in spite of the crowds.

"Come on, Róisín," said Jimmy.

Why was he looking at me like that? Did he expect me to go into hysterics on the spot?

We went to a film. I can't remember. It might have been a

western with Jimmy Stewart. And then we went to Searson's in Baggot Street and he bought me drinks I didn't want. My eyes smarted from all the bloody smoke and the contact lenses I'd only got in October. At least I wouldn't have to put up with glasses as long as everything else, I had told Lorcan. Whenever they wanted to make even Grace Kelly look plain in the pictures they shoved a pair of glasses on her. He had laughed and said I was not plain anyway, even if I wouldn't believe it. Easy for him saying that, with one foot on the plane already for the priesthood unknown to me, a bloody idiot gabbling about contact lenses.

"Sure you won't feel it until it's time to go home for Easter," said Jimmy Lavelle.

"No, no," I said. "Never feel it." Only three months away, and today alone felt like a year. I never knew it to take so long to get to lights on and off and "Time, gentlemen, time." And this a Sunday and early ten o'clock closing.

"That's the girl," said Jimmy, smiling. "Sure you'll be so busy you won't have time to be lonely."

Lorcan was gone about three weeks when I knew something was wrong. I had felt wretched but put it down to general misery. However, when I missed my period I told Teresa.

"Holy Jesus, Róisín," she said. "You know what the books say? Pregnant, until proven otherwise."

She had the test done for me as soon as she could – and what do you know, it was not otherwise.

Of course, Harry had to be told. But no one else until the sixth month – there are some advantages to being the size of an elephant. Harry wanted to get on the next plane to Rome and drag Lorcan before the Pope himself, after he had half killed him first. Teresa talked him down while I stayed out of his way until he was used to the idea. And I was adamant: no one was telling Lorcan. I had been bad and wicked and done everything to encourage this predicament, while Lorcan had done everything to avoid it.

Two weeks of this I was fine, then I fell apart. Nightmares, crying, helplessness. I couldn't even get up for college.

"Come on," said Teresa. "You can't afford to miss time now. You might have to later."

"I'm sorry, Teresa, I can't."

"Don't be sorry. No use being sorry. Just tell me how I can help."

"I don't know."

"I could kill him," said Teresa.

"It's not just him. It's everything."

Teresa hugged me, or tried to, a leaden weight in my chair.

"I'm sorry," I whispered, unable to cry, unable to hug back, unable to move.

"Poor love," she said and brushed my cheek with the backs of her fingers. "You really are out of it. I could kill that bastard."

"It isn't him," I said again. "I don't think it is."

"I have an idea," she said. "Something that might help."

Half an hour, or maybe two days, later, she came back with the Fly.

I can only remember bits of it. Not being able to eat. Sleeping, sleeping. And every time I opened my eyes, the Fly beside me. I felt remote. A wall between me and the world. I didn't know what time it was, what day.

I do remember the Fly stroking my hair, kissing me, crooning. The velvet feel of her voice and touch. Telling me where she was and how much she wanted me to come to her. Most of all, I do remember that. I might have lost my footing, lost my way, but she was here, still right here, it's all right, you're all right. Over and over until somewhere deep inside I knew I would indeed be all right.

I lay there and said nothing. It was painful to watch, Teresa told me afterwards. Hours I stared at the ceiling or the wall, she said. I did remember when she told me. The feeling of being cut off, in another reality. I could see and hear them around me. Talking to me. Concerned. Teresa crying. But whatever had connected me to them was gone. Severed.

The Fly was a long time coaxing gently, often in total silence. I wanted to believe her, to go to her, but I did not want to go back where I was. Scared I might be, but there was something I sensed I did not want to lose.

When the Fly did finally manage to get me to speak, Teresa said later she half wished she hadn't succeeded. Merciful hour – the language.

"It wasn't too bad to start with," Teresa said. I was in a boat somewhere and it was black night. I was lost in the pitch dark and my compass was pointing in all different directions. Every image, every landmark I knew from birth had shifted. Everything I thought I knew had moved. I was utterly lost.

Then I really took off from the deep end. Jesus and John were homosexuals. Mary's cloak was reversed – blue jokes, blue movies. The world was cockeyed, hell-bent on destruction. From soft green fertility to blue ice. Earth not to earth, but to the moon.

I went backwards in time, backwards. Now at the Crucifixion, now the Passover. Back, back, all the way through rings to a sheaf of wheat. Forwards, spiralling, boundless through ages and continents, people and animals. Searching. Was it lost? Was it ever there? What was it anyway?

Some island had disappeared, I told them. I couldn't find it. Teresa told me I said a lot more besides and a lot worse, if I wanted to know. I didn't particularly. I wanted to sit in the same room as the Fly again.

"She didn't bat an eyelid," said Teresa. Not her. I could have been reciting the six times' table. Teresa supposed after her few stints in Harlem, anything I could come up with would be tame.

No, on and on the Fly had me ramble. "Like getting all the pus out of a wound," Teresa said. And when I was absolutely beside myself with bewilderment, with Teresa nearly as bad as me by now, she said, still the Fly wouldn't stop. "Enough, enough," Teresa would plead with her. "Can't you see she's in bits?" But over and over the Fly silenced her: "Patience, not yet, patience." Only when Teresa despaired of there ever being a change, did my eyes open suddenly and focus on them, and I stretched out my arms to be held. Only then did the Fly herself finally begin to speak softly.

"You have taken the east from me; you have taken the
    west from me,
You have taken what is before me and what is behind me;
You have taken the moon, you have taken the sun from me,
And my fear is great that you have taken God from me!"

I do remember that. And I knew then that just at the very time
I was so alone, I was also closest to never being alone again.
That countless souls had struggled this way. I could hear them
in the Fly's soft voice as she whispered the verse over and over.
For the first time I could feel warm soothing tears begin to
wash me clean. A sadness that was very close to joy. I remember forever the fertile warmth of those tears. As if I'd left the
barren wastes of solitary confinement and found communal,
strengthening mourning. All the pain of the human condition
profoundly connected.

This was not permanent. Soon my natural irreverence took
command again. I wanted to know if that was bloody old Yeats,
and what would he know.

" 'You have taken the east from me'? No," said the Fly. "Not
Yeats. But someone who felt just as you did, centuries ago. 'Grief
of a Girl's Heart,' she called it. She wrote in Irish. We don't know
who she was."

"Doesn't matter," I said.

"No," said the Fly smiling. "It doesn't. And Yeats might have
known more than you think: 'What is the flesh I purchased with
my pains, This fallen star my milk sustains . . . .' His own beloved
Maud had two children without the benefit of a husband. Not his,
of course," she added.

"Oh no, not Saint W.B.," I said then. "Didn't get the chance,"
as far as she knew. Well, of course, we never would know, would
we. If they did teach us things like that in school, as well as the
risings and the battles, then both we and the country would be a
sight better off. Whereupon the Fly turned to Teresa and said that
whatever about the country, she did believe I was a sight better.

But she would not leave me until I could smile.

"You probably don't believe me yet, Róisín, but it's all right. You'll be fine. And you certainly won't believe that this actually happens to the best of us."

"What?" I was still struggling to understand what indeed had happened.

"Mmm. Me for instance. Or something like."

"I bet you say that to all the nuts."

"When it gets bad, remember T.S. Eliot: 'Wait without thoughts. You are not ready yet for thought.' "

"I can't."

"Yes you can. When you don't like the way your thoughts are taking you, stop and wait. We can only bear the truth grain by grain."

Her calm settled on me. "I'll try," I said.

"That's better, Róisín. Now, what are your plans?"

"I don't know. Ask Teresa. She's been talking away but I haven't heard a word she says."

"She should be all right for this year," said Teresa. "Won't show too much before June and the baby is due late September."

"So she'll be all right for October," said the Fly.

"Yes. Lucky timing."

"Do her parents know?"

"Heaven forbid!"

"Are you sure? Parents often surprise you . . . . "

"Not hers. We're very sure and all agreed."

"You won't tell Lorcan, Róisín?" the Fly asked then. "They don't come any better than him, you know."

"No!" I said. "No."

"He would come back."

"Don't I know it."

"Won't you at least give him that choice?" she asked.

"Wouldn't be a choice, would it?"

"No. Well, you may change your mind, but if you don't you will have all the help we can give. For now, we'll leave well enough alone. I want you back in my front row, if you please. I won't mind if you doze off."

"Some chance of that at your lectures."

"Róisín is to stay with me during the summer while her parents think she is in England," Teresa said. "We'll send a few letters over for posting."

"Looks like you're all organized," said the Fly. "I'll get your reading lists as early as possible, so you can have your books over the summer and be off to a great start next year. But we're ahead of ourselves. First things first, will I see you at lectures tomorrow?"

"Yes, I'm better now," I said. "Thank you."

God, it sounds so easy when I say it – "better." It all sounds so bloody easy. It was anything but. I wouldn't have remembered a word that was said, only for Teresa's telling me later. Over and over. And if I looked like slipping off again, I got a dose of T.S. or W.B., or someone else the Fly had invoked. She had sure converted Teresa – the pair of us cried and laughed for the Fly's unlikely saints and wondered would going to theatre ever be recognized as going to church.

And it was Teresa who told me the Fly didn't leave my side for three days. Not for mass on the Sunday, not for her lectures on the Monday. Not until she was sure I was okay.

Bit by bit, Teresa told me it all . . . . I was finished, I kept saying. I was done for. Not at all, the Fly would smile. What were ashes for, if not for a little phoenix – if I didn't kick it to death before it got started. This would keep me calm for about five minutes, when I'd be off again. I never shut up about leaving some room or some loom or something, and yowling about curses and smashed mirrors. And Lorcan was so good and perfect and so wonderful and kind – Teresa did an imitation of a plaster saint.

Well, horsefeathers to all that, the Fly kept saying. She would assure Teresa that I would be okay. That my subconscious was a sight wiser than I – and would put up the father and mother of a fight in the face of such codswallop. Imagine the Last Day – the Almighty flanked solely by clergy. Upping his hand for silence: Excuse me and hard luck to the rest of you, but out of all my creation I only like Roman Catholics? Dear knows, the Fly told Teresa, but she hoped she was working for a better God than that.

I hoped so too, but one thing I knew: the Fly and Teresa saved my life. And old Harry for letting them at it. I felt that as surely as if they had pulled me from the tide. And in an old-fashioned way I now owed them a good life. Never again could I say I did not know what it is to be loved profoundly. To be given rebirth. To be mothered.

I would not claim you. I dared not. I would not claim the head and back that butted and the sharp heels that drummed under my rib cage. Even in the last weeks when you were too big to move and I lay there wondering was it time for you to venture forth. I moved you carefully with me when I turned over in bed. And halfway I would lie on my back where I could feel your body and weight best. I laid my palms by your sides and wished you courage for your journey through life.

There was never a chance of my keeping you.

I see you everywhere.

We never talked about the baby. Teresa made all the arrangements for the birth and adoption.

After my second-year exams, she got me a job through one of her patients, knitting fishermen *báiníns* for Gaeltarra Éireann. At least I could earn my keep while marooned for the summer, like a beached whale in her little flat. She delivered the finished jumpers, picked up more orders and wool.

I knit and thought of all the mothers and wives who worked their own family patterns in case that was all that would identify a body too long in the sea. I knit for the loony who didn't even have that mark of love.

I bought the bare minimum of maternity clothes because I had no business in the world looking well at a time like this. The tent dresses, catapulted out of their brief moment in fashion, were dirt cheap and ideal.

I could never say to God I was sorry for what I did. God knew better. God is no idiot. I don't know what God is, but it's good whatever it is. Definitely not an idiot.

In many ways I was never more content. You and I flourished. I knew this would be my only time with you and I could not show you enough.

I did "Up the Airy Mountain" for you and "Rafferty's Pig." I told you about the island. I told you about everybody, everything I knew. I played my favourite music; some you loved, some you didn't.

I told you stories too. I didn't tell you about Fionnuala and the swans, because I couldn't bear to. You told me that was okay, as long as I came across with some other good ones. You loved Hans Christian Andersen. You made me tell you "The Little Matchgirl" six times.

You made me wonder if the lights the little girl had weren't the stories of all the centuries. And if we could only find her and get her to light them again, they would light the way to everyone's grandmother.

Even hymns got to us. Psalms mostly. But there was one hymn I remember in particular: "In Christ both north and south, in Him both east and west . . . . " Ridiculous, isn't it? Yet, bawling we would be, and I was never prepared. Each time I thought it an isolated incident and never had a tissue for next time. There we'd be in the back of the church, bawling like idiots. You were okay. They couldn't see you. And you didn't care what I looked like.

Not that it mattered, really. No one minded. Because we weren't at Teresa's local Ballsbridge parade – Haddington Road Church.

No, the Fly stayed home that summer, and one of her habits was to take me to a new church she was helping to establish in Tallaght. I said it must be easier than Harlem anyway, but she said sometimes she wondered.

Sundays she played the organ and led a few singers in hymns I didn't know. Not ones I grew up with. But whatever they were, I cried in that little shack of a church as I never would have in a cathedral. Not out of misery. No, more out of fellow feeling. Readings, as well as hymns, sounded different – more immediate.

As if referring to events to come as well as those of eons ago.

Some priests, when they spoke, hit the tear ducts too, while others exasperated. I asked the Fly did this happen to her.

"All the time, Róisín. Things are never either-or. Think all, Róisín. It all belongs somewhere."

"But some of it makes me want to scream."

"Well, remember you came from that. We come from our worst, as well as our best. Sometimes I think Original Sin is simply exclusion, Róisín. I hate what has happened to women, but I still love men . . . ."

She didn't often lecture me. When she did, and we were in her car, she drove faster and more lethally.

"Those lights were red, Sister. I suppose killing this child is one way out of it. But we'd make all the papers."

"Vixen. I just want you to understand where exclusion has got us. And I do know what you mean. Sometimes I get more out of Paul to the Liverpudlians than I do out of Paul to the Corinthians."

"The pharmaceutical psalms?"

"Now, now. What have I just said about exclusion. And there's many a lad thinking he's clever with words, but truth will have the last laugh. There's comfort in the most unlikely places."

"That reminds me – Yeats and his unlawful pregnancy, indeed. I looked it up. That was the mother of God he was talking about."

The Fly laughed so much I thought we'd be dead again. She could barely both reach the pedals and see out at the best of times.

"You wouldn't have listened to me, then," she said. "You were only interested in fallen women and scarlet harlots. As I told you, Róisín, I'm only trying to broaden your viewpoint."

"There's a limit, Sister."

"Why? Tell me something. What does 'be it done unto me' mean to you?"

"Meekness. Drippy passivity."

"I see. Now, tell me something else. Was there anything meek, or drippy, or passive about your own experience?"

"No, Sister, that's the last thing there was," I said, blushing for the memory.

The Fly then said she might even sing, if she only had a little help from her friends.

I awoke one morning a week before time with a piercing ring of pain. I knew from the books Teresa brought me there was no hurry. No sense in waking Harry until I had to.

The pains were every fifteen minutes by half past seven, so I woke Teresa. She called me all kinds of an eejit for not waking her sooner. She telephoned Harry to get himself over, and fast.

Harry had me out of his car and through the side door of Holles Street Maternity Hospital so quickly I didn't know where I was or which end was up. Not that you could tell. But Harry wasn't going another inch where he might be recognized. Or worse, taken for the father.

Teresa stuck with me through admission until they made her leave. They didn't even like husbands around in those days in Holles Street.

A nurse was assigned to me when they brought me up to a room near the delivery suite. O'Donoghue her name was and she told me she came from Oughterard in Galway. She had gingery hair, tied back in a bun under her cap, and an ice rink of a starched chest. She could have been twenty-five or forty; there was no telling with all that dimpled freckled flesh.

But she was nice to me and that was all I cared. Not sticky goody-good nice either, that would have made me feel worse. Just unconcerned about the awful thing it was to be here without home or husband, having a baby to give up for adoption.

She checked me, she checked the baby, and she kept up a great stream of chatter about other babies she had helped deliver. "Nothing to it," she said. "Falling off a log. Did you not go to your prenatal classes, Róisín? Aren't you the bad girl."

She shaved me. Gave me an enema. I delivered myself completely to her will; a sheepish, foolish girl who had brought everything upon herself. No indignity was too much to suffer without question. Even welcome.

Back on the hard bed in the little cell of a room I was put on a drip. A young red-haired doctor came in long enough to stick a syringe in me.

"Pethedine," whispered Nurse O'Donoghue. "Better than gin. It will help the pain."

"What's in this?" I held up the back of my hand with the drip inserted.

"Pitocin. To hurry things up. We promise every mother a baby six to eight hours after labour starts. No hanging about here. You would have learned all this in prenatal."

An older doctor came and, pushing up his sleeves, announced he was going to break the waters. I was put up in stirrups, but not before a gaggle of students clustered at the door. And probably half the passersby from Mount Street, for all I knew. I looked at the ceiling from my side of the mountain and tried not to imagine the view from the other side.

He poked and probed until suddenly a thunderous cascade hit the baby's bath placed below. To think I used to wonder might I have broken or lost the waters unknown to myself. Fancy that in Roches' stores or a 7A bus.

"Four centimetres," he said to the students, and they all moved off to the next stirrup case, with more centimetres to offer.

The pains came one tidal wave on top of another then. No position lessened their vice grip. There was no more chat with the nurse. She kept monitoring the baby, moving me to get a better check. Angering me because the movements were added torture.

Never has the centimetre meant more to me. I yearned for six and eight. The magic ten. Silently screaming for a respite from the agony. But there was none. At least there's a dentist's command of a little rinse when drilling an abscess without freezing. A few seconds free of pain.

When I could show the magic number of centimetres, I gained entry to the delivery suite.

"You must be almost ready to push," said O'Donoghue.

"Okay," I said, believing everything readily.

In the delivery suite I could at least see the sky because there were windows. It was a leaden cloudy sky, and under it Dublin people were doing ordinary things, like going for lunch in Davy Byrne's. Making phone calls, catching buses. All while the most momentous thing was going on here. Amazing.

"Shallow breaths, Róisín, as I told you. Do you not feel ready to push?"

"No," I said, "but I will if you want me to." Always ready to oblige.

"Use your contractions to push. Shallow breath again, just like I told you. Here now, this way. In control. In, out, in, out. That's it. You are almost ready. Yes, I think I see the head."

She listened to the baby again and suddenly she became alert. She listened again.

"Foetal distress," she shouted. She rang my bell. "Don't push," she said as she ran out. "Just don't push."

I hadn't really intended to. The pushing was all her idea in the first place. I was just carrying out orders.

The doctor came back with her. He listened to the baby, and poked and prodded again.

"Forceps," he said to O'Donoghue. She nodded.

"Your baby is face first," said the doctor. "In that position you can't push because of the angle of the neck. We have to lift your baby out safely. Don't worry."

The forceps arrived and the doctor gestured the audience of students back a little.

"This is going to feel like I'm pulling you off the bed," he said. "We'll give you something to help."

He braced one foot against my bed and positioned the forceps.

A mask descended on my face at the very same instant I felt I was being torn apart.

The next thing I remember is being shaken gently. Someone trying to wake me . . . another holding up a bundle of towelling with a livid squashed head. And then I was out again.

I woke up in a ward of chattering women. They seemed mostly old, and luckily I was down in the end bed where there was a wall on one side at least.

"What are you in for, child?" said the woman in the next bed. She had a leathery face, a fresh perm, and clutched a crocheted bedjacket with bony hands as she hung out of the bed to talk.

"A baby," I said. Was she stupid? This was a maternity hospital. "To have a baby."

Experimentally I felt my bump: a hill of wobbly jelly. As for the jagged pain in my bottom, that was a nasty surprise. Even the thought of a bathroom made me wince.

"Ha, ha," crackled the old biddy beside me, showing a mouthful of grey loose-fitting false teeth. "That's a good one. Thinks she's havin' a baby. This is the gyney ward, love. No babies here." She sniggered to cronies around and twisted at a screw in her forehead to tell them I was not only a gyney case but a nut case as well.

I turned to the wall.

A nurse came and checked me, but she knew nothing. She didn't know whether it was a boy or girl or even whether it was healthy.

Hour after hour I lay. Tea-time came and went, and then visiting time. Husbands and sons and daughters poured in with flowers and chocolates, shouts and laughter.

At last Teresa came. I clung to her and poured out the tale of woe.

"I have to see the baby," I said. "I have to at least see and know it's okay. I don't even know if I had a boy or girl."

"Come on," said Teresa. "I know a few girls working up in the nursery. Pretend you're just going to the loo if we see anyone."

Weakly I hung on to her, up the two terrazzo flights. She found me a chair while she went to fix it with someone she knew. They wheeled out a cot.

Inside a baby lay, the head all distorted, hair matted with blood and blackened face. My heart grew so big and heavy in my chest I could barely speak.

"I knew there was something wrong when no one would come and tell me," I said. "I knew it."

"What are you talking about? She's a beautiful healthy girl, you silly ape," said Teresa.

"Well, why is she all battered and bloody, and why is her head like that?"

"Forceps deliveries are always like that. They never wash any of them for twenty-four hours. She's lovely. You'll see. Didn't someone tell you?"

"They told me nothing. Can I hold her?"

"Not now. I have to get you back. But I'll fix it up, I promise."

I nearly fainted going back down the stairs. Teresa had to open a window and hang me out.

The nurse in my ward had missed me and was waiting for us to sneak back.

"Sorry, Sister," said Teresa, winking at me behind her back as we passed. "As if she'd have given you permission to go."

It was only afterwards I realized there was no time for the dreaded moment. The moment I worried about all along. When I first saw my child, that I might never be able to let you go.

I called you Róisín because I knew I was handing over part of myself. I knew then there would never be a day I would not think of you. I knew too they would change your name, but I called you Róisín first because some day you would know that and might wonder why.

You did not look like me. No, you inherited the slenderness of the O'Donnells. The nurses marvelled at the narrow length of your hands and feet and laughed when I asked if this was not the same with every baby. They said your eyes might change, your face and head definitely would, but those long, narrow limbs were yours for life. I knew your eyes would not change, no matter what the nurses said. They were blue-violet, black-ringed, with specks of gold like pansies. My mother's eyes. She would have been so proud of you – had the circumstances of your birth been different.

Who are you like now, I wonder.

The Fly and Teresa held me together when they took you. One on either side of me, holding my heart and my soul in my body from following.

The Fly took constant care of me for a while after. Teresa had to work every day; they weren't about to leave me alone.

We had a few weeks until term started. The Fly got me odd jobs in her department. Or I spent the time with her, preparing her work, researching, indexing, sorting, anything.

So I did get by with some help from my friends. Actually, I barely got by – and it was only because of so much help from my friends.

Bishop Lorcan Burke sprinkled holy water on his mother's coffin. He paused and looked out over the crowd before he spoke:

"You knew me O Lord before I was born . . . . "

'Twas he who said the mass in black the morning that she died . . . . 'Twas he, indeed, only he's not wearing black at all but the white of the Resurrection.

Your father and your grandmother. And your mother in the back rows.

"Now I return my soul to You, for You are my maker." Lorcan's voice rose and then fell. "My sins, Lord, make me afraid."

Ah yes, his sins. My sins. No place like a church to remind me. Out the doors I run to escape them: Lovely day, Mrs. Dempsey, not a bad sermon today. And up to the rafters they float suspended. There they wait to descend and hover once more. And the farther I run, the less escape. I might run to Timbuktu, only to have dreams worse than the reality.

Lorcan was still speaking: "May Christ who called you take you to himself. May angels lead you to Abraham's side."

Christ, angels, Abraham. Always the right channels. In this church alone, a cast of hundreds: Majella for pregnancy, Cupertino for exams, Anthony for lost objects, and Jude for lost causes. I could spend my life praying. Elect myself to the ranks of the sanctified by currying and scurrying among minions. Without ever once raising my heart to the source of the mystery.

Is that it, Fionnuala? Not even well-meaning earthly churches before God? That's it, isn't it, Fionnuala? If we know whom we are worshipping we are already wrong. Eye hath not seen, nor ear heard. Is that it? As soon as it is imaginable it is a false god? As soon as it detracts from the mystery?

So how should we pray, Fionnuala Fitzgerald? To whom it may concern? Irreverent giggles threatened; it was just as well Lorcan Burke rose then to face the congregation.

Bishop Burke gave the crowd his final blessing. He stretched his arms up and out and spoke firmly past all those sins in the rafters:

"Give her eternal rest, O Lord. And may Your light shine on her forever."

I bowed my head with the rest.

And so it was over. Lorcan followed his mother's coffin out of the church and the congregation began to flow after them. "Lovely, wasn't it," said one Child of Mary to another. "Lovely and simple, and isn't he a beautiful speaker?"

He stood briefly outside, hugging, shaking hands, thanking, the centre of a huge crowd. I could not have approached him even if I wanted to.

"Róisín, come with us." It was Teresa, pushing her way towards me in the crowd.

"I don't think I'll go to the grave at all, Teresa," I said.

"All right. You know best. I'm so sorry," she said, squeezing my arm. I knew it wasn't Mrs. Burke's death she meant, or even the presence of Lorcan close by. No, she was remembering you. She and Harry waited five years for one of their own, and I could see the sorrow grow in her eyes until we were of no comfort to each other. By the year, that anguish grew until at last she had a baby of her own. But my pain never lessened.

I tried to fight my way out of the crowd.

"Róisín! Róisín, it is you. Hello, dear." My father and mother stood towards the back. My father seemed stooped and shrunken since I'd seen him last. For the first time ever I noticed he was an old man. My mother looked perfect in her tailored coat and tightly swept up hair. She could have been a retired ballerina. She was still stunning, and she knew it.

The effort, lifelong, to present such a perfect picture.

"Deirdre and Harry and all the children are here," she said. "There's to be a luncheon for everyone at the Imperial, and whoever's there first is to keep a table for all of us. You'll be there? You might have told us you were coming, dear . . . . " She was all smiles and enjoying herself hugely.

"I don't think I will be there," I said, "but I'll probably see you all later at home."

"You always were a law unto yourself, weren't you?" she said. "Never wanting to do anything to please anyone else."

I left and wandered down through the town towards the sea. I had the street to myself; all the shops were closed for the funeral.

A notice in Miss McAloon's handwriting informed the public of her planned return at half past three, approximately – she was not going to miss out on luncheon at the Imperial. Due to the sad occasion, et cetera, et cetera.

Twenty years.

Frank O'Laughlin owns our house now. He runs the local supermarket and has a squad of kids. Married to a bank girl who – Miss McAloon says – never gets up before eleven. He is pasty and pompous and looks at me as if I missed the Throne of England in O'Laughlin's Spar Grocery.

He missed the Master's daughter, but he got the Master's house. Owns the door I once closed in his face. The Master has a bungalow now. Too many stairs in the old house and too few children. Frank has remedied that. *Where do you do it? In a Volkswagen. How many children will you have? Twenty-three.* Well, looks like he's on his way without me.

One of Sergeant Egan's daughters has Kathleen Gibbons's house. Bernadette slid into oblivion; she'll hardly do an encore now. Not as a siren anyway. Is she a housewife in Scunthorpe, or maybe a madam, still on the government's blacklist? Or did she – as Miss McAloon regretted to note – slip into something worse? Like a bottle. Sober enough at her poor mother's funeral, but roaring by Mullingar on the way home – having kept the cork in as long as she possibly could.

Abstinence is the clue, Miss McAloon said. The giveaway. Not a sip of brandy against the cold of her mother's funeral. That and the indecent haste of abandonment of her mother's house to rack and ruin. And, of course, the unseemly show in Mullingar, witnessed by one of the brethren in the Department of Post and Telegraph there as she made arrangements for her onward journey home.

Found guilty on all forty-six counts they could think of, by Miss McAloon and Mrs. Grimes.

Jimmy Lavelle got the his-and-her teaching jobs Lorcan and I used to talk of sometimes. He is headmaster in some little town with more syllables in its name than streets within its boundaries. Not Termonfeckin or Ballymoreustace, but something like that. His lady wife is said to terrify students of chemistry even more than she terrifies Jimmy Lavelle. But I wouldn't know.

Fitzgerald's Bakery as neat as ever, its fresh peppermint paint and precise rows of dainty goods relentless in their orderliness. Big and little tragedies swept well out of sight.

I saw Mr. and Mrs. Fitz briefly at the church. Old and shrivelled now, wizened into their own gingerbread men, they still do not want to see me. No, I remind them of untidier times when emotion and illness cracked the shell of propriety. Pushed the rows of lemon tarts and éclairs all out of rank. I am not complaining. Well, I am, of course. I would have liked someone to mourn Fionnuala with me. It would have been good, had someone accepted the disorderliness and untidiness of that.

There was a memorial card centred in a huge black satin bow on Burke's shop door, and all the blinds were drawn. The track of an old hand there, suspicious of the church's new-fangled joy in the face of death. Some old crony of Mrs. Burke's confident in this, at least, she knew more of the dead woman's wishes than the bishop himself.

The seafront was less depressing than the town, in that here at least nothing had obviously worsened. You could pretend there were nice family hotels and guesthouses up the town. You could pretend there were still the lively cafés where music was played on real instruments in the summer. You could pretend all the old-fashioned wood-scented shops had not gone the way of video arcades. You could pretend this was still a nice seaside town. A place nice people could come every year and bring home gentle memories. You could pretend.

The seafront was as on any of a hundred grey March days when Lorcan Burke and I chased each other home from school: the rank pungency of seaweed blending with a thousand illegal pees, clinging to the dark walls of the cement shelters. The wooden laths of the benches up the cliff path still rotting around rusted bolts on cement supports. The same cracks in the same paving stones, with lusher, stronger weeds between. More of Cleary's Steps were rotted away.

The houses and caravans of the town squatted stubbornly in a sudden squall. Clusters of faded conversation lozenges, or the eggs of some monster alien sea bird. Rain lashed dark, unpainted houses black, their stark windows gaunt.

I still think this place is magical. I did bring you here. And I told you about Lorcan and me. I showed you the exact spot on the island. Spring it was the last time, and I'd have been a right mess if the tide caught me there in that cold. But then I had you on my mind. As I have now. As I have always.

I brought you because I felt that you, too, belong here. That you were thought of – here with me and Lorcan when we were only six years old. We belonged to the island. Never since have I known a time I felt so utterly connected. Other moments came close – kneeling on the beach that morning around the loony none of us knew except by heart. And when Fionnuala was slipping away from me. And with the Fly that time I was lost myself.

Róisín.

I could have sworn I heard Fionnuala's voice.

You did.

Nonsense. I'm not an impressionable child anymore.

Pity. You were so easy to reach then.

I'd say the dead arose, but it would be appropriate for once.

Black humour, Róisín. One of your great defences.

Never got the hang of any other. You do pick your moments, don't you, Fionnuala? Why don't you go and liven up the gathering at the graveside?

They won't listen.

So I'll have to do?

Afraid so.

I'm beginning to get the hang of you lot, Fionnuala Fitzgerald. You just don't answer when it doesn't suit you, do you? Heaven forbid there might be any reassurances. Any certainties. Sometimes

238

I wonder is there any such thing as belief, I can love an idea, hope it is true. But belief? Belief in what?

No answer.

See? No help. I don't know from Adam what to say to my girls. And I know I'm not the worst of teachers. I remember what the Fly did for me. And M-Cubed.

Still no answer.

The girls don't listen, anyway, of course. I doubt if any of them fell in love with Mr. Yeats because of my teaching.

All the better, Róisín, he is still yours.

Don't be ridiculous. But I was smiling at the echo of a long ago tug-of-war over a Welshman.

The Fly and M-Cubed, yes, but who first put Yeats in your head?

Don't know. I suppose every English teacher I ever had took a crack at him, but I didn't hear them.

Long before that.

Suddenly I could remember one horrible day long ago when I was five. One unforgettable day my daddy tried to pull out of the fire:

> Come away, O human child!
> To the waters and the wild
> With a faery, hand in hand;
> For the world's more full of weeping
> than you can understand.

And those words were so lovely I couldn't bear to think they weren't my daddy's own . . . so I gave them to him. How did I lose hold of him after that? He let me go, didn't he? Right then and there. It was that very day my daddy realized he could never right my wrongs for me . . . fight my battles. All these years . . . Daddy . . . .

If I have forgotten that, what else have I forgotten, Fionnuala?

There was silence then, but it was a silence I knew well. It was the finger on the lips, conspiratorial hush of Quarant-Ore.

And then I knew. I remembered a promise. I remembered Fionnuala's dying face, pleading with me wordlessly. I began to see why.

The silence was more present than ever. I began to think and remember. Over the early years, nothing, nothing. No unaccountable, unfinished moments. Not even while she was ill. Not while she was alive. But when I began to relive the aftermath of her death I knew instantly. I could feel again the unease, the terror, the anger, the raw grief until M-Cubed taught me how to start living with it.

The legend. Of course – Fionnuala's story. What would set her free? The story was everywhere, in every nursery, version after version, and most ended with the bell. The bell of Christianity, the bell of Elevation.

But the story I fell in love with was Lady Gregory's. Taken closest to source, from the remotest Gaeltacht peasants, who knew only Irish and so had the last grip on old folklore.

The bell is only half the story, Fionnuala. What about the rest? Where Fionnuala and her brothers would only be set free when . . . when the Man of the North joins the Woman of the South. Yes.

East is East, West is West, and ne'er the twain shall meet . . . . The four corners of a round world . . . square peg in a round hole . . . speaking from four directions . . . . Witch of the East, wicked Witch of the West . . . the land of Oz.

Oz, O's – rings! Circles!

Circles! When the Man of the North joins the Woman of the South. No, when opposites – no, when polarized opposites join in harmonious circles.

That's it, Fionnuala: WHEN POLARIZED OPPOSITES JOIN IN HARMONIOUS CIRCLES – WHEN THE MAN OF THE NORTH JOINS THE WOMAN OF THE SOUTH.

It was quiet. The wind hushed, as if listening, as if holding her breath.

And I heard then, not Fionnuala, but the dying Beast call for Beauty from his winter garden. Saw Beauty, dead with sorrow.

The call – weak, weaker. Beauty hears it, not dead but asleep. Rising from her leaves in the lake. Through the glass case, hacking away the hundred years' growth. She hears him. Her tears flow like a river now, she summons the strength of those sleeping years. Her arms reach, she catches something and launches herself, pushing, straining. Swings wide, wider, higher. Makes a great arc in the air, stretching, flying.

Weaker the call comes, fainter. Like an exhausted trapeze artiste, Beauty tries to make that circle all by herself. She arcs through the air, desperate for help.

I knew then that nothing else counted. Nothing mattered but this – not sickness, not death, not famine, not disaster. This was the source of the symptoms.

I begged then that whatever was so intrinsically wrong might be put right. And that Fionnuala might be set free. Not as easy as it sounds, because I didn't know who was north or south or good or bad anymore. So I asked that all our opposites might join, all our banished outcasts come home.

Even Lucifer?

Lucifer? Get thee from me. Behind me, Satan.

Then galloping towards me, I saw Ben Thompson's chalked rider on the pavement. Blue, green, the lady of my dream. Shining front, obscene back, light and dark. Get behind me, Satan. Not a banishment, but a rescue. The camel through the eye of the needle.

The Fly and her Original Sin – exclusion. Lucifer – what a circle that would make . . . . No more house divided . . . the most prodigal, the most defiled. The most essential. Quarant-Ore. For the souls farthest from God.

What was Lucifer but Fionnuala's farthest soul from God?

I hesitated no more. Especially Lucifer. Sure we need the light!

It was then the terror set in. That I was overwhelmed by the impertinence of what I was thinking. What did I know? From my little corner on one piece of the jigsaw? I was bound to miss something, get something wrong, trip, and not even know I had done it. My terror grew by the second until my heart was thumping like an engine.

And I felt another rhythm: *Róisín, Róisín*. My old friend, the ocean, calling me home. We redeem ourselves and each the other or no one can. I knew now where Fionnuala found the courage to die.

My heart slowed down. No, the best I could do was my own

part, whatever that was, in a scheme of things I would never understand. So I offered all I had, or ever could have, in case this might help in some way I couldn't see. To whom it may concern, and no matter what.

That's my line . . . .

Fionnuala! Were you there all through that and never even helped?

Ah Róisín, Róisín.

I remember now, Fionnuala. How could I forget?

How, indeed. A winter afternoon I brought my girls to the art gallery in Parnell Square, bringing them into the Garden of Remembrance on the way home . . . .

The Children of Lir were there, towering over the waters in the Crucifix of Reflection. On a whim, I asked the girls to tell me the legend of the Children of Lir. Half could tell me little or nothing. The other half knew only of the bell of Christianity.

Not one could tell me about the Man of the North marrying the Woman of the South. And none had that beautiful detail that should draw tears from stones: the battle-flying formation of the four swans in burial.

From nowhere, I was overwhelmed with grief. Bereft, I sat on the cross and wept.

The girls tried, but I was inconsolable. As if half our very selves had been robbed by omission.

Mortified, the girls gathered tightly around to protect me.

"Miss . . . this is the Garden of Remembrance," said Terry Hayes very gently.

The others tittered, both in embarrassment and at the obviousness of what she said.

But its very simplicity calmed me at once. I thanked her. There were always one or two kindred spirits in every class.

Every detail of that scene came back now. Only just as sorrow and despair had enveloped me then, it was joy's exuberant turn now.

I knew at last the swan song was not in vain. Because from the very time of the swans up to the present minute, their people have quietly insisted on the marriage of the Man of the North to the

Woman of the South. Through all the long centuries since, a ring encircles the crucial heart of every Celtic cross.

A cross like that wouldn't let you down. *Wouldn't leave you halfway to paradise. So near, yet so far away.*

I didn't know whether to smile or cry. *I want to be your lover, but your friend is all I stay.*

First Ben and then Lorcan.

> *When he who counts pain and loss*
> *Gave to you the Rose . . . .*

I named our child and I never even thought of that.

When the Man of the North joins the Woman of the South . . . .
When the priest of Rome joins the serpent woman . . . a Rose is . . . .

A Rose is a Rose is a Rose . . . .

Fionnuala, Bernadette, Lorcan, and I in the waves, Ben looking on from the island. Join hands. Ring a-ring a-rosies. Join hands . . . .

> *Ring a-ring a Rose is . . .*
> *A pocket full of posies*
> *Asha, asha, we all fall down.*

I searched in my handbag for paper, something to write with and a tenpence piece. With two fingers holding the coin steady, I traced around it. Inside the circle I wrote – a rose is a rose – in small letters until the letters met.

I saw it at once:

Arose Is. Ad infinitum.

And there, where I least expected it: the island. The hapless arose in the palm of the is. The unfathomable pas de deux of the gormless and the formless.

I knew what to do. I set off, half afraid I might lose the island again. But the waves reminded me I might well lose the feeling, but never memory. I calmed and slowed pace at once in obedience.

As I started down the path, a figure trudged stolidly towards me. Not wearing black now either, but the gin-bottle shoulders bobbing towards me were unmistakable. Lorcan Burke.

Something in that figure bespoke twenty years of more despair than the newspapers and television showed.

His head was down. One of the King's men, soundly defeated.

Then I knew one thing surely as I know my own name.

He wants to know your story. He gets up in the morning wondering, and his last thoughts at night are questions. I can feel it in my bones.